"WHAT DO YOU WANT, CHLOE?"

She knew what he meant even in her innocence.

"We're practically strangers. I don't know you," she responded.

"Yes, you do." Travis moved a pace closer. His voice was low, intimate. He grasped her with a look, held her without touching her. "I'm the one you can't get off your mind. When you wake up deep in the night from dreams that leave you edgy and restless, I'm the one you're reaching for."

Thunder sounded again, nearer this time.

He moved closer until his breath stirred fine strands of her hair.

"You know me. And I know you. I know every curve of your body, the silky feel of your hair when it's brushed out." He reached out and removed her hairpins, combing the long strands with his fingers as they fell to her waist.

"That's not true," Chloe replied. "You've never touched me. You don't know anything about me."

"Let's find ⎯⎯⎯⎯⎯⎯⎯⎯⎯⎯⎯ he felt his soft li

HOMEWARD HEARTS

by

Alexis Harrington

A TOPAZ BOOK

TOPAZ
Published by the Penguin Group
Penguin Books USA Inc., 375 Hudson Street,
New York, New York 10014, U.S.A.
Penguin Books Ltd, 27 Wrights Lane,
London W8 5TZ, England
Penguin Books Australia Ltd, Ringwood,
Victoria, Australia
Penguin Books Canada Ltd, 10 Alcorn Avenue,
Toronto, Ontario, Canada M4V 3B2
Penguin Books (N.Z.) Ltd, 182–190 Wairau Road,
Auckland 10, New Zealand

Penguin Books Ltd, Registered Offices:
Harmondsworth, Middlesex, England

First published by Topaz, an imprint of Dutton Signet,
a division of Penguin Books USA Inc.

First Printing, May, 1994
10 9 8 7 6 5 4 3 2 1

Copyright © Alexis Harrington, 1994
All rights reserved
Topaz Man photo © Charles William Bush

Topaz is a trademark of New American Library,
a division of Penguin Books USA Inc.

Printed in the United States of America

Prologue

At the crossroads of eternity and isolation stood the dying town of Misfortune, Oregon.

Once it had been a prosperous, brawling mining town, waltzing the line of law and order with clumsy strides. Gunfights, knifings, and drunken chaos were standard every night. But the passage of twenty years had seen the gold mines go bust, the population dwindle to a clannish few.

Now, in the velvety darkness of warm summer nights, all that could be heard were the soft calls of chirping crickets, an occasional barking dog, or maybe strident but muffled voices engaged in domestic disagreement. Icy winter twilights brought the lonely moan of frigid, snow-laden winds blowing down from the Canadian Arctic.

While a few old-timers still pecked away at claims in the low hills surrounding Misfortune, the town inched along in its desolation year after year. So when an outsider was spotted within fifteen miles of the main street on that hot blue day in 1894, the news spread quickly and caused a lot of head-scratching speculation.

After all, there wasn't much reason for a stranger to come to Misfortune.

But one was on his way.

Chapter 1

Chloe Maitland silently cursed the July heat. Her beige muslin dress had been fresh and crisp with starch this morning but now the skirt hung in limp folds. The sun was a silver-white disk as she closed her front door and set out for DeGroot's Mercantile to buy groceries for Saturday dinner and to pick up her mail. Her basket on her arm, she glanced at the drooping, stunted flowers in the planter boxes that stood on either side of the porch. The lawn was a yellow, mangy mat, worn to bare dirt in some places. Now and then, a hot breeze would kick up, lifting and rearranging the dust. Rain, she knew, was still three months away.

Maybe a letter would be waiting for her today. She didn't know where her optimism came from because every Saturday for ten weeks she'd walked to DeGroot's, hoping for a response to her advertisement. Each week she'd come away disappointed.

Three months. Chloe could scarcely believe so much time had passed since she'd placed an advertisement in the Baker City newspaper, forty miles away. She realized her chances of finding an experi-

enced blacksmith were not very good, especially
since she could pay no wages, only room and board.
But she'd never once imagined there would be no
response at all. There had to be at least one man in
the county willing to do an honest day's work in exchange for good food and a roof over his head.

As Chloe headed down the boardwalk, she tried
to ignore the rundown buildings and deserted stores
that cast cool shadows on her path. Her attention
snagged on a tumbleweed rolling down the center of
the dusty street. True, it wasn't hard to understand
why the world wasn't beating a path to Misfortune.
But the town wasn't dead.

The same anxiety that kept her awake nights suddenly descended upon her. If she couldn't find a
blacksmith, she didn't know what she'd do. The
washing she took in generated only enough money
to feed her. There was nothing left over for a debt as
big as a mortgage. If her circumstances didn't
change soon, she'd lose the house and have to leave
Misfortune. And go where?

Looming ahead on the other side of the street was
the silent, abandoned building that had once been
Misfortune's fanciest saloon, the Rose and Garter.
She averted her eyes—she didn't need to see beyond
its dusty, web-draped windows to remember the mir-
rored back bar, lined with bottles. It had been a long
time since she'd heard the jangling piano music and
noisy laughter that had rolled past the swinging
doors, day and night. A long time since Frank
Maitland, Misfortune's only blacksmith and the saloon's best customer, had slumped at the mahogany

bar letting grief chase him to the bottom of a whiskey bottle. Some people inherited money or property or heirlooms. Her father's bequest to her had been a heart full of grim memories.

Albert DeGroot's big wall clock was softly tolling four o'clock when Chloe pushed open the door to the mercantile. There was a mingling of scents in Albert's store that always reminded her of when she was little, of the pickle barrel and coffee and leather harness. The shelves reached nearly to the ceiling and bore tin cans and glass bottles and porcelain jugs. Sacks of rice, flour, and sugar were propped up against the back counter, and brass spittoons graced each end. As a child, Chloe had thought the only thing better than DeGroot's was Christmas.

Today three men lounged against the counter to catch up on the latest events: Albert, Tarpaper Bolen, and Dr. Miles Sherwood. Their conversation ceased as she walked to the counter, her heels sounding on the old wooden floor in the uncomfortable silence.

She was a tall woman and she knew that alone commanded attention. She also knew she was a popular subject of gossip and it was not beyond possibility that they'd been talking about her again.

"Hello, Albert, Doc." Chloe nodded at the men leaning on the counter. She made a point of standing upwind of Tarpaper Bolen, a grizzled prospector who bathed only on his birthday and Christmas Eve. "Tar." The flat acknowledgment was descriptive of the old man's lack of personal hygiene.

She pushed her shopping list toward Albert along with her tea tin. "Just a few things today, I think."

Albert scanned the list, then peered over his spectacles and took a longer look at her hair. "You know, I got in a new order of curling irons. Nice ones, too, with painted porcelain handles."

Albert DeGroot was one of the least tactful people Chloe knew. If she'd been younger and still capable of blushing, he would have turned her face scarlet with his remark. Getting older did have its blessings, though. For one thing, it gave her the ability to bury her hurts so deeply she hardly felt them anymore.

Curled hair wasn't for a woman who spent the majority of her day bent over a scrub board. There'd been a time when all that fussing had seemed so very important but now she wore her red-gold hair twisted into a bun at the base of her neck. Functional, Chloe had learned, was more important than frilly. She straightened her shoulders and lifted her chin just a bit.

"Just what's on the list, Albert."

Sure of step and firm of jaw, she knew she intimidated some people. In some cases she preferred that. Her mirror told her she didn't possess a classic beauty, but at least her features were even. Her long nose was straight on her oval face, properly aligned between high cheekbones.

Albert nodded and shrugged. He turned to reach for a box of starch from a high shelf when Tar prompted anxiously, "What was you tellin' us about a stranger?"

"Oh—right. As I was saying, I had it from Andy Duykstrom, Caleb's boy," Albert said, turning back to the counter, the starch forgotten. "We got a stranger headed this way."

When Chloe heard that she sighed inwardly and she knew she was in for a long wait. After *The Misfortune Observer* had published its last issue five years earlier, Albert had taken to holding court on Saturday afternoons to dispense the latest news to anyone who'd hold still and listen.

"Albert, please, I'm in something of a hurry."

"Right away, Chloe, right away. This is really interesting," Albert replied, putting his elbows on the counter.

She doubted that. Albert, his wife Mildred, and Mildred's closest friend, Bertha Preston received and dispatched information—gossip, to the more discerning—with the efficiency of a daily paper. Chloe seldom found their announcements the least bit interesting.

The balding little man pushed his spectacles farther up his nose and continued with grave importance. Chloe knew there was no stopping him now.

"Andy said Caleb talked to a stranger walking down the road along the west edge of his spread. He wanted directions to Misfortune. Caleb tried to find out where he was from, but couldn't get anything out of him, not even his name. When Caleb asked him where his horse was, the stranger said he didn't own one. Caleb offered to let him spend the night in the barn but the man turned him down flat. I 'spect by the time he gets here he'll have been walking a long time." Albert paused here for this fact to be fully appreciated by his listeners.

Indeed, it was an amazing suggestion since Misfortune was surrounded by miles of desolate, nearly treeless terrain. Bitterly cold in winter, mercilessly hot and dry in summer, it was suitable for the wheat that grew well in its soil but not for the support of a lone human life attempting to cross it on foot. And with the lack of nearby towns, Albert's comment was correct. For a person to get this far, no matter where he'd come from, he would have been walking for quite a while.

"He's probably just passing through," Chloe suggested as she studied a bolt of yellowing lace in Albert's display case. A new face in the area *was* interesting—even she had to admit that—but she had never shared her neighbors' fascination with others' business.

"There's no place around here to pass through to," Tar put in, clearly suspicious of the outsider's intentions.

No, Chloe thought, that's true. Misfortune was the end of the line. She placed her basket on the counter, hoping to hurry Albert along.

Albert sprinkled tea onto his scale, then stood back, hands at his sides. He always made a point of proving to his customers that the weight of his thumb was not included in the price of their goods. He poured the tea into the tin Chloe had brought with her and with all the subtlety of a cow flop, he said, "Looks like another Saturday night dinner with Evan—he does like his tea, doesn't he?"

Chloe felt annoyance roil in her. Oh, the clacking, wagging tongues—did they really have nothing better to do than chart her activities? She could imagine them at their windows on Saturday evenings, noses pressed to the glass, watching Evan walk through town toward her house, carrying his usual bouquet for her.

"I'll bet he can't wait to move out of that attic at the Tollivers'," Albert prattled on. "When do you expect him to pop the question, Chloe?"

She supposed she should be grateful that Albert at least refrained from adding the general feeling of the townspeople: Chloe Maitland, with her sharp tongue and bossy ways, had better marry Evan Peterson—the schoolteacher was her first and, no doubt, last prospect.

Tar's brows flew up at the shopkeeper's prying foolhardiness.

Doc Sherwood merely shook his head at Albert's rude presumption.

Chloe gave Albert a cold steady look before replying. She wasn't about to stand here and discuss personal matters with this nosy fool. Anything she said would be all over town by tomorrow's breakfast. "I guess that's my business, now, isn't it?"

"Oh, sure, Chloe, sure." Albert had the good grace to appear ashamed of himself. "I'll just get that baking powder."

Chloe heard Doc's low chuckle. She flashed him a look and a small private smile. She was especially fond of the old physician. He was one of the few who'd never once commented about the loss of her "glowing beauty" after her mother died and her father started drinking. And once, it got back to her, Doc had taken the sheriff to task for saying he'd rather try to arrest a drunken buffalo hunter than deal with her.

A can of baking powder was thumped down on the counter in front of Chloe.

Evidently undaunted by his earlier blunder, Albert said, "I'll put all this on your account, Chloe."

She was tempted. She thought about the few coins in her bag and how nice it would be to keep them a while longer. But, no. Debts had a nasty way of growing quickly. Credit, she felt, was a luxury designed for those who didn't need it rather than those who did.

"No, thank you, Albert. I'll just take my mail."

He turned toward the pigeonholes that served as his post office, his hand extended.

Chloe held her breath.

Then Tar, ever worried about claim jumpers, frowned through his greasy beard and brought the conversation back to the topic of the afternoon. "Well, that drifter best not have any ideas about workin' my Pony Gal. I'll bean him with my shovel if'n he gets too close. I've done it before."

Albert stopped short of completing his task and gave him an impatient look. Tarpaper, so called in honor of his first mining shack, had lived in the hills for nearly thirty years and it had made him peculiar. Although his claim, Pony Gal, had never yielded enough gold to let him do more than barely survive, he was certain his one big strike was coming any day. All the old prospectors felt the same way about their claims.

"Nobody is interested in that picayune stake of yours, Tar," Albert pointed out. "You've been scraping away at that thing since Moses was a boy and it ain't made you rich yet. Nobody is interested in mining these parts at all. The big money was taken out of here years ago." Then he added, "The one time you got into a scuffle over that patch of dirt, you were full of the Grover sisters' moonshine." He jerked a thumb at the row of jars on the shelf behind him. "And you're lucky you didn't get killed."

Chloe felt all eyes in the room shift to her uncomfortably, then skitter away.

The old miner shifted his tobacco from one jaw to the other, then broke the awkward pause. "It wasn't my time to leave this earth, and it ain't yet. I reckon I'll keep my eyes open for this stranger, just the same. What's he look like, Albert?"

"Well, Andy didn't say, exactly," Albert admitted. "He said Caleb told him the man takes after the devil, but we know Andy tends to be a mite addled sometimes. I suppose we'll find out soon. The man asked where Misfortune was and Caleb sent him off in this direction. Without a horse, I don't imagine he'll be here for another day or so."

"If the heat doesn't kill him first," Doc Sherwood put in, mopping his forehead with a large handkerchief. He was a tall, elegant-looking gentleman with a full head of snowy hair and a luxuriant mustache. "This is the hottest July I can remember around here. A man would have to be a damned idiot to try to walk anywhere in heat like this."

"Albert," Chloe prompted firmly, "my mail?"

"Hmm? Oh, right—mail."

Albert finally turned back to the pigeonholes, then returned, shaking his head. "Nothing this week, Chloe."

Disheartened but unwilling to show it, she paid her bill and said goodbye, waving to Doc Sherwood. When she stepped outside, she glanced up at the hot sky. Doc was right: a man would have to be a damned idiot to travel on foot under a sun like this and she had no time to spare for idiots.

Miles away, Travis McGuire shuffled to a stop on a low rise. He lifted his eyes to gaze over the vast rolling plains surrounding him. Like a castaway set adrift on a strange yellow sea, his sole point of reference was the broiling sun overhead. He reached for his canteen and listened as he shook it, then tipped it over his open mouth to drain the last swallow of stale water.

The prying farmer he'd talked to early last evening had said he'd find Bad Luck or Hardship, or whatever the name of that town was, out here if he maintained this course. He was beginning to think he'd be in Wichita before he found it.

Fatigue made his legs shake now that he was standing still. He considered sitting down for just a moment but changed his mind; he wasn't too sure of his ability to get up again.

His cheekbone and brow throbbed, a reminder of

the punishing blow his face had taken yesterday morning when his horse snapped a foreleg in a gopher hole. The horse had sunk heavily with the fracture and he was pitched over the animal's head, landing on his chest and face against earth as hard as concrete. His eye had begun to swell shut even before he got to his feet again. Blood had run from the scrapes on his face and dripped on his torn shirt.

The horse had thrashed and kicked, trying to stand. Seeing the broken bone, something very close to grief had twisted his heart before he squelched the feeling. He'd drawn his Colt revolver and fired two shots, shattering the utter silence of the prairie and ending the life of the only companion he'd had in years. Then he'd pulled off the saddle and saddlebags and started walking. He carried the saddle for a while but as he trudged over barren miles it became a pointless burden and he abandoned it.

Now he stood looking at the infinity before him, resting his weight on one hip. A sigh rose in his chest. The saddlebags containing all he owned in this world lay heavy on his shoulder and he shrugged against the load, shifting it. He recognized that he was only a scrap of humanity on this plain, that his life could easily be snuffed out and its passing not even noted. Worse than being on foot, having no water reduced considerably his chances for survival.

But he had one thing going for him that gave him an advantage, something that had seen him through the last five years. A thing he nurtured and polished and carried before him like a shield against the world.

That one thing was grim resolve.

* * *

"Miss Chloe, you've outdone yourself again," Evan said, spooning up three-quarters of the mashed potatoes. He heaped them on a plate already burdened with a biscuit and most of a roast chicken.

A stiff breeze blew this evening, lifting the snowy lace curtains and brushing them against the wallpaper filled with the figures of cabbage roses. It was too warm to close the windows but Chloe could feel a fine grit under her shoes and knew it was settling on everything in the dining room.

Where was he putting all that food? Chloe wondered, taking what remained of the dinner she'd cooked onto her plate. She supposed the odd jobs he did around the Tollivers' farm in exchange for his keep might give him an appetite. Yet while he sometimes gobbled her food like a starving man, barely tasting it, on other evenings he'd pick suspiciously at the meals as though they were poisoned.

"Did you hear about the drifter on the Duykstrom property?" he asked, skewering peas on his fork. He chased those he missed, clinking the tines on his plate and pushing a few peas off onto the embroidered tablecloth. "Albert told me he'll be here any day and that he's disfigured."

"What?" Chloe exclaimed. "That's not what he told me. Oh, I don't even know why I bother to wonder. Each time the DeGroots repeat a story it becomes more exaggerated."

Evan stuffed a buttered biscuit into his mouth. "Albert swears it's true," he stressed, eyes wide.

She shook her head. "I don't care. Unless that drifter is bringing me a bag of gold dust for the mortgage payment, he doesn't interest me."

After dinner Chloe sat with Evan on the porch swing to watch the sunset and have their tea and dessert. She was content to rest here, pondering the low hills on the faraway horizon, painted blood red by the sun falling behind them. The wind rustled the dry leaves in the maple in the corner of the yard and sent the yellow tops of the grass bobbing.

Evan pushed the swing into motion with his foot, reminding her he was there. Glancing at him, she knew he wasn't the kind of man who made a woman's heart flutter. He was slightly built and approaching his fortieth year. His sandy hair had surrendered to create a horseshoe effect around his head, leaving the top shiny and bare.

He had appeared at her door one afternoon shortly after her father's death, bearing his laundry, a box of chocolates, and a wilting bouquet, to offer his condolences. She'd been feeling blue and asked him to stay for dinner. A man for whom habits were written in stone, he'd since appeared for dinner every Saturday with unflagging regularity. He provided quiet companionship and that was enough, she told herself. Although this evening she could feel him fidgeting next to her, fussing with his collar, his cuffs, brushing lint from the lapels of his somber black suit.

Chloe didn't want a man who was opinionated or had bad habits and Evan was guilty of neither. If only she could soothe the conflict that sometimes churned in her.

He was a nice man, she would argue with herself, one side trying to convince the other, the usually silent side of her that questioned her judgment and made her want to pull away from him.

But now both sides in this debate cringed when, without preamble, Evan leaned over and clumsily groped for her hand with clammy fingers. Lunging his face at hers, he tried to place a damp peck on her mouth, making the swing tilt sharply. Sensing what was about to happen she turned her head away suddenly and the kiss caught the corner of her upper lip. The unappealing smell of chicken and mashed potatoes on his breath made her wonder why anyone thought kissing was a gratifying pursuit.

Evan quickly released her hand and stared straight ahead, turning several shades of red, his back as stiff as a broomstick. Astonished, Chloe could only gape at him. He'd never tried *that* before. She fought the urge to wipe her lip.

"I'm very sorry, Miss Chloe," his words stumbled out. "I don't know what came over . . . it's just that sometimes . . . I most humbly beg your forgiveness."

His awkward discomfort only reinforced what she already suspected. Romance, with its complicated maneuvers and crude, embarrassed fumbling, was not necessary between them.

Recovering, she reached for the teapot and, using her most sensible voice, responded, "We don't need to go through all that sparking nonsense, Evan. We're not children on a hayride trying to hold hands and steal kisses. We get along just fine the way things are." She refilled his cup.

"Of course, you're right," he agreed. "I hope you're not angry with me."

"No, Evan, I'm not angry at all," she replied, wishing he wouldn't pursue the subject. "Please, let's just forget it happened."

He seemed relieved. Still, she could not help but notice that he'd unconsciously begun to sharpen the creases in his trousers with his short fingers.

Just as his teacup was filled, he stood abruptly, pulled out his watch and announced loudly, "Why, look at the time! I really must be going, Miss Chloe. I wouldn't want to overstay my welcome."

Not upset to see him go, she rose from the swing. "I'm glad you were able to come for dinner," she prompted.

Although he faced her, he always seemed unable to look directly at her, and his pale, nearly lashless eyes were fixed on a spot just above her head.

"Thank you for inviting me. The only time I eat a decent meal is in your home." His lips twitched into the semblance of a smile. "Mrs. Tolliver means well, but her cooking . . . I really look forward to these evenings."

The obvious but unnecessary hint for an invitation to dinner next Saturday hung in the air like a tangible thing. Taking her cue, Chloe asked, "You will come again, won't you?"

"I would like that very much." He beamed, staring at the button on her collar. "Shall we say next Saturday?"

Satisfied with this ritual she had come to expect, she agreed. "That would be nice. I'll plan on it."

The clock was striking ten when she put out the lamps and climbed the stairs to her bedroom. The night was quiet.

After she changed into her nightgown, she stood before her long mirror and thought about what had happened on the porch. She certainly hoped she'd relieved Evan's mind about the nature of their relationship. That business of kissing—she just wasn't comfortable with the idea.

Or holding hands, either.

At that thought, she held up her hands and inspected them as though they belonged to someone else, tokens representing what her life had become. Even in this low light she could see their red dryness. Nothing she tried seemed to heal them. The laundry she did every day, in hot water and harsh soap, left them so irritated, they just hurt. It wasn't that she minded working hard. Work never hurt anyone. But she was offended by the unwelcome intimacy required of the chore. She'd never expected to wash and iron strangers' clothes, to sort their stockings and underwear, to support herself.

Knowing she was perilously close to self-pity, she shook off the thought and released her hair to give it its nightly one hundred and one strokes. Unbound and brushed, the heavy locks tumbled down her back to her waist, catching highlights from the single candle burning on her nightstand.

Leaning closer to the mirror, she spied one strand

that protruded from her head like a piano wire. Puzzled, she pulled it out with a snap and carried it to the candle to look at it. It was white. She stared at it stupidly for a moment as it lay across her palm, and suddenly she felt her throat tighten and her eyes burn.

With a deep sigh that was almost a sob, she held the strand over the flame and watched it dance and wither until it was gone.

Chapter 2

Under the blistering noon sky, Travis McGuire moved in a shambling, tottering manner, the way a horse will stumble when it has been run beyond its endurance. Was this Saturday? Tuesday? He'd lost track of the days; they'd all become one in his mind.

Exhaustion, thirst, and too many hours in the pitiless sun made him doubt his eyes when he saw a collection of buildings a mile or so ahead. He squinted at the sight through the shimmering heat waves. The image didn't become much clearer, but it didn't disappear, either.

"Thank God," he croaked to the scorched landscape, his throat unbearably dry.

From the marrow of his bones he pulled forth the last trace of energy he possessed and hastened his wobbling progress. The pulse throbbing in his ears all but drowned out the sound of his spurs. As he neared the first building, which was set some distance from the rest, he read the word BLACKSMITH, painted on its weathered side.

"Thank God."

Chloe stood in the backyard, scrubbing at a stubborn coffee stain on a tablecloth. The sun was high and her back ached from bending over the washboard for so many hours. She'd wanted to be finished before lunch but now she heard the clock in the parlor striking one o'clock. Letting the cloth drop into the water, she straightened and put her hands on the small of her back to relieve the stiffness.

She'd always done wash on Monday, but now every day was Monday. She stared wistfully at the silent blacksmith shop across the yard. The extra money that shop could earn would make all the difference, if only there was someone to work it. Impatiently, she lassoed her thoughts. No amount of wishing was going to change anything and she had hours of ironing still ahead of her.

As she reached into the tub again, she heard someone fumble at the latch on the gate behind her that separated the yard from the road. Turning, she was startled by an apparition staggering toward her. The head was bowed and she could not readily see the face.

No one she recognized, she decided. She didn't know any man that tall. His physical presence dwarfed the yard and gave her a sense of sudden danger.

He's blind drunk! she thought indignantly as he lurched to her on long legs, spurs ringing at his heels. And at this hour of the day! That alone gave her reason to feel fear, aside from his height and apparent strength.

He wore a pair of denims, although they were so

dust-covered, they no longer looked blue. His boots were equally dusty and his shirt was an indefinite color. Its sleeves were ripped off at the shoulders, revealing arms formed with sinuous muscle. A hat concealed most of his dark hair and a blue bandanna was tied around his neck. He carried a saddlebag slung over one shoulder.

There was nothing between her and this intruder but five feet of dry grass and the hot afternoon breeze. She backed against the washtub, feeling it press sharply into her thighs, and unconsciously clutched the wet tablecloth to her. It soaked her dress front from neck to knees. She thought of her grandfather's rifle, loaded, but in the parlor, and wanted to kick herself for not bringing it to the yard.

When he raised his head to look at her, she pressed a hand to her open mouth and stood transfixed, eyes wide.

His face, shadowed by several days' growth of dark beard, was puffy and bruised, as though it had connected with an angry fist. One eye was almost swollen shut and his lips were cracked and peeling.

"Excuse me, ma'am," issued a hoarse, almost whispering voice from those cracked lips. "Is this Hard Luck?" He reached into his shirt pocket and pulled out a tattered piece of paper.

"Not Hard Luck, it's Misfortune and—"

He weaved unsteadily and waved the paper in his long hand. "I'm here about the job."

She looked him over and her heart sank. What she didn't need was another drunken blacksmith, and one who brawled, besides. "I'm the one you want to talk to, but I don't think—"

He swayed on his feet. "I don't mean to interrupt, but could I trouble you for a drink of water? I've been walking for a while." His head moved slightly in the direction of the tin cup hanging on the pump spout.

He's not drunk, Chloe realized with a start, he's sick. The request jolted her into action and she nearly fell backward into the washtub in her haste to get to the pump to fill her bucket.

She dipped the large cup in the icy water and held it out to him. As he reached for it with two shaking hands, she warned him, "That water is very cold. You'd better drink it slowly."

But she knew her words were ignored when he lifted the cup and drank the water down in one greedy gulp, spilling part of it down his bloodstained shirt. He was about to hold the cup out to her to re-fill when he suddenly turned away from her and threw up the water and whatever scant secretions his empty, cramping stomach had managed to produce.

Chloe stood shaking her head in pity. When the bout subsided, he slowly straightened and turned back to her, his head down, unable to look her in the face.

"I'm sorry—" his words sighed out and she watched in horror as his eyes rolled back and his knees buckled. The cup slipped out of his nerveless hand. He fell facedown at her feet, his hat rolling across the yard. She dropped to a crouch and struggled to turn him over. Perspiration rapidly beaded on her forehead and the back of her neck as she wrestled with his dead weight. Losing her balance, she toppled over and landed on her backside in the mud around the washtub, then scrambled to her knees while she pulled on his arm in an effort to turn him.

When she finally accomplished the feat she put her ear to his chest and was relieved to hear his heartbeat. But it sounded too fast and his breathing was shallow. She looked around frantically. There wasn't a living soul on the street, which wasn't surprising. Her house was located away from the core of Misfortune and not much traffic found its way down here. The man needed Doc Sherwood and she would have to get him herself.

But what to do with this poor wretch while she was gone? He was lying in the harsh sun and although he was bone lean, he was well over six feet tall. She knew she couldn't drag him to the shade of the only tree standing in the far corner of the yard. She'd had enough trouble just rolling him over.

As she looked around she spied a bed sheet she'd hung on the line to dry. Jumping to her feet, she yanked it from the clothesline and stuffed it into the water bucket to soak it. She pulled it out dripping wet and flung it over his inert body, covering him so that only his boots stuck out.

She backed away to the gate, feeling miserable about leaving him, especially because so shrouded, he looked like a corpse.

He might become one, she told herself, if you don't hurry.

Heedless of her wet dress, which clung to her bosom, she jerked the gate open so hard it banged against the fence and she flew down the street toward Doc Sherwood's house on the opposite end of town.

When she reached DeGroot's Mercantile, she poked her head in the door to make sure Doc wasn't there, but only Albert's wife, Mildred, was in the store, sorting hair ribbons. Chloe slammed the door shut again and heard its overhead bell bounce to the floor.

Behind her she heard Mildred call after her from the boardwalk, "Chloe, that dress looks like you've been making mud pies." She disregarded the woman's useless observation and kept running.

When Chloe neared Doc's house, she began yelling for him. "Doc!" she screamed. "Doc Sherwood!"

The doctor pulled open the door of his examining room to meet her in the hall.

"Tell me," he commanded.

"A man—" she panted. "A stranger in my yard—he's dying. You've—got to come."

"I'll get my bag," Doc said. "Lucky for us I just hitched up the horse.

They rushed out the door again and jumped into his buggy.

"What's wrong with this man? Can you tell?" the doctor asked, flapping the reins on his horse's back.

"He came into the backyard asking about the blacksmith's job. Doc, his face is so beaten. Anyway, I gave him the water and told him not to drink it too fast, but he did and it came right back up. Then he just dropped over in the dirt."

32

"Were his clothes wet? Did he look like he's been sweating?" Doc questioned.

Chloe thought hard but she couldn't remember. "I didn't notice. What difference does that make?"

"Could be he's got sunstroke. That can be very serious—fry a man's brain like an egg."

When Doc and Chloe arrived they found the man lying under the sheet just as Chloe had left him, with just his long boots showing.

"Jesus, Chloe," Doc murmured. "He's not dead already, is he?"

"No, no. I couldn't move him out of the sun so I soaked a sheet in cold water and threw it over him."

"Good girl," Doc nodded approvingly, then stepped up to the form and pulled the sheet off. With only a scant glance at the battered face, he ripped open the man's shirt and touched his throat, searching for a pulse. After a brief examination he announced, "It's sunstroke, no doubt about that. We've got to cool him down or he'll die. Even if he doesn't die, his kidneys could fail or his brain will cook and he'll be an idiot—a worse fate in my opinion. Drag out your bathtub. We'll fill it and soak him in there." He gestured at the unconscious form. "But we'd better get him into the kitchen first. He's been in the sun too long as it is."

Doc pulled on the limp arms and then slid behind him to hook his own arms around the other man's chest. Chloe gripped the stranger's ankles, taking care to avoid the sharp rowels on his spurs.

"Ready?" Doc asked.

She nodded and they lifted him. She wouldn't

have guessed that hard muscle and bone could weigh so much. He seemed very heavy for a person with so little spare flesh and getting him up the back steps was not easy. When they were in the kitchen, they laid him on the table. The slack face looked more dead than alive.

Chloe hurried to the pantry and pulled her big galvanized bathtub from its hiding place. She then grabbed the water bucket that stood by the door and filled it from the pump at the sink. Doc took it away and poured the water into the tub. She pumped until her arm and shoulder ached.

"All right, we've got enough," Doc finally announced. "If you've got a fan, we could use that, too." She nodded and found her mother's old painted Chinese fan in the sideboard.

They lifted the man from the table and carefully lowered him into the tub, bending his knees sharply to make him fit.

Chloe fanned the man's bruised face and after they watched him for a few minutes, a low groan escaped the cracked lips and his head rolled to rest on the edge of the tub.

"What do you think?" Chloe whispered, as though she might disturb their patient. "Is he getting better?"

"Too soon to tell yet, but this much I do know. He's going to have to be put to bed right away and I'd rather not move him. It's going to be dangerous in his condition."

The unspoken suggestion that she keep him stopped Chloe's fanning in midswish. A strange man sleeping in the house? And she here alone? A funny shiver darted through her, raising goose bumps on her arms. Although the man was slender—too thin, really—he was nothing but lean muscle. His chest was broad and covered with soft, dark hair. Embarrassed to have even noticed, she moved the fan with determination and saw how that chest hair fluffed in the resulting breeze. Her eyes returned to the bruised, lean-jawed face. It was so haggard she couldn't tell what kind of man owned it. He just looked sick, hurt, and uncared for. And he didn't look as though he were in any condition to give her trouble. She could not refuse him the nursing he plainly needed.

"I suppose it would be all right if he stayed here," she offered tentatively.

Her moment's hesitation brought her a quizzical look from Doc and then, with a slap on his knee, he said, "That's right, you're alone here now."

"That doesn't matter. I'm not worried about it."

"No, no, this isn't a good idea. When folks around town learn of it, there's bound to be talk."

Her decision made, Chloe pushed back a straggling curl. "They talk about me already, and it's the least of my troubles. This man needs my help."

"Evan will hear about it."

"Doc, I don't need a devil's advocate. Certainly, Evan will understand."

She felt Doc's eyes scan her dishevelment and knew she must look ridiculous in her wet, muddy dress and ruined hair. But she lifted her chin with stubborn determination.

"The matter is settled. I'll keep this man here until he's well," she affirmed.

Nodding, Doc began issuing instructions to her. "And for the next few hours put a pinch of salt in the water you give him. Are you sure you can handle all this?"

"Yes, I can manage," she answered, lifting her chin again.

After a half hour had passed Doc suggested, "Let's see how he's doing." He put a hand on the forehead and then grasped the lifeless wrist.

"We can move him now. He's cooler and his heartbeat is slower and stronger. I think he'll mend."

While Chloe made up the sickbed, Doc cut off the stranger's shirt and jeans with her sewing scissors, then covered him with a clean white sheet. She decided to put him in the little nursery adjoining her room, thinking it would be easier to tend him there. Between them, Doc and Chloe managed to get him upstairs, but the task was much harder than the trip from the yard had been. Chloe almost lost her hold on the stranger's ankles once and nearly sent the three of them rolling back down to the parlor.

When they finally had him on the bed, another groan sounded from the man.

"I don't know what you're complaining about," Chloe huffed breathlessly to the still form. "We've been doing all the work." She pushed aside her old rag doll sitting on the rocker and lowered herself to the seat.

Doc dropped into a chair that faced the window. "I'm getting too old for this kind of thing." After a moment he got back to his feet and stepped over to the bed, flipping the light blanket over the sheet-clad body.

"I'll come by tomorrow morning to check on him. He'll probably survive."

"I thought you said he'd get well!"

"Yes, I did say that and I believe it. His face is too banged up for me to tell, but judging by the general appearance of his body and hands, I'd guess that he's young—maybe twenty-six or twenty-seven. And that helps. But sunstroke is a tricky thing and he's still unconscious. Now, do you remember everything you are to do?"

She recited the instructions he'd given her.

The doctor nodded, satisfied, and patted her arm. As they headed downstairs he gave her a measured look and said, "Don't forget to look after yourself, too. You're quite a sight, child."

For the first time since the man lying in bed upstairs had walked into her backyard, Chloe stopped to think about mending her appearance. "Yes," she agreed, looking down the front of her dress. "I guess I am."

"No, I don't mean your clothes," he said. "You look worn out. I want you to start being a little kinder to yourself, Chloe."

Her heart lifted with his thoughtfulness and she smiled. As many worries as she had to handle, no one fretted about her. "Thanks, Doc."

After Doc left, she pumped water into a pitcher and put a spoon of salt in it. Then she stood in the center of the kitchen contemplating the mess they'd made. Nothing worth saving was left of the drifter's clothes; Doc had hacked them to ribbons. His boots were soaked from the dunking in the tub, and probably ruined. Chloe was putting them on the back porch to dry when she heard a crash overhead. Grabbing the water pitcher, she ran through the parlor and up the stairs. In the nursery she found her guest in the grips of delirium. A candlestick lay on the floor, apparently knocked off the nightstand by his outflung arm.

She hurried over to the bed and pressed hard against his shoulders to keep him from rolling off the mattress. At her firm touch, he reached up and threw off her hands. He jerked bolt upright to a sitting position, the sheet and blanket sliding down to reveal nearly all of his lean torso, his eyes open but unseeing.

"Let me go!" his hoarse voice snarled angrily. "I didn't do it. You know I didn't, you lousy bastards. You've got the wrong man."

Chloe was horrified at the ease with which he'd flung her off. Somehow, he seemed bigger now that he was moving and closed in this room with her than he had at any earlier moment, even when he'd walked into the yard. His clothes had camouflaged the broad sweep of his shoulders and furred chest and the narrow strip of dark hair that shot down the center of his flat belly.

There was only one way out of this room, through her bedroom and down the stairs. She poised in the corner, watching him, ready to jump. Glancing at the distance between herself and the door, she wondered if anyone would hear her scream from this lonely end of town.

The weak and sick patient she'd so stubbornly insisted on taking care of had suddenly become unpredictable. And in a flash of insight she remembered one of the first rules in dealing with any threatening creatures: never show fear.

She swallowed hard and approached the bed, putting her hands on his shoulders to press him against the mattress again. "Don't fight like this. You're very ill and you have to lie quietly and rest." How was she going to control this fever-crazed man? "Stop it!" she demanded firmly. "Stop it right now and lie down!"

Either her commanding voice penetrated the deep recesses of his brain or fatigue conquered him once more because his eyes closed and he flopped against the pillow, breathing as though he'd been running for his life.

She yanked the sheet back over him. Then, watching for a moment to be sure he was going to stay put, she hurried to her room and got a glass to pour a drink for him. Maybe she could coax him into taking a sip.

Bending low, she slipped her arm beneath his pillow to raise his shoulders, but his size and weight made that impossible. The most she could manage to do was lift his head, then she tipped the glass to wet his lips. She pulled it away to see if he swallowed and when he did, she let him sip again.

His puffy eyes opened the merest slit and fixed on

her face. Beyond his confusion and disorientation, his piercing, intelligent gaze grasped her.

As he continued to stare at her, she asked quietly from a drying throat, "Who are you?"

His look of bafflement increased at her question and he did not respond.

Oh, God, she fretted, thinking of what Doc had said about this man turning into an imbecile. Doesn't he remember his name?

His frown deepened, as though he were trying to decide if he should say. "Travis," he finally murmured wearily. "Travis McGuire." His eyes closed again and she watched his injured face grow slack before she lowered his head.

It was slow in the Queen of Hearts Saloon, with only one card game going in the corner and no customers at the bar. Ben Winstadt didn't much care for hot, quiet days like this—it made time drag and left him with not much to do but polish glasses and refill the pickled egg jars.

But this sleepy afternoon made it easy for Ben's attention to stray from the pickled eggs to a man who appeared at the doorway. The stranger wasn't a big man—he was just tall enough to be seen over the swinging doors. He walked in, spurs ringing faintly, and stood there for a moment, perhaps waiting for his eyes to adjust to the smoky gloom.

Nobody from the corner table bothered to look at him, but he coolly surveyed each face there from under the wide brim of his hat.

Ben gaped, the egg in his hand forgotten. He

didn't get too many of this type in the Queen. In fact, none of Prineville saw many bounty hunters. But this man's profession was as unmistakable as was Lottie's, upstairs. He moved with a watchful deliberateness that was inborn, not learned. He wore a long duster that reached nearly to his heels and when the coat parted, it revealed a big gun belt, another unusual sight in this town. His dark hair fell below his shoulders and while his face was surprisingly young, he had cold blue eyes that looked as old as the grave.

It was that contrast of innocence and iniquity that gave the man away and Ben suddenly realized who had just walked in. Wait till he told the boys about *this*—Jace Rankin was in his saloon.

Rankin made his way to the empty bar where the bartender stood watching him.

"A shot and a beer," he ordered, pushing money toward Ben. His voice was husky, his tone, low.

"Yessir," Ben replied, swamped with a primitive sense of danger. He set the mug of beer, a bottle, and a glass in front of the bounty hunter. He wished there was a way to get the card players to look over this way, but they showed no interest.

Rankin took a tentative sip of the whiskey and scowled at its raw edge.

"That's prime whiskey," Ben offered nervously. "Comes all the way from Portland." He swallowed. The blue eyes resting on him were unforgiving, remorseless.

"Yeah, in kerosene barrels," Rankin growled. He dropped the shot glass into the mug to kill the taste, then swallowed half the beer. Pulling a silver dollar from his pocket, he became absorbed in balancing it on its edge on the countertop. "I'm looking for someone. Maybe you've seen him. A tall man, probably a good head higher than me. He's thin, dark hair, light eyes, pale as a fish belly—prison does that to a man." Rankin looked up from the stabilized coin. "He's a woman-killer."

When Chloe went outside to collect the laundry she'd begun earlier, she found the tablecloth where she had dropped it. Bertha Preston's beautiful tablecloth! It was her best and it was covered with mud, most of which had dried. It will never come clean, Chloe despaired, trying to imagine how she might pay for it if it didn't. She put it back in the washtub and scrubbed until her hands were raw. Then she re-washed the sheet she'd used to cover McGuire.

When both were rinsed, she hung them on the clothesline and gathered the dry wash. Walking back across the yard, her arms full, she tripped over the saddlebag McGuire had dropped when he collapsed. Putting the laundry in the wicker basket, she picked up the saddlebag and slung it over her arm so she could carry both inside.

In the kitchen she stared at the saddlebag, battling with her conscience. Don't snoop, she told herself. It wasn't right to go through the man's personal belongings. But she only wanted to find his extra clothes. Practicality won out and she emptied the bag on the table. She found a razor and a shaving brush, a gun belt with a long-barrel Colt revolver, a box of shells, half a bottle of whiskey, a ten-dollar gold piece and change, and a comb, but no clothes. Not even extra underwear.

What kind of man came to a town like this on foot, with no possessions, willing to work for room and board? A man who had nothing, she realized.

She shook the bag again and heard something metallic clanking at the bottom. She pulled out the object. What she saw nearly took her breath and she reached for a chair to sink into. In her hand were a pair of heavy manacles with a two-foot length of chain connecting them. The locks were smashed. The last wearer of these restraints had broken them off rather than opened them with a key. She dropped them on the table and recoiled.

A dozen thoughts collided in her mind. An outlaw? An escaped prisoner? Who was this man? What had he done?

Chloe had never met anyone who had even been arrested. Since Misfortune's decline the jail had stood empty. Oh, there was Morris Caldwell, the town drunk who was sometimes kept overnight on Saturdays by Sheriff Winslow. But that was only to prevent Morris from sleeping on the porches of the town's residents, which he was apt to do if not supervised. For the past eleven years, Morris had been the only person to occupy the jail cell in Fred's office. But Fred didn't put handcuffs or leg irons on Morris.

They put manacles on criminals, dangerous criminals.

Her gaze fell to the big revolver laying on the table

in front of her. Had this McGuire shot someone? Stolen something? Or—real terror nudged her— raped a woman?

She rose and paced in circles around the table, alarm and a sense of vulnerability rising in her. Fear of another person was an alien emotion for Chloe and she didn't like it. Her first impulse was to run back to Doc's office and tell him she couldn't keep this man in her house, that he'd either have to put Travis up himself or find other accommodations for him. She felt foolish for her earlier bravado when she'd insisted that Travis stay, especially when Doc had given her an opportunity to back out of her offer. Of course, at the time, she rationalized, she'd had no way of knowing such a nasty skeleton hung in McGuire's closet. She'd only known that he was sick and shouldn't be moved.

Chloe remembered what McGuire had shouted upstairs when she'd tried to subdue him—that he didn't do it, whatever *it* was, and that he was the "wrong man."

Her conscience stirred as she recalled him collapsing at her feet and the deathly look to his unconscious face as he'd lain in the bathtub while she and Doc ministered to him. Doc had said McGuire was too sick to be moved. He had even implied that the man might die if he couldn't stay here. Chloe glumly accepted that she couldn't demand that the drifter be removed from her house. Not yet. Not while his condition was still so uncertain. For the time being, she'd have to risk her safety with him.

Smothering her fear, she stopped pacing and returned McGuire's belongings to his saddlebag. When only the Colt and its box of bullets were left, she paused. Picking up the heavy revolver she flipped open the chamber. It had been fired. Four, not six, rounds were in it. She unloaded the bullets and wrapped them in her handkerchief and hid the small bundle and the box in the pantry behind the rows of jars on the shelf. The gun she locked in her father's desk in the parlor. Removing the key, she put it in her pocket, deciding to keep it with her. Risk was one thing. Complete foolhardiness was another.

Satisfied with the weapon's hiding place, she climbed the stairs and went to sit with McGuire.

Chapter 3

The day was nearly gone when Travis McGuire came swimming back to consciousness with a sluggish jolt. Jesus, what horrible dreams he'd been having.

In his disjointed nightmare, he'd been arrested and dragged away to prison in the worst snowstorm he'd ever seen. It was bitterly cold and he'd had no coat or hat. The way the guard had prodded him along made him slip and fall into a slushy puddle that immediately soaked his hair and light clothing, freezing him to the bone. The guard had jerked him upright by his belt and thrown him into a chair where he shivered in misery.

Even now Travis wasn't certain he was awake. The first thing his eyes focused on when he opened them was a barred window. A cell? He fought the confusion clouding his brain. After a moment he realized he was looking at a window through a spindle-back chair.

Where was he? He surveyed the room and saw flowered paper on the walls and lace curtains at the windows. The bedding smelled like sachet. No prison was decorated like this. Even he felt washed.

Laboriously, he rolled to his side, the effort bringing sharp pain to every muscle in his body. His head ached so much he wondered if he'd been horse-kicked. And thirst—his tongue was stuck to the roof of his mouth.

When he looked past the edge of the mattress his gaze came to rest on what appeared to be a pair of knees covered by a dirty gray skirt. Glancing up, he saw a middle-aged woman asleep in a rocking chair beside the bed, her work-reddened hands folded around a rag doll that sat on her lap. She was a God-awful plain-faced thing and her dress was covered with dried mud. Her straggling hair looked as though birds had been nesting in it and there were purple shadows beneath her eyes.

Panic momentarily seized him. He jammed his hand under the pillow, looking for the gun he always kept with him when he slept. It wasn't there, and he felt defenseless and naked without it. He groped around in his mind trying to unravel the puzzle but his memory failed him. Where the hell was he and how had he gotten here? And why did he feel so rotten? This was worse than any hangover and he couldn't recall getting drunk.

He saw a glass of water on the nightstand and was sure if he didn't get a drink, he'd shrivel up and die. Hoisting himself up slowly on one elbow, he grasped the glass and took a sip. He frowned at the salty taste but drank it anyway. A wave of dizziness washed over him and when he tried to set the glass down it fell and shattered on the hardwood floor.

Chloe woke with a start. For a moment her eyes locked with his. Those eyes were as gray and threatening as a winter sky, she noticed. She had to look away from their dark scrutiny.

"I'm sorry," she began, "I guess I fell asleep." Now that he was awake she felt uncharacteristically timid.

Her statement told him nothing except the obvious. "Who are you?" he demanded, his voice still hoarse. "Why am I being kept here? As a matter of fact, where is 'here'?"

Conquering her reluctance to get too close to him, Chloe knelt and picked up the broken pieces of glass. "You don't remember what happened to you?" Putting the shards on the nightstand, she perched nervously on the edge of the rocker. She couldn't forget how quickly he'd moved earlier, or how easily he'd pushed her away.

"If I did would I be asking?" he snapped, a sharp frown creasing his scraped forehead. He felt he should recognize her but couldn't imagine why.

His rude hostility tweaked Chloe's temper. "Mister McGuire, I don't like your attitude. I'm only trying to help you." Where was the polite man who had begged for water in her backyard only a few hours ago?

He shot her a flinty, suspicious glance. "How do you know my name? Damn it, lady, I want some answers!"

The severity of his furious gray stare pinned her to the rocker. She remembered the manacles in his saddlebag, that he was a dangerous man, and her anger faded to apprehension, which she knew showed plainly on her face.

That look both annoyed and satisfied Travis. He'd get to the bottom of this damned quick.

"My name is Chloe Maitland and you're in Misfortune."

"Tell me something I don't know."

She suppressed a sigh. "The name of the *town* is Misfortune."

He looked at her a moment, searching his memory for the reason this sounded familiar. Then he hit on it. "Oh, yeah. Hard Luck."

She ignored the remark and went on to relate the day's events, stressing how seriously ill he had been and still was. When she had explained what he wanted to know, his memory was sufficiently nudged to recall what had happened and his frown diminished a bit.

"That still doesn't tell me why you know my name," he reminded her.

That he'd almost died didn't seem to trouble him nearly as much as her knowledge of his identity. At this point, she thought it was an unreasonable thing to be upset about, but the hard glint behind his swollen lids told her he expected an answer.

"You told me your name not more than four hours ago, right here in this room."

Travis found this very hard to credit. He never told anyone his last name if he could possibly avoid it. His survival might depend on it. There was only one other way this dried-up hag could have learned who he was.

"You're lying. Where's my saddlebag?" he asked, his tone demanding and surly again.

"Downstairs in the kitchen," she responded. Chloe could only hope she sounded casual. That saddlebag with the damning evidence she'd discovered because she'd snooped. It didn't matter that her intentions had been innocent.

"And did you look in it?"

Chloe had sensed the question coming and fearful guilt bloomed in her. She'd obviously learned something he didn't want anyone to know. Should she tell him the truth and risk his almost certain anger, or should she lie and perhaps even save her own life? There was no way of telling what form his fury might take.

Dodging the direct question and trying to appear unruffled, she replied, "I make it a point to mind my own business. I know your name because after Doc and I carried you up here, you seemed to wake up for a moment. I gave you a drink of water and asked you your name. You told me."

Travis dimly remembered that except he thought it had been part of his nightmare. He sank wearily to the pillow, satisfied for the moment.

Feeling the sheet brush his bare hip, he lifted the covers and looked down. Their eyes met for a moment, then he let the sheet drop and crossed his arms over his chest. "And did you undress me, too?"

This was too much! Resentful of his question and unnerved by the memory of his long, muscled torso, her outraged modesty made her answer without thinking first. "Of course not! Doc had to cut off your clothes and I was not present when he did it!" The words were out before she realized she could be adding fuel to his cooling anger.

"Cut off my clothes!" He would have been shouting if his voice were not still hoarse. "And tell me, Florence Nightingale, what the hell am I supposed to wear? They were the only ones I own!"

Now that his clothes were gone, so was the chance for a quick getaway, she assumed.

He jerked himself up to his elbow again and leaned forward, his eyes fixed on her face. "Who told the sawbones to do that?" he demanded. But as quickly as his rage flared it left him, the exertion costing him the little strength he had. He flopped back against the mattress and closed his eyes.

Chloe had shrunk back into her chair, her heart thudding in her chest at his outburst. But when he appeared to lose consciousness she jumped up and placed her cool hands against his face.

"Ouch!" He winced and pulled away.

Fearing another dose of his wrath, it took her a moment to catch herself. Why should she be afraid of him? And how dare he speak to her like that? She certainly was not going to let him think he'd have the upper hand with her.

"Mister McGuire, I don't know why you are so angry with me. If I had refused to let you stay here you might be dead by now. You came into my yard, uninvited, looking for a job and a drink of water. You passed out on my lawn and took five years off my life trying to die in my kitchen. I've answered your questions. Now I have one. Why in the world should I hire a man as rude as you?"

He eyed her carefully, properly scolded, but not cowed. "Because you won't get anyone else to work here for what you're offering. And I'm one hell of a lot better than nothing."

She stood over him, uncomfortable with that assessing stare of his and astounded at his gall. Why, he was insufferable! She was especially annoyed because she could think of no rebuttal to his glaring truth. Three months had passed since she ran her advertisement. She may as well have stood on her front porch and sung "Yankee Doodle" for all the response she'd gotten. But she wasn't desperate enough to invite this fugitive to stay.

"I think you overestimate your value, Mister McGuire." Her tone became commanding. "Now I'm going to change my clothes and fix some broth for your dinner. Please stay in that bed until I get back."

"I won't get far dressed like this, will I?" he asked, his voice tired but sarcastic.

"Forget your clothes for now," she advised, her patience dangerously low. "We'll work out something later."

"I don't have much choice," he muttered.

She sighed in exasperation and fatigue. "Must you always have the last word?"

With sullen stubbornness, he rolled over to face the opposite wall, silently dismissing her.

Chloe stared at his naked back for a moment,

confounded by his behavior. And in her mind a clock began ticking by which she would measure his progress till the day he was well enough to leave.

"Don't worry about thanking me for my help, McGuire. I would have done the same for any sick animal that wandered into my backyard."

As soon as he heard the door close, Travis Patrick McGuire rolled over again and stared at the ceiling. Looking at the wall reminded him too much of the other one he'd stared at for five years.

Misfortune. What a fitting name. It didn't matter to him that the town was in the middle of nowhere. Except for a couple of brief years, he'd felt like an outsider for as long as he could remember, full of anger and later, bitterness, no matter where he was.

When he read about this job it had sounded close to ideal, although six months earlier he'd sworn to himself he'd never go near a forge again. But desperation could drive a man to break all kinds of promises. He needed a corner of the world to hide in.

A clean scent wafted over him from the bed linens and he lifted the hem of the sheet to look at it. How long had it been since he'd slept in snow-white bedding like this?

Not since Celia.

Celia, Travis recalled darkly, just before sleep overtook him. That beautiful, unfaithful, nagging bitch he'd married when he was eighteen, the last woman he'd ever allow to get close to him.

Celia, staring at him from their bed with astonished eyes, still crystal blue even in death, his belt cinched around her slim, creamy throat.

After Chloe washed her face, repinned her hair, and changed her clothes, she went downstairs to fix dinner. She was at the stove, simmering beef bones for Travis's broth and mulling over her patient, when she heard pounding on the frame of the screen door.

"Miss Chloe! Are you there?"

Oh, dear God, she thought. Evan. Word had spread faster than she'd counted on. "Yes, Even, I'm coming," she called as she crossed the parlor to let him in.

"Miss Chloe, what's this I heard about that desperado attacking you in your yard?" he demanded as he stepped in.

"That's ridiculous, Evan. No one attacked me."

He looked at her with disbelief, as though she were plainly bruised and abused. "Mildred DeGroot told me she saw you running down the street, screaming, with your dress torn. She said you must have been beaten."

Damn that Mildred DeGroot, Chloe thought. It was bad enough that the woman and her husband blabbed incessantly about everyone, but they might at least get their facts straight before they started talking.

"Do I look like that?" She held her arms wide, inviting his inspection. "You should know better than to listen to the gossips, Evan. A stranger came into the backyard while I was doing the wash to ask about working in the shop. He was very sick and he collapsed. I was afraid he was dying and I ran to get Doc Sherwood." For the second time that day she explained their frantic efforts to revive Travis. She was careful to omit her discovery of the manacles. Just why she kept that secret, she wasn't sure.

"Well, where is he now?"

Chloe hesitated. Despite her confident remarks this afternoon, she really wasn't sure Evan would understand why Travis was asleep upstairs. Still, she plunged ahead. "He's staying here for the time being. Doc said it would be dangerous to move him."

Evan stared at her incredulously, his thin lips parted. "Here? Miss Chloe, that certainly is not proper! I don't approve of this arrangement and—and I forbid it! You can't live in this house alone with a strange man. You'll have to stay with the DeGroots or the Prestons while he's here."

Chloe's brows locked. He looked so proud of himself for standing up to her. She hadn't expected him to choose this time to assert his will over hers and it was irritating.

"For heaven's sake, Evan, the man is too sick to get out of bed. There's nothing indecent about him being here and I can't leave him alone while I stay somewhere else. I can't just let him die. Surely you wouldn't want me to do that."

"No, of course not," he responded without conviction, and then more vigorously, "but how does this look? What will people say?"

Ah, so that was it, Chloe realized, piqued. What will people say? Her patience had reached its end. She had been working all day, she'd had to deal with the perplexing, hostile Travis McGuire, and now Evan was lecturing her about moral propriety. If he knew about the manacles, she could imagine the howling he'd set up.

"If the opinion of this town is so important to you, then I don't care what you tell them," she snapped. "Naturally, I can understand that you wouldn't want to be disgraced by the scandal of my saving a sick man's life. Now I ask that you excuse me because I am very tired and I haven't eaten my dinner. Good evening, Mister Peterson."

Even stood rooted to the spot. She'd never spoken to him like this and she could see the effect of her words. Trepidation made his Adam's apple bob up and down.

"P-Please don't take offense, Miss Chloe. I didn't mean to insult you," he gulped, as though trying to unstick the sides of his dry throat. "It's just—I didn't intend to suggest that your purposes were—are immoral."

"Good night, Evan," she repeated, on the verge of tapping her foot to stress her desire that he leave.

"Uh, yes, well—good night, Miss Chloe," he stumbled, his brave moment at its end. He backed out the door, still making apologetic noises as he crossed the porch. She hooked the screen door to lock it and went back to the kitchen to fix a dinner tray for Travis.

The nerve of the man, she thought, slamming the silverware and a clean glass on the tray. How dare he question her actions and sit in judgment on her? He hadn't thought anyone might find it improper for him to have dinner alone with her all these months.

And Mildred DeGroot. Torn dress? Screaming? Leave it to the town crier's wife to assassinate her reputation.

Then there was her houseguest, she continued to fume. What a delightful person he was. Sullen, rude, argumentative—and an outlaw besides. And he wanted her to give him a job. At least he was conscious. As soon as he was well enough, she'd send him packing, saddlebag and all.

Her anger gave her a spurt of new energy and she marched up the stairs with the tray, as mad as she could remember being in years.

She entered the little bedroom and was relieved to find Travis awake and alert. His dark hair and beard were stark contrasts to the bedding's snowy whiteness. He looked menacing and out of place in the lace-edged room. She took a deep breath and forced herself to approach the bed.

When Travis saw the tray he dragged himself to a half-sitting position, wondering if he was in store for another tongue-lashing. He hadn't meant to be so short with her earlier. His temper showed itself most easily when he was cornered or frightened; he'd awakened in a strange place, sick, weak, and scared. Fiona McGuire had once compared her son's bad temper to a boiling kettle and warned it would bring him grief if he didn't pull it off the fire. He'd still not learned to control it very well. And he'd never learned to apologize with any grace so he didn't try.

Instead he asked, "Who were you arguing with

downstairs?" The muffled sound of her voice, tinged with vexation, had reached him, but he'd been unable to distinguish the words. The voice of the other person, a man, Travis thought, had been nothing but a low hum. He didn't know if he'd been able to throw Jace Rankin off his trail with that detour around Prineville, but if Jace had made it to this backwater, Travis would be leaving, sick or not.

His question startled Chloe. Had she and Evan been speaking so loudly? Hoping he hadn't heard the content of their conversation, she responded coolly, "I wasn't arguing, Mister McGuire. I was just visiting with a neighbor." She spread a napkin across his chest and put the tray on his lap.

Travis studied her for a moment. She didn't have the kind of face that could easily hide a lie so he let the matter drop. Now that she was cleaned up, she looked a little better, but still careworn. And she smelled good, kind of like sunshine. She wore a brown skirt and white blouse with a high neck. Her hair was a nice color, somewhere between red and blond, but it was bound to her head as though she were afraid it might be stolen.

"Do you want me to feed you or do you think you can manage it yourself?" she asked.

The question made his temper rumble but when he caught the scent of the broth, hunger triumphed and he let it slide. "Just give me the spoon," he said and impatiently yanked it from her hand.

Chloe sat on the rocker again, watching the spoon travel from the soup bowl to his mouth back to the bowl. "As soon as you've finished your dinner, I have to clean up your face and put some ointment on it. You're fairly scraped and bruised.

He'd just bet he was, after landing face-first on sunbaked dirt. He nodded and continued to spoon the rich broth into his mouth. He was beginning to feel stronger already, fortified by the simple meal.

Chloe wanted the answers to a dozen questions but hesitated to ask him anything after the way he'd behaved just because she'd learned his name. Still, there were certain things she felt were her right to know. She opened with a subtle inquiry.

"Are you from around here, Mister McGuire?"

Travis shook his head as he swallowed. Now the prying would start. "I've never lived anywhere for very long." He shot a glance at her. Did she know he'd been a guest of the state for almost five years?

"Is your husband the blacksmith?" he asked.

She stood and poured him a glass of water from the pitcher on the nightstand. The sunshine fragrance drifted to him again. "No, it's my father's business."

"Does your husband work here, too?"

Now it was Chloe's turn to feel defensive. Somehow he'd turned the conversation and put her in the position of answering questions. "I'm not married, Mister McGuire."

Another blacksmith's unmarried daughter, Travis thought sourly. He was struck by the overwhelming sensation of living a recurring nightmare. This was bad news all the way around. If he didn't need this hiding place, he'd be out of here as soon as he could put one foot in front of the other.

"Well, thank your father for letting me stay."

How easy it was to be polite to someone he'd never met, but he couldn't be civil to her, she smoldered. "You're stuck with having to thank me. Since my father died last spring, I'm the only one here." She could have bitten off her tongue for revealing that information in her haste to spite him.

Travis answered with like sarcasm. "Don't worry, lady. You're not my type."

Scorched with embarrassment, Chloe jumped from the rocker and snatched the barely finished tray from his lap. "I don't know what you're talking about."

"No? Well, you've just admitted that no one is home but you, you're blushing like a twelve-year-old, and you seem pretty peeved." He took a big drink of water and scowled again at the salty taste. "I admit it's a brave thing to do, taking a strange man into your house when you're here all alone. After all, I could be an escaped criminal or some other kind of outlaw." He threw out this last comment just to see how she'd react, but her face simply registered annoyance. "And I mean only to ease your mind. As I said, you're not my type."

Chloe slammed the tray on the dresser and reached for the tin of ointment and the water basin. Not his type, she simmered, telling herself she was glad. What possible interest could she have in a long-limbed, wide-shouldered man with hair on his chest? "I'm relieved to hear that, Mister McGuire. I'm sure my fiancé will be equally relieved when he learns of it." Fiancé? She could scarcely believe she'd said that.

Travis was skeptical, too. Was there a man who would willingly shackle himself to this woman? When she'd been younger, maybe—

She approached the bed with the basin and a towel. "I'll try not to hurt you." That, she thought with perverse satisfaction, will be nearly impossible.

"Well, come on, let's get it over with," he coaxed irritably. The little strength he had was fading and he wanted to get her out of the room. Dealing with her was exhausting.

Setting the rocker next to him, she dipped a corner of the towel in the water and touched the biggest gash on his cheekbone. He nearly flew off the bed. The sheet fell again, not even covering his lap. Chloe jumped back, his nudity firing embarrassment and wicked curiosity in her.

"Goddammit!" he croaked. "What's on the end of your hand? A wire brush?"

"I'm sorry," she replied, holding up the towel, now stained pink. "Let me try again. I promise I'll be more careful."

"Forget it, sister!" Travis lay down and dragged the sheet up. This pinched-up female would just have to find her fun someplace else, maybe by pulling the wings off a fly or something, but she wasn't going to touch his face again. "I'm not going to die from a few scrapes."

Chloe stared down at him with tremendous agitation. "Your face is a mess. I've got to put this medicine on it."

"*My* face is a mess! You're not exactly the first breath of spring, you know. Can you close your eyes to sleep at night with your hair skinned back and screwed down to your head like that?"

Automatically Chloe put a hand to her hair, surprised that a stranger's rude remarks could hurt so much. Her mental clock ticked louder. By God, she vowed, she'd snub him to the bedpost if that's what it took to get the medicine on his face. She wanted him patched up and out of her house.

Glaring at him, she went to her room and grabbed her silver hand mirror. She marched back to his bed and shoved the glass at him. "Look at yourself and tell me which of us looks worse."

He regarded her through the swollen slits of his eyelids.

"Go on." She shook the mirror at him again. "Take a good look!"

He slowly reached for the handle and looked into the glass. He stared at himself for several seconds, surprise and worry holding his attention. His right eye and most of that side of his face was as purple and swollen as an eggplant. Various raw abrasions still contained sand and dirt he'd picked up when he fell. Maybe this was serious.

Lowering the mirror, he mumbled, "I guess you're right."

"Excuse me, I didn't hear you," she pressed.

"I said you're right."

Mollified, Chloe continued, "Shall we try again?"

He nodded.

She sat on the edge of the mattress and dabbed at

the wounds with feathery strokes. Then she smoothed the ointment over them. His beard was prickly beneath her fingertips and his skin was hot. Under her hand, she felt his jaw clench and she didn't think he drew breath the whole time she worked on his face, but he remained still long enough for her to finish.

Wiping her hand on the towel at the washstand, she faced him. "I'm going downstairs to have my dinner now, but I'll be back afterward." She turned and pulled the door closed.

"Thank you."

It was said so quietly she wondered if it was meant for her.

A few minutes later, Chloe stood at the front door, breathing in the coming twilight. What a horrible day it had been.

She dragged herself upstairs and carrying her bedside candle, went to the nursery to check on Travis. She stood in the connecting doorway and looked at him. What had she been thinking of to put him in here, in such intimate proximity, with no way out but through her bedroom?

He was asleep on his side with his back to her. He'd kicked off the blanket and only the sheet was wrapped around his middle, leaving his long legs uncovered. One foot hung over the end of the bed. Chloe stared with curiosity at a red stripe encircling his ankle. In the low light she couldn't make out what the mark was. Tiptoeing closer, she held the candle higher. The shiny red line appeared to be a newly healed wound. Over the bone the angry scar was especially deep, as if something had rubbed away the flesh.

Something like a manacle.

Suddenly she remembered all she knew and didn't know about Travis McGuire and fear rose in her again. But as he lay there, reluctant compassion elbowed aside her apprehension. The thought of him wearing iron manacles that ground off his flesh made her heart contract. And with a touch that was no more than the brush of a moth's wing, she briefly pressed one cool fingertip to the scar.

Then she went to her own room, leaving the door ajar.

She didn't hear Travis McGuire's weary sigh.

Chapter 4

After Chloe blew out her candle, she slept like the dead but she was awake at six the next morning. She put on a plain gray dress and, standing before the mirror, began to twist her hair into its knot and then stopped, her arms in midair. Travis McGuire's remark had stung more than she cared to admit, but it had been so long since she'd worn her hair any other way she didn't know what else to do with it. Tentatively, experimentally, she wound the shiny red-gold length instead of twisting it. She stood there a minute, holding it like that until she was hit with a bold inspiration.

Moving swiftly through the hall and down the stairs, she retrieved her sewing scissors from the parlor. Back in her bedroom, she stared with concentration into the glass and severed fine strands across her forehead and at her temples. Then dipping her hand into the pitcher, she dampened the tendrils and watched them curl. Again she wound her hair, but not so tightly this time, and pinned it in place on the crown of her head. The total effect was flattering to her face and made her feel very feminine.

Travis's baiting may have been partially responsible for this change, but from now till he left, she resolved, she would not let him bother her. She would just ignore his sarcasm and barbs. If he had no one to argue with, he'd give up. She took one last glance at her hair and smiled at herself in the mirror.

Travis was still asleep in the darkened nursery when she checked on him before going down to the kitchen to fix their breakfast and she had to wake him when she brought his tray.

"Good morning," she called as she stood next to his bed.

His face looked only a little better but he stretched and was able to sit up so she could set the tray on his lap.

"Morning," he responded. He looked at the dishes and found thin oatmeal, dry toast with strawberry jam, apple sauce, and weak tea. "It smells good," he said without enthusiasm.

"It's light food, but it's better for you right now."

Chloe moved around the little room raising the window shades to let in the early sun. As he munched the toast he took in her appearance. He realized she was younger than he'd originally thought. The purple smudges beneath her green eyes were gone and even her hair looked a little different. And along with her sunny smell, he thought he detected a touch of some flowery fragrance. Her skirt and blouse were plain but she moved well in them; they seemed to flow with her. She was taller than most women, but she had a willowy grace, accentuated by her long waist and softly rounded hips.

He'd seen less attractive females, he grudgingly admitted to himself.

"How are you feeling today, Mister McGuire?"

Mr. McGuire again. Every time she called him that, it rankled. If he hadn't been out of his head, he knew he never would have told her his last name. "Travis."

"All right, then. Travis."

"Better, I think."

Then maybe he'd be more civil today, she hoped. She resumed her post in the rocker and started the chair in motion while they studied each other.

He was so different from any man she'd ever met, so irritating and threatening, she didn't know how to deal with him. Those long limbs, those pale gray eyes—

"You've changed your hair," he said, gesturing at her head with his fork.

Startled out of her thoughts, she fidgeted and looked at her lap. Now that he'd noticed, she felt a little foolish. She certainly didn't want him to get the idea that his criticism had made her hurry to alter her hair. "You caught me on a bad day, yesterday. I always wear it like that when I do the washing."

"It looks nice," he continued, his eyes returning to his breakfast. "Looser or something."

It occurred to her then that he might be apologizing for his previous insult. "Thank you. I'll change your pillowcase after you eat and put more ointment on your face. You rubbed most of it off during the night."

The prospect of more ointment made him frown at his plate. When he looked up, he caught her staring at the outline of his legs under the sheet. He waited for her to ask about the scar on his ankle she'd discovered the night before.

That wound was the last thought on Chloe's mind as she looked at his legs. Embarrassed at the disturbing turns her thoughts had taken when she glanced at him, she blurted, "I was wondering how you got this far with no horse, no water, starving, beaten."

Relieved, he supposed it was a fair question, but he didn't know what to say that wouldn't reveal that part of his past he wouldn't discuss. After a minute of chewing and thinking, he said, "I didn't have any choice. I had a horse, but he stepped in a gopher hole about forty miles from here. He broke his leg. I had to shoot him. I was thrown when he went down and landed on my face."

For her own peace of mind, Chloe gave him the benefit of the doubt, hoping that might explain why there were only four bullets in his revolver.

"I hated having to put him down," he continued pensively, "but I couldn't help him. So I started walking and I ran out of water before I ended up here."

Just then a knock sounded at the front door downstairs.

"That must be Doc," Chloe said, rising from the chair. "He said he'd stop in the morning to see how you're doing."

When she left the room, Travis sighed, glad for the interruption. He didn't know how long it would be before she started asking more pointed questions. In fairness to her, he had to admit she wasn't as nosy and gabby as some would have been under the circumstances. He leaned over and set the tray on the table next to him just as a tall, elegant-looking man with flowing white hair came into the room.

"Well," the man said, appraising him. "Looks like you might make it after all. I wasn't sure yesterday." He approached the bed and held out his hand. "Miles Sherwood. I'm the doctor in these parts."

"Travis is my name," he replied, taking the man's hand. "I want to thank you for what you did yesterday. I can't say I remember any of it."

"Hell, son, if Chloe wasn't as quick-witted as she is, I couldn't have saved you." The doctor asked a few questions about how he was feeling and then examined his face.

"You're recovering faster than I thought you would. You'd better stay in bed for now," Doc summed up, "but you can have dinner downstairs in a couple of days, if Chloe doesn't mind. You should be up to it by then."

Getting out of bed sounded good to Travis, but he couldn't do that without pants. He shrugged. "I won't be going anywhere until I get some clothes. I heard you had to cut them off."

Doc sat in Chloe's chair and crossed his legs. "Sorry about that, but I couldn't see any other way to get you out of them. It's not easy to strip wet denims off an unconscious man. And I couldn't very well ask Chloe to help. She has a sassy tongue sometimes, and she might seem to have enough grit to hunt bear with a switch. Don't let that fool you. She hasn't had an easy life, but it's been a sheltered one."

Travis had seen almost nothing in this woman of the blushing shyness that would indicate a protected life. "It's hard to tell," Travis replied.

Doc stared at him for a long, uncomfortable moment. Travis stared back.

"Son," Doc began, "right after I graduated from medical school, the War Between the States got started. I ended up working as a surgeon at Andersonville—maybe you've heard of it. Anyway, I was there long enough to see what leg irons can do to a man's ankle and I know you're too young to have been involved in the war."

Travis felt the blood rising to his face and he looked away from the man's intense scrutiny, fixing his gaze on a bright square of sun on the hardwood floor.

"Now I don't know what kind of trouble you're in and I suppose it's none of my business, so I won't ask. My job is to patch you up. But I will tell you this. Chloe talks tough but she's one of the finest people I've ever known; fair, honorable, and trustworthy. She offered to take you into her home because I thought you'd die otherwise. God knows she has enough on her hands doing folk's laundry. And I would hate to think you'd take advantage of the hospitality you've been given here, if you know what I mean."

Travis gave a short nod, but kept his gaze averted and said nothing. Fury boiled in him. Did the doctor think he'd jump on that female and rape her? Or maybe steal the silver? He cursed his continuing bad luck, this time for letting the man see his ankle. Every time someone figured out he'd been in prison, he was on the road again. He'd always be running and would always be treated as though he were less than human, either because of Rankin or because of his past. It wore him out to think about it.

Doc continued. "Now you follow Chloe's instructions and cooperate with her. She'll have you back on your feet in no time."

"That's fine with me," was his sullen reply. "I want to be out of this bed as soon as I'm able." He wanted to add that he didn't want the silver and he sure as hell didn't want that old maid's virginity.

The doctor stood. "That won't be for a while yet. I'm not going to tell Chloe or anyone else about this conversation. If you want to that's your business."

Travis looked up at him and the hand that was offered. He saw no judgment in the doctor's eyes, only kindness. Slowly, he reached out to take the extended hand. "I appreciate that, Doc. Thanks."

Doc was already in the hall when Travis heard, "And the next time you decide to go for a walk, take some water with you."

Travis almost smiled.

Chloe was putting away the last of the lunch dishes when she heard a hesitant knock at the front door. She hung her apron and went to the parlor.

Silhouetted in the screen door she saw Evan Peterson holding a shaggy bouquet. She'd been thoroughly annoyed with him yesterday but now as he stood there, she was touched by his woebegone, lost-soul expression and her irritation faded.

"Hello, Evan," she said, opening the door to him. He came in and thrust the flowers at her like an embarrassed ten-year-old boy, his face pointed at the bright rag rug under his feet.

"Hello, Miss Chloe," he mumbled, raising his eyes only as high as her collar.

For an instant, Chloe thought Evan was staring at her bosom but discarded the suspicion. Evan Peterson? No one could accuse him of improper behavior.

She took the withered bouquet. "Goodness, Evan, these are lovely but you must have cleaned out Mrs. Tolliver's flower beds."

He looked up then, vehemence animating his face, and she almost stepped back from its strange intensity. "I wish they were more. I'd do anything for you." He took her elbow and directed her to the settee. "Please, I-I'd like to talk to you."

This new and unsuspected facet of his personality caught Chloe off guard. "Well, yes, of course, but let me put these flowers in water first," she replied. "I'll bring some iced tea, too."

She went to the kitchen and found a tall cut glass vase and pumped water into it, wondering all the while what had gotten into the man. When she came back to the parlor, she brought a napkin-lined tray with a pitcher and glasses and set it on the oval table in front of Evan. She looked at Evan a moment, then handed him a glass of tea and sat on the end of the settee, wishing she could shake off the creepy feeling he was giving her. She felt as though someone else's eyes, a stranger's eyes, were staring back at her through Evan's face, just watching. Her muscles tightened and she took a quick breath—

that was a silly notion. Nervously, she smoothed the doily on the arm of the settee.

He took a long, noisy drink from the glass, then blurted, "Miss Chloe."

She looked at him and as she did he grappled for her free hand with his damp fingers. Mild foreboding rose in her as she looked at him. She really didn't want a repeat performance of his embarrassing attempts to kiss her but he was behaving so oddly, she didn't know what to expect. Her senses narrowed and focused and without knowing why, she felt she was about to be faced with something unpleasant.

"Well—uh, we have known each other for several years, and uh, I have been formally calling on you for almost six months now . . ."

Evan paused here and swallowed. Chloe suddenly realized what was about to happen, the thing she'd dreaded and yet had felt curious about all this time. She was reminded of when she was a child and had turned over rocks in the garden, fascinated and at the same time repelled by the insects that scattered when the sunlight hit them. What a thing to remember now.

As she looked at Evan, his eyes occasionally met hers and then darted away.

He spoke again. "We seem to get along quite well, and since neither of us is getting any younger—"

Her brows lowered ominously.

Amending his poor choice of words, Evan said, "I mean time has a way of slipping by, and I have worried about you having no male protector . . ."

She saw a look of panic cross his features. The more he talked, the more he botched the whole thing.

"Miss Chloe, I want to marry you. And the sooner the better."

The words were out and lay between them like a shapeless lump of dough. Chloe felt her eyes widen and Evan hovered expectantly for her reply.

Knowing that some kind of response was required, Chloe said, "Yes, it's true we've known each other for quite a while, but your proposal comes as a surprise."

And it did, too. Although she had thought of it as an inevitability, hearing the words spoken came as a shock. It was like when Emma had died. She had known her mother could not get well, and yet when the end had come, she was still stunned.

As slim as her vanity was, it would not permit her to believe that fear of gossip was Evan's sole motivation for his proposal. Yet while she hadn't expected to feel ecstatic joy when he asked to marry her, she was surprised by the vague depression settling over her. It was all so cold, so businesslike. And she had only worried that he might try to kiss her again.

"Please don't be offended, Evan, but I would like to think about it before I give you an answer. I hope you understand."

"Naturally, you should think about it," Evan began weakly, then stressed, "but don't wait too long. I want to spare you from the rumors that are sure to crop up now that a drifter is living in the house. And while your—visitor—is here, perhaps I should come by every evening for dinner. It will give you a sense of security."

She clutched at the idea that he wanted to protect her, hoping she would feel heartened. She forced a smile and replied, "I suppose you're right."

He returned her smile then, obviously satisfied, and crossed to the door. "Then I'll see you this evening." He reached for her hand again, and suddenly leaned over and grazed her mouth with his dry lips. "Until then, Miss Chloe."

"Goodbye, Evan," she said as she watched him go down the steps. When he was out of sight, she went back inside and sank to the settee. A feeling of terrible emptiness enveloped her as his musty smell floated to her from the cushions.

The next morning before church Chloe was at the stove stirring tapioca when she heard a rustling noise and the sound of bare feet on the wood floor behind her.

Travis stood in the kitchen doorway, wrapped in his sheet. By the time he reached the table he was soaked in cold sweat and grabbed for the back of a chair.

Chloe saw him begin to weave on his feet and she rushed forward to press her shoulder against him until he could lower himself to the chair. She had forgotten how tall he was. And how warm he felt.

"Travis," she huffed, "I can't keep propping you and lifting you. You're just too big. Doc and I got you upstairs, but I can't carry you up again by myself."

She reached down and tightened the sheet across

his lap, her touch unintentionally intimate through the fabric. Mortified, she snatched her hand away and then compounded her mistake by glancing at his face. She saw a flare of something compelling in those gray eyes as he stared back, a restrained energy, and her face heated with a scorching blush.

"Excuse me—I didn't mean to—why are you downstairs, anyway?" she demanded irritably.

Travis waited a deliberate moment before releasing her from his gaze, savoring her embarrassment. Then he raised a shaking hand to rake his hair off his forehead. He was a lot weaker than he'd thought when he began this trip to find her. "I want my saddlebags. You've got them and I want them," he said.

Those things again! she thought with annoyance, her embarrassment forgotten. Her anger rose in spite of her vow to check her temper around him.

She strode to the pantry, returned with the bags and threw them across the table to him. The tablecloth wadded up beneath them and slid askew. "You can wear them, you can sleep with them for all I care! Why you'd keep those broken shackles is beyond me!"

His dark head came up sharply.

"Yes, yes," she continued impatiently, with no thought for what she was saying. "I knew about it the first hour you were here. I went through these things trying to find your extra clothes. I didn't mean to pry. But it didn't require many brains to figure out you escaped from jail, and it wouldn't surprise me to see a posse ride up to my front porch any day. Personally, I don't give a damn about your name or your saddlebags or who you are. You aren't doing me any favors by gracing me with your presence. So far, all you've meant to me is aggravation and more work."

"There's no posse—" he began, but she cut him off as though he hadn't spoken.

Jabbing him in the chest with her index finger, she continued. "But I locked up your revolver because you are a stranger and I'm alone with you in this house. Even you must agree that given the circumstances, I'd have to be a simpleton to let you keep a loaded gun tucked under your pillow!"

Travis stared at her, eyebrows lowered. "Don't you want to know what kind of crime I committed so you can blab to your other busybody friends?"

Chloe's wrath was working up to a full boil and it felt wonderful to vent it on the cause of her frustration. She stood before him, feet planted wide, voice raised. "I told you, McGuire—oh, I beg your pardon—Travis, I'm truly not interested," she lied, "and if you knew me you'd also know better than to suggest I'm a busybody. You don't matter enough to tell anyone about!"

God, but she had a temper! A temper as hot as his. Her face was pink with anger and her eyes were snapping. He might have been a little rough on her but she dished it out with twice the passion.

"Doc's right. You do have a sassy tongue."

Chloe stared at him, her mouth open in preparation to further defend herself for going through his belongings. This was the last thing she expected him to say. She heard the pitch of her voice increase significantly.

"Miles Sherwood said that about me?" How dare he make such a remark to an outsider, especially this one? Now she felt like smacking Doc as well as Travis.

Travis massaged his aching forehead, careful to avoid his right brow. "Yeah, and I agree with him. Somebody ought to take you down a peg. You've got a tougher crust than a bad pie."

He stayed calm but Chloe sputtered with indignation at his criticism. "Down a peg? I'd like to see you try!" She ground out the words.

"Huh, not me, thanks. I'm not interested in a job that hard. I only shoe horses, which I can't do dressed like this."

"You are far ahead of yourself, mister. I didn't say I would hire you. As a matter of fact, I don't plan to."

"You'll change your mind."

"Oh, really!" She couldn't believe the gall of this man, dictating terms to her.

"Even if you don't, I still have to get something to wear. There's money in here"—he gestured at the offending saddlebag—"and I was going to ask you to buy me some pants and a shirt. This sheet isn't my size."

Chloe's anger deflated a bit. "But Doc said you won't be well for a few more days."

"He also said I can have dinner downstairs when I feel up to it and I'm going to feel up to it tomorrow night. I'm not used to lollygagging and if I don't get up pretty soon, I'll lie in that bed forever. I don't think either of us wants that."

Oh, that was just fine, she thought, nettled. Evan would be here for dinner. She regretted telling Travis that Evan was her fiancé, but he'd goaded her into it. And now he wanted to eat downstairs. A jailbird sitting down to eat with her and Evan? It was one thing to take a dying fugitive into the house to save his life—it was quite another to have him sit down at the table with her. Heaven knew what vicious crimes he'd committed.

"And coffee," he added. "Take part of that money and buy a pound of coffee. I'm sick of that everlasting tea."

"Are you sure you're ready? To come downstairs, I mean? Tomorrow night seems so soon." Silently, she willed him to deny it.

Travis watched as the wheels turned in her brain, then gave her a dark-gray look. "I suppose I could find the dry goods store myself if you don't want to help."

Cornered, she held out her hand for the money. "DeGroot's won't open till tomorrow morning. And you need new boots, too."

"'And I looked, and behold a pale horse: and his name that sat on him was Death, and Hell followed with him,'" thundered Reverend Adam Mitchell from his makeshift pulpit, his fleshy face red with exertion. He stood at the head of the schoolroom, pounding his fist on the lectern. He came through Misfortune once a month, whether the town needed him or not, to save souls, perform weddings, and speak over the dead.

The reverend was a pompous, haughty man whose depressing sermons dealt primarily with the wages of sin, the importance of Christian charity to avoid damnation, and the necessity of prayer.

Every six months or so, Mr. Mitchell felt duty-bound to step up his efforts and would set out a dragnet to pull in any wretched stragglers who might have wandered from the paths of righteousness. Today's joyless monologue warned of burning in the fiery pits for transgressions too numerous for him to cover. Holding the congregation's attention by the sheer volume of his voice, his intimidating gaze fell on each face in the school, rousing feelings of guilt where no real guilt existed.

When his eyes lingered on Chloe, she shifted on the bench. She'd been listening with only half an ear, due in part to her confrontation with McGuire earlier. Her attendance had fallen off since her father's death. A person seeking hope and solace in Reverend Mitchell's church was bound to come away disappointed. The wrathful God Reverend Mitchell presented did not agree with what her idea of what God was like. Surely He had more tolerance for human failings.

Frank Maitland had thought Reverend Mitchell was decidedly lacking in the skills necessary in a spiritual advisor and usually referred to the man as God's Windbag. Frank had hung this title on the reverend after he came to the Maitlands' to deliver a temperance speech.

She could imagine her father watching her from wherever his spirit had flown, counting himself lucky to have escaped another of Mitchell's come-to-Jesus-or-else sermons.

By the time the blessing was pronounced, Chloe's tailbone ached from prolonged contact with the hard bench and her legs were almost numb. She made her way toward the door where the reverend was already bidding goodbye to his much-relieved flock.

Trying to escape unnoticed, she was on the bottom step when she felt a hand clamp down on her shoulder.

"Chloe, dear," Mitchell said. "I was hoping to speak with you."

Her stomach clenched. Something about Adam Mitchell made her distinctly uncomfortable. She knew other women in town flocked around the bachelor like brainless twittering birds, parading their marriageable daughters, inviting him to Sunday dinner, organizing bake sales to fund a real church building, and blushing like schoolgirls when he favored them with his attention.

Chloe was not among that group of slavish admirers. She sent a brief, desperate glance around the dusty school yard, looking for anyone she could draw into the conversation, but it was hopeless. He had her cornered.

"I can't tell you how pleased I was to see your lovely face with us today," he said. Although his words were innocent enough, his tone and manner felt too personal to Chloe. "We have missed you in these past months since Mister Maitland's passing."

She gave a short nod, hoping to keep the conversation brief.

"The reason I wanted to speak with you, Chloe, is because I was talking with Grady Hewitt at the bank yesterday. He said you might be interested in earning some money."

Grady was the bank president. Chloe could scarcely believe what she was hearing. Was her every movement and waking breath common knowledge? Did the entire town know she owed money to the bank? She sighed. Probably, and they probably knew how much as well. Everyone's business was everyone's business in Misfortune. Still, she considered it extremely ill-mannered of Mitchell to bring it up, especially in front of everyone.

"Mister Mitchell, this is hardly the time or place to discuss—"

"Now, now, my dear," he clucked in a low voice, patting her hand. "Of course we won't talk about it now. I'll be in the area for a few days. What I'd like to do is come by one afternoon next week. I think you may be interested in what I have to propose."

Chloe doubted that. A very brusque reply formed in her mind but it was tempered by a childhood remnant of respect for his position as a clergyman. "Really, that isn't necessary—"

Just then, Sylvia Westerman came up, her seventeen-year-old Eula lumbering behind her. Rumor had it that one late evening at the Twilight Star, Albert DeGroot had observed that the chief difference between Eula and his mare was that his horse had the prettier face.

"Mister Mitchell, you positively must come to dinner this afternoon. Eula has learned a new hymn on the piano and she's just dying to play it for you."

Chloe saw her chance for escape and took it,

mentally thanking poor, awkward Eula while she hurried down the street toward home.

The clock marked the hour of half-past eleven that night as Chloe sat at her father's rolltop desk, pen in hand, shuffling papers while she again reviewed her financial situation. What was she going to do? The mortgage payment was due in sixty days and she had no idea where the money was going to come from. Evan, she knew, had no assets. His teaching job paid only sixty dollars a year. It would be up to her to provide a home for them if they married.

She put the pen down and rubbed her forehead, her eyes tired from working under the harsh lamplight.

Why couldn't her life have been different? she wondered, not for the first time. In a rare moment of self-pity, she thought it seemed like she either had bad luck or no luck at all.

Her sense of helplessness was doubled because she couldn't find someone to work in the shop. Since Frank's death, everyone around Misfortune had been getting by with their own blacksmithing, and making a poor job of it from what she understood. Even though the town was far past its prime, she wouldn't suffer from a lack of business. But who was there to do the work? Room and board were not much compensation but were times so prosperous that even one man didn't need such basics?

One such man is sleeping upstairs right now, she reminded herself.

No. Travis McGuire was beyond consideration. Aside from the fact that he was in trouble with the law, an unacceptable drawback in itself, his quick anger and rudeness would make him impossible to deal with.

And, of course, there were those other disquieting traits about him that sparked feelings in her she shouldn't be having at her age.

The stairs creaked suddenly and her head snapped up. Beyond the reach of the light a ghostly white figure was descending. It took her a moment to realize it was her patient.

"Why are you sneaking around like that?" she demanded, fright and discouragement sharpening her voice. "You shouldn't be down here at this hour, anyway. You're sick."

Travis approached the desk, wrapped in his sheet like a Roman at the baths. Any other man would look ridiculous in such a getup. He didn't. "I wasn't sneaking. It's hard to stomp barefoot."

He was much steadier on his feet than he had been this morning. The clean scent of him, subtle yet distracting, drifted to her. "Well, do you want something?"

He glanced at her ledger and at the wads of paper littering the desk. She looked tired and pinched again, like she was worried.

"I want a decision from you. Do I have a job or not?"

Chloe couldn't believe her ears. This man, this outlaw, had insulted her, abused her hospitality, and tried her patience in a dozen different ways. And still he thought she might hire him.

"I believe I made myself very clear about that this morning. It just wouldn't work out."

He gestured at her ledger. "Things are going that well, are they? Looks like you can't afford to be so fussy about this. You need me." And he needed to be here.

She slammed the book shut and leaned back in her chair. Why did he seem to know things without being told? It was unsettling. "No, things are not going that well." She hated explaining her money problems to a stranger but frustration pushed her to it. "A mortgage payment is coming due on this property in two months. I have ten dollars to my name and I've never been in this kind of fix in my life."

She sat forward again and folded her hands on the desk, her shoulders hunched. "I need a blacksmith to work in the shop to help me make that payment. But I want a nice man who won't insult me at every turn, a man who'll appreciate my help. I don't need a convict." She looked him directly in the eye. "As bad as things are, I'm not that desperate."

He took a step backward then, out of the circle of lamplight, but not before she saw his expression. Ice-cold anger shone from his eyes, but there was something else, too. For just an instant she saw a flicker of injured pride and a tiny dart of guilt jabbed her. His voice came to her from the shadowed side of the parlor, hushed but heated.

"You say you want a 'nice' man to work here. What you really want is someone so miserable and down on his luck you can bully him. Some poor bastard who'll grovel at your feet like a stray dog for every bone you stoop to throw him. You're right, lady. That's not me."

Chloe was speechless. Nobody dared talk to her like that.

He turned and crossed to the staircase, his sheet rustling along the floor. Then he paused on the bottom step. "Don't forget to buy those clothes for me in the morning. I'll need them if I'm going to leave."

"You won't be leaving *tomorrow*," she countered. "You're not well enough."

"No, but since I won't be working here, I plan to be out of here as soon as I can." He didn't wait for her response before going up the stairs.

For several minutes she sat staring at nothing, the papers at her elbow forgotten. If she needed another reason to get Travis McGuire out of her house, she had it. Imagine him suggesting she was a bully when he was the one who gave her so much trouble. If fate was going to send someone to pass out in her yard, why couldn't he have been the one she needed instead of the hellion she got?

She looked down at her column of numbers and refigured them again and again, hoping to find an error in her favor. The total remained unchanged. Her gaze lifted to the darkened room, to all the modest furniture and possessions accumulated over generations, and she thought of them belonging to someone else. That was a real possibility.

Frank Maitland's troubles had ended last spring. His daughter's were just beginning.

Chapter 5

The next evening Chloe set the table for two, then hurried to fling porch chops, peas, and mashed potatoes on a plate for Travis. Evan would be here any moment and she wanted this chore behind her. She looked over her shoulder every couple of minutes, expecting to see the tall, dark-haired man standing in the kitchen doorway.

It just wasn't proper, she told herself again, to have a man of Travis McGuire's background and position sitting down to eat with her and Evan as though he were an honored guest. The very thought had her so flustered, she hadn't done anything right all day.

Then she'd hit upon a possible solution. It was a flimsy idea but it was all she had: she simply wouldn't wake Travis. He'd been asleep most of the time since he arrived; she'd just let him sleep through dinner. She'd take him a tray so if he woke, at least he'd have something to eat. But she'd also remove the new clothes she'd hung over the end of his bed to make sure he couldn't come down.

Her cooking had been rushed and nothing turned

out well. She'd spent the afternoon bent over the scrub board, then at DeGroot's buying Travis two complete sets of pants, shirts, socks, underwear, and a pair of boots. And since he'd complained so much about the tea, she had bought coffee for him, too. But she'd paid for that. Truthfully, she was getting tired of tea as well.

As far as tonight's dinner went, the only thing she felt good about was the chocolate cake she'd made this morning for dessert. She'd have to serve Evan the dismal meal. He wouldn't complain, of course. He'd eat a boiled string mop if she told him to.

Travis, she knew, wasn't so agreeable. She stared at the burned, leatherlike chops on the tray, wondering what to do about them. Finally she cut them up into small, manageable bits and carried the tray upstairs.

She stood in the doorway between her room and the nursery, watching him. He *looked* asleep. She tiptoed in, her skirts swishing. To her ears it sounded like the wind stirring a hundred acres of wheat. Why did a person make the most noise when they wanted to be quiet? she wondered. She set the tray on the nightstand, her heart pounding as though she were afraid of being caught in the act of an atrocious crime.

Suddenly Travis rolled to his back and sighed. Chloe froze. When he didn't open his eyes or move again, she pressed her hands to her skirts and glided from the room. She felt very clever.

* * *

The room had a warm somnolence to it and it was easy to drift in peaceful suspension where there were no memories or nightmares. The shades were pulled against the late afternoon sun and Travis lay on his back, eyes closed, his pillow hugged to his chest with one arm.

He thought he heard a rustling, like the whispering of petticoats, but he ignored it until the noise stopped. Finally a combination of scents stirred him; of meat and potatoes, of feminine fragrance. Glancing around he saw that Chloe had left a dinner tray on the nightstand next to him and his mouth began to water. The hellcat had brought him real food at last. Since coming here she'd had him on broth, porridge, and bread, and before that, he'd survived on skimpy food that traveled well, beef jerky and the occasional rabbit. Thank God, she'd given him coffee, too.

He sat up and lifted the tray to his lap, looking forward to his first full meal in weeks. Then voices floated to him from the main floor and he remembered he was going downstairs for dinner tonight. But the tray on his lap indicated that Chloe had other ideas. Upon closer examination, he saw she'd taken what appeared to be pork chops and cut them up into pieces so small she must have thought he was as toothless as a newborn. Next to the bits of meat was a cold, loose blob of mashed potatoes mixed with dried-up green peas. He poked the mess around the plate with his fork and even tried a taste or two before giving up in disgust. If this was a sample of her cooking, it was a good thing he wouldn't be working here. She'd offered room and board in her advertisement. He'd assumed the board would be edible and this sure didn't qualify. On top of all that, his nakedness trapped him in this room.

It was then he noticed the new clothes draped over the end of the iron bed. He put the tray back on the nightstand and closed a hand around a leg of the jeans.

If she wanted her romantic little dinner for only two, she should have fed him something better than this.

"Will you have more potatoes, Evan?" Chloe asked with a straight face. The potatoes had a consistency of wallpaper paste.

"Yes, thank you," he replied and took the bowl from her.

She was glad to see that Evan's appetite was voracious again tonight, soothing her regret for the quality of this dinner. She'd looked forward to spending some quiet time with him. He wasn't a prince on a white steed, but at least he respected her and didn't threaten her in the dark, troubling ways Travis did. She was thinking of her decision not to hire the drifter when she heard the ominous thumping of boot heels moving across the floor overhead.

Both she and Evan looked up at the ceiling, their gazes following the path of the sound as it headed toward the staircase. Oh, damn! she thought. She'd been so worried about waking up Travis that she'd forgotten to move his clothes. It would seem he'd found them.

"Wonderful," she said under her breath, then put

her napkin on the table. "Excuse me a moment." Ignoring Evan's puzzled expression, she rose from her seat to head Travis off in the parlor.

She saw him at the bottom of the stairs, carrying his tray like it was a box of scorpions.

His transformation was both intriguing and disturbing.

His face was not yet healed and since he hadn't shaved, his dark beard masked his features more each day. But he was somewhat combed and his new clothes fit very well, distractingly so. The denim pants hugged his long slender legs and backside as though they'd been tailored for him. The shirt she'd chosen, a plain chambray, stretched across his broad shoulders and tapered along his narrow waist. No man had the right to look that good, she thought.

"I didn't think you'd feel like getting up yet," she said, trying to will him back to the steps. Evan didn't need to meet Travis. Not just yet anyway.

"You *hoped* I wouldn't feel like getting up yet," he corrected. He frowned at the mess on the tray and launched into his complaint. "You couldn't keep a chipmunk alive with food like this."

"Will you keep your voice down, please? My fiancé—" she caught herself but not in time. "I have company in the dining room," she hissed and glanced over her shoulder.

It was then he noticed that she was dressed up. Her hair, pulled softly to the loose knot on top of her head, gave her a less rigid appearance. She wore a crisp pale blue blouse with enormous sleeves and tight cuffs that reached her elbows and gave her femininity a much-needed boost. A cameo fastened her high, close-fitting collar. Her skirt was cream-colored and that surprised him—Chloe Maitland struck him as the kind of woman who'd never wear such a color because it would only get dirty. All this fancy dressing must be due to her special caller. His curiosity was kindled. Travis wanted to get a look at the man willing to take her on. He'd have to be tough enough to wear sandpaper for underwear.

"Well, maybe I'll get something better than this if I join you," he said and started to push past her.

"No, no, you can't do that," she replied, panicky. She did not want to get into the complications of having the two men meet. What if Travis said something at the table to make Evan believe she'd accepted his proposal when she hadn't? And how would Evan react to this intimidating stranger?

"Besides, what I gave you is no worse than what we're having. You may as well just take this food back upstairs." She pushed the tray more firmly into his hands.

Why was she so skittish? he wondered. It might be this Evan was a hulking buffalo with a jealous streak who would make all kinds of wrong assumptions. "Maybe your intended won't like my being here," Travis ventured.

"Miss Chloe, is everything all right?" Evan called from the dining room.

Truthfully, Travis didn't care whether her company liked it or not. He was hungry. He stepped around her and made his way to the table. If there was going to be a problem with the fiancé, he'd face it head-on.

Seeing Evan, he nearly laughed aloud at his wildly inaccurate mental picture of him. This juiceless milksop looked as though he'd be afraid of the dark. But as Chloe introduced them and Evan extended his hand with obvious reluctance, Travis felt every hair on his body rise. His appetite drained away and a peculiar aversion overtook him. The sensation was so powerful Travis could only stare at Evan, who twitched under the inspection.

"Peterson," Travis acknowledged brusquely. After the teacher's damp, limp handshake, Travis barely suppressed the urge to dry his hand on his jeans.

The tension in the room was so heavy, Chloe swore she could see it. "Shall we eat?" she suggested weakly.

The meal proceeded at a snail's pace. As dishes were passed among the three, Travis was watchful and silent, Chloe struggled to keep conversation going, and Evan yipped out one-word responses to her dinner table remarks. In all, it was the worst hour she'd ever spent. She was so annoyed she failed to notice that Travis never tasted one bite until the meal was nearly over.

The evening did have its blessings, she noted as she cleared the table. Evan was too intimidated to ask Travis any questions about himself. Travis's closemouthed hostility prevented him from talking to Evan and possibly revealing the lie Chloe had told about their supposed engagement. And the outlaw's presence almost guaranteed she would not have to sit on the porch swing with Evan after dinner.

Indeed, as soon as the last dish was removed from the table Evan was up and on his way to the door. Travis had succeeded in scaring him off and Chloe was mortified.

"I hope I'm not being too rude, Miss Chloe, to eat and leave so quickly, but I have to be up before daybreak tomorrow to help Ben Tolliver." His eyes flickered to Travis, who sat unmoving at the table, his gaze steady upon the teacher.

"Why, no, Evan, I understand if you feel you must go. But I have chocolate cake and coffee for dessert. Are you sure you can't stay for some?" She followed him to the front door.

"No, really, I have to be on my way," Evan stressed, his hand already on the screen door. "Perhaps I can drop by tomorrow afternoon—when you've made tea." He glanced pointedly at Travis again, then back at Chloe, as if to say, *I hope he's gone by then.* "Will you save a piece of cake for me?"

"Of course. I'm so glad you could come tonight." Chloe had never felt more humiliated.

Travis rose from his chair and began walking toward the kitchen, then stopped. Looking back at Evan, he said, "Nice meeting you, Peterson."

To Chloe, it sounded like, "I'll see you in hell."

Chloe stormed into the kitchen. "Couldn't you have tried a little harder to be pleasant? First you barged in on our dinner, then you practically ran

Evan off. I have to believe your mother taught you better."

Travis was leaning against the back doorjamb, sipping a cup of coffee. He turned a flat look on her, which did not frighten her as it had Evan. She expected him to shout back. Instead, he pushed himself away and walked toward her. He paused, his face just inches from hers, and held her with that same closed expression.

"My mother didn't teach me anything about snakes, but my old man did."

Chloe gazed up at him, suddenly mesmerized by a primal force she hadn't noticed in him before. "Snakes?"

"He said never turn your back on them, and get rid of them as fast as you can." He put the cup in the sink. "Thanks for the coffee," he said, then turned and strode to the parlor.

Chloe stared after him, her mouth slightly open, knowing only that for one instant, she did not control the situation. Travis did. And she wasn't completely certain she disliked it.

Travis lay naked on his narrow bed in the dark, the hot night close around him. Only the faintest breath of air stirred the curtains. He'd left the door ajar between his room and Chloe's to catch the occasional cross draft, but it wasn't helping much. Anyway, the small room felt too much like a cell when the door was closed. He couldn't stand confining spaces and now that he was getting well, he was more aware of the walls around him.

While the clock downstairs chimed only ten times, he felt like he'd been lying there for hours, restless and edgy, chasing sleep that remained beyond his reach. It often did.

Tonight it was because he couldn't get Evan Peterson out of his mind. The teacher lurked there in the shadows of his thoughts, nagging at him with a vague sense of dread, worry—something—and he didn't know why. Travis only knew he didn't trust the man.

God, let it go, he told himself. He had enough problems without adding to the list.

He could see the dim silhouette of his clothes where they hung on the end of the bed. One more day here and then he'd be gone. This time he'd head west for the Silver Creek Ranch near John Day. Before he'd seen Chloe's blacksmith advertisement, he'd heard they were looking for a few hands. If he could sign on with the ranch, the job would probably last through fall roundup. Then he'd move on again. With the exception of a few years of marriage and prison, he'd never lived in any one place for more than several months.

Frustrated, he got up and sat on the chair by the window, propping his feet on the sill. Below, the yard lay frosted in moonlight and crickets called from the shadows. He let his head drop back against the chair's high back and closed his eyes.

He'd found that given the right amount of time and effort, a person could escape just about anything, good or bad. Loneliness, love, financial obligations, imprisonment of the body or spirit—there were ways around these and more. He'd seen people manage it many times. But memories were not put off so easily. They popped up anytime, invited or not, regardless of evasive mental maneuvers.

Sitting here in the darkness, his past rose in his mind and he saw his parents. Originally immigrated from famine-stricken Ireland, they had been good, loving people. But his father, possessed by a wander-lust and the unlimited promise of America, had taken his mother, brother, and him zigzagging from one side of the country to the other. Always the new boy wherever he went, and so a target to be chal-lenged, Travis had gotten into more than his share of fights.

This existence had turned him into a loner, an outsider who'd watched the secure lives of others with a painful longing that, in time, he'd been able to subdue but never conquer.

Travis was sixteen when his parents and younger brother died of cholera in a desolate Oregon Val-ley. Driving the wagon away from three unmarked graves, he'd not only been stunned by the loss but struggled with both guilt and relief that he'd myste-riously been spared. On his own now, he'd vowed to settle in the next fair-sized town he came to. He wanted the one thing his parents had not given him. He wanted a normal life—he wanted a home.

Three weeks later, he'd arrived in Salem and gone in search of his dream. He found Lyle Upton, a local blacksmith with a good business, and persuaded him to take on an apprentice.

His work with Lyle had been hot and hard, but

Travis thrived. He revealed a true talent for fashioning horseshoes, kettles, and wagon wheels. Finally, he'd settled down.

Then, too, there had been Lyle's daughter, Celia—

Suddenly he heard Chloe's footsteps in the next room and he opened his eyes. She'd get a real surprise if she decided to look in on him and found him sitting here, without a stitch on. And she apparently hadn't noticed that the door between their beds was ajar. Her candle flame threw a wedge of light on the floor next to him. He was getting used to her routine just by listening to her. The rustle of fabric reached him as she changed her clothes, the splash of water in her washbasin, the whisper of her brush through her hair. What did her hair look like when it was loose, flowing down her back? he wondered. Was it only as long as her shoulder blades or did it hang lower? Did it wave like an ocean of gold and copper wildflowers? Maybe it fell like a satin drape, heavy and lustrous. And her skin, it would be soft like the inside of white rose petals, smooth and yielding under his touch . . .

His sat up with a start when he realized the direction of his thoughts. He must be losing his mind if he could even *imagine* anything appealing about Chloe Maitland.

He waited a few silent moments after she blew out the candle. Then he went back to the old bed and lay down with an irritable huff to search for sleep again.

* * *

Chloe pushed her dust rag over the old sideboard. She remembered the dreadful, awkward dinner last night, and the scene that followed in the kitchen, and wondered if she'd imagined it all. Her jittery uneasiness had turned her hands so cold they looked blue. From the yard she heard the dull sound of hammer on wood where Travis was fixing one of the kitchen chairs. This was his first full day out of bed, and to have him up and around and well, *around*, was so intimidating she could barely keep her mind on her work.

Having him come downstairs to dinner had been bad enough. But last night, the sound of those screeching bedsprings had given him a new status, an extra edge of danger. She knew he'd been out of bed, maybe even watching her from that darkened room. She thought she'd gotten accustomed to him being there, on the other side of the wall. And she had, too, but as a patient. Now, an invalid no longer, he could prowl around his room, *her* room—the entire house. The possibilities had her so rattled, without thinking she rubbed her forehead with her grimy hand.

This morning he'd come downstairs, dressed, looking for things to do, and had taken it upon himself to mend the chair. He'd said lying around for a week had made him creaky and he wanted to stretch his legs because he'd be leaving tomorrow. And not a moment too soon, as far as she was concerned. Her orderly life had been in utter turmoil ever since he got here.

She was on her hands and knees, dusting the legs of the china cabinet when someone knocked on the screen door. She dragged herself out of the corner, and it occurred to her that in the last week she'd had more people coming to see her than in the whole six months since her father's death. Several had dropped by, she suspected, hoping only to get a look at "the stranger." Their neighborly interest in her welfare was too sudden to be believable.

But when she went to the front door she was disturbed to see Reverend Adam Mitchell on her porch. He was dressed completely in black, making her think of death. With everything that had happened in the past few days, she'd forgotten he was planning to come over. "Mister Mitchell, this is a surprise."

"Chloe, dear, I hope I haven't come at a bad time," he said, his hand on the door pull. His smile was broad and ingratiating, his voice as smooth as oil. "I know I didn't tell you which day I would be dropping by."

She pushed at her hair, loose in its pins. "I'm afraid you've caught me cleaning this morning. You'll have to forgive my appearance."

She wore an old faded dress she saved for housecleaning. Catching a glimpse of herself in the mirror on the hall tree, she saw a big smudge on her forehead.

"Nonsense, Chloe," he said, stepping in and removing his hat. "I think you're as lovely as a rose."

It was another of those personal comments that made her feel so uneasy around him. As he said it, his eyes traveled beyond her and around the room, as if he were looking for something. Or someone.

She motioned him to the settee. "Can I offer you tea or lemonade?"

He sat down and patted the upholstery next to him in invitation. "No, no, I don't want to put you to any more bother. I understand you've had a busy week. Your guest has created quite a stir around town."

Chloe stifled her irritation as she sat at the far end of the settee. There was no escape from Misfortune's curiosity and McGuire's arrival was probably the biggest event to happen here since the last gold mine went bust. She was just going to have to accept that.

"Mister McGuire came here in answer to my advertisement. But we decided that it probably wouldn't work out."

"Ah, that's a pity," Mitchell nodded sagely, "but it brings me to the proposal I want to discuss with you." He settled back more comfortably. "I know you've had quite a struggle since Brother Maitland passed on."

Chloe bristled at the familial term. There had been no love lost between her father and the reverend. In fact, they'd exchanged strong words on at least two occasions; once when Mitchell took it upon himself to reprimand Frank for his wicked life, and another time when he wanted a donation.

"I've managed," she answered carefully. "Things could have been easier, but I have a good roof over my head and I'm not starving."

Mitchell reached over and patted her hand. "You

know, I'm quite fond of you, dear. Your courage is in-
spiring. It makes me want to help you all the more."

As he spoke, she heard the quiet squeak of the
back door hinge. Soft footfalls, that could have easily
been mistaken for house creaks, sounded in the
kitchen. Mitchell appeared to notice nothing and in
an intimate tone, prattled on about her pluck. She
wondered where this conversation was headed. She
also wanted to pull her hand back, but it would
seem too rude.

"I've given a lot of thought to your predicament
and I've prayed and prayed, begging the Lord to
show me a solution. I believe He has finally answered those prayers."

Beginning to feel cornered, Chloe glanced over
the back of the settee and saw Travis in the kitchen
doorway, one shoulder braced against the jamb. His
arms were crossed over his chest and his eyes were
riveted on the back of Adam Mitchell's head.

"I appreciate your interest, Mister Mitchell, but
really—"

He continued as though she hadn't spoken, his
tone one of grave concern. "Hiring a stranger to live
and work here is very risky business, especially since
you're here alone. You would know nothing about
him. And think of the gossip you'll stir up." He
leaned toward her, as though to impart the wisdom
of the ages. "Now, I myself have a room in a boardinghouse in Vale and I was thinking I could rent a
room here just as easily and pay you the money.
Then every three or four weeks when I come to Misfortune to minister to my flock, I would stay here."

Chloe gaped at his jowly face. "You say *God* gave you this idea?"

He gave her a modest smile, as though she were overwhelmed by his genius. "I thought it was quite resourceful myself. We could work out a price that would include laundry and, oh, a few other personal services. Not having a wife, there are some— conveniences—I miss. And who knows," he smiled, his expression as oily as his voice, "if the congregation's needs increase, I may have to visit more often. You could do far worse, my dear. Life can be diffi- cult for the unworldly and unprotected, as you are discovering." He squeezed her hand, then pressed a wet kiss on it.

Chloe wrenched her fingers from his grip. Every suspicious feeling she'd harbored about the minister congealed within her. What a lecherous fraud, pass- ing himself off as a kind and decent man. He dis- gusted her.

"Mister Mitchell," she retorted, "my life may be 'unworldly' as you say, but I grew up in a mining town and I'm not naive. I need someone to work in my blacksmith shop. I'm not opening a boardinghouse—or a whorehouse—for you or any- one else. I would dig for gold in the hills, and starve to death if I failed, before I'd consider your revolting proposition." She jumped from her seat. "I want you out of my house, right now."

At her forthright response, Mitchell's expression turned flinty, his face red. "My dear, I enjoy your spirit, I really do. It's your most attractive quality. But you had better not be so hasty," he replied. "You

don't appear to be in a position to turn down my offer." He reached out and tried to grab her hand
again.

Furious words tumbled one over the other in her
throat, rendering her speechless.

"Miss Maitland asked you to leave."

Chloe turned toward Travis as he strode into the
room, his bruised brow creased with a frown. She'd
forgotten he was there, watching, waiting. He was
tall as it was, but suddenly he looked as big as a fir
tree, commanding and intimidating. His battered
face gave him a fearsome edge.

Startled, Adam Mitchell's head swiveled around to
look at the man who'd eavesdropped on his proposition. But he covered his astonishment and rose to
his feet. Travis deflected his imperious gaze as it
swept over him, taking in the minister with a dark,
assessing glare.

Travis leaned over and grabbed Mitchell's hat
from the settee and jammed it into the man's hands.
"Don't forget your hat," he said with a frightening
smile. Then he bent forward a bit and said in a low
voice, "One more thing. The next time you talk to
this lady, if there is a next time, she's Miss Maitland
to you, not 'Chloe', not 'dear', do you understand?"

Mitchell walked to the door, obviously trying to
maintain his dignity while hurrying. "I'd hoped to
save you, Chloe—Miss Maitland," he said, falling
back on self-righteousness. "But I'm afraid you're already lost."

Travis shut the door and Chloe heard the man's
footsteps as they crossed the porch and went down

the stairs. She dropped to the settee again, waiting for her nerves to calm. She glanced up at Travis, expecting some remark from him, but he only returned her gaze for a long moment. Then he turned and walked back through the kitchen. That he'd bothered to get involved at all was surprising. He definitely did not impress her as the kind of man who would step forward to help anyone. He was too cold-blooded and distrustful.

Chloe knew she had done nothing, *nothing* to give Adam Mitchell the idea that he had the freedom to make such an outrageous suggestion to her. She thought of all it implied and a shudder racked her from her scalp to her ankles.

She looked around the room again, at the faded furniture and papered walls. This was home and she had to find a way to save it, without the kind of "help" Mitchell had offered.

That evening when Evan came for dinner, she kept the events of the afternoon to herself, although she was preoccupied while she searched her mind for a solution. Asking him for advice was an option she'd discarded long ago—she had to find the answer by herself. She was used to that from years of practice with her father. Besides, Evan had so little grasp of her predicament, he wouldn't be able to help. He seemed to think things would work themselves out.

"Miss Chloe, I don't think you've heard a word I've said. Is that drifter still here?" he questioned, as she poured his tea.

"What? Oh, yes, but he'll finally be leaving tomorrow," she replied, tucking a stray hair behind her ear. "Doc said he's well enough to go. I think he's still surprised Travis lived. He said he must have an iron will to have pulled through."

"He's too mean to die," he said.

Chloe gave a delighted laugh, heartened that he'd tried to cheer her. "Evan, you made a joke."

He simply stared at her. "No, I didn't. I never joke."

"Oh." She glanced at her plate and twiddled with the corner of her napkin, momentarily discouraged. No, he never joked.

"At least we didn't have to suffer the man's company at dinner," Evan continued.

Travis had already eaten in the kitchen and was now upstairs, asleep again. He wanted to get an early start in the morning, he'd said.

"I just wish he'd been someone I could hire to work in the shop," she fretted, more to herself than Evan.

He reached for the sugar and put two heaping spoons in his tea. "I'm glad he wasn't. I wouldn't want him around here."

Chloe sighed. Carrying this burden of worry by herself sometimes wore her out. Even if Evan couldn't help, maybe talking about it would make her feel a little better. "I don't know what I'm going to do if I can't turn things around soon. I could lose this house."

His bland face became sympathetic and another spark of hope flared in her heart. "I know how hard this has been for you. I think you're the bravest woman I've ever known." He squeezed her hand in his fingers. "But try not to worry so much. I know you'll do whatever it takes to find a way out of this."

Of course, he was right. The answer was here somewhere. She just hadn't discovered it yet. She began to collect the dishes to take them out to the kitchen while her mind raced on, trying to grasp the elusive solution.

Abruptly, Evan put his spoon down and rubbed his temples, his expression oddly wide-eyed and attentive, as though listening for something.

"Oh, dear," Chloe said. "Is it another one of your headaches?"

At length, he nodded.

Evan had begun having headaches a couple of months earlier. Sudden and apparently severe, they were getting closer together, now occurring once or twice a week.

"I'll get an aspirin powder," she said, rising from the table, dishes in both hands.

He stopped her. "No, no, don't bother. Aspirin doesn't help. This will be gone soon."

Chloe sat again and looked at him doubtfully. "Have you talked to Doc Sherwood about this?" she asked.

"No!" he snapped, his expression suspicious. "No doctors. They don't know anything."

"All right, all right," she agreed, baffled by his attitude.

He did submit to a cold cloth on his forehead and when he finally left, Chloe felt drained by both the event and his presence. There were so many things in her life to worry about. So many things.

Later, long after Evan had gone back to the farm, Chloe sat at the desk in the parlor, wishing again for a nice man to answer her advertisement, the kind of man Travis had ridiculed. But for all her thinking, only one reality came to her mind.

No nice man was going to come along in time, if ever, to help her save her home. No amount of wishing would make that different. She would have to take in this drifter for now. If she could just get past this current crisis, it would give her time to find someone else later.

She took a low deep breath and let it out. Then she placed her palms flat to the desktop and pushed herself to her feet. For that moment she felt like a very old woman as she struggled with the only choice desperation left her, and it was a galling choice. It felt only slightly better than it might have if she were forced to accept Mitchell's offer. She carefully stacked her papers, closed the desk, and went upstairs.

She hung back in the doorway to the nursery, watching Travis. The candle flame from her nightstand revealed his shape on the bed. He lay with one muscled arm thrown over his eyes and his breathing was slow and even. Chloe was grateful for the dim light because the corner of his sheet covered only one slender hip and just barely anything else, and she could see where that narrow strip of hair on his belly went. Why couldn't he keep the sheet over himself? She quickly averted her eyes to his face. This naked, dangerous drifter—she must be out of her mind to consider hiring him.

Go on, she urged herself. She took one step closer to the bed, then another. When she stood next to him she reached out a tentative hand to shake his shoulder, but withdrew it. Finally she gave the leg of the bedstead a hard kick, making the springs twang.

He woke with a jerk and pulled himself up to his elbows, sleep-fogged. "What the hell are you doing?"

She stood with her arms crossed over her chest. "I'm willing to take you on, for a while, anyway. You'll start work tomorrow. I'll fix up the spare room in the shop for you." Then she turned and left the nursery, pulling the door closed and making sure it latched this time.

"Will that be all, Your Highness?" he called irritably through the door.

"It's enough," she called back. Being forced to hire an outlaw was more than enough.

She added another black mark to Frank Maitland's list of misdeeds.

Travis woke at dawn the next morning tangled in a snarl of sheets. Trying to turn his long frame on the narrow bed during the night had him wrapped like a mummy. He'd been dreaming again, this time about snakes that could assume human form, and he knew Evan Peterson and Adam Mitchell had triggered the vision.

He hadn't meant to get involved in that scene yesterday with the minister. He'd heard a male voice in the house and, always alert for Jace Rankin, he'd crept in to learn who it was. When he'd heard the drift of the conversation he listened, more in amazement than anything else, waiting to see what Chloe would do. For all he knew, maybe she wouldn't mind being kept in her own house by that bastard. As far as Travis could see, it was a toss-up between Mitchell and Peterson as to which was the worst choice.

But when he realized she wasn't interested and that the situation could get ugly, he had to step in. In all his years on the road with his family, he'd seen too many of that type: the hypocritical preacher, spouting damnation and cursing sin, then trying to seduce any vulnerable young woman available.

At least it hadn't been Jace Rankin in her parlor.

He thought of the last close call he had with the bounty hunter. He'd been in Sodaville, planning to hire on at a logging camp, but Rankin had gotten there a couple of days ahead of him. Rankin talked around and two nights later, after meeting the camp foreman, Travis had been galloping toward the forests of the Cascade Mountains, observed only by the Milky Way and an occasional owl.

To be chased was bad enough; to have his pursuer outguess him was hell. Even if Rankin weren't hunting him, he'd done enough damage just by talking with people. No one would even give Travis a job after they learned he'd been in jail.

In groggy frustration Travis worked himself loose of the sheet and sat up on the edge of the mattress, rubbing his nose with the back of his hand. By leaving a confusing, meandering trail, he hoped he'd finally lost Rankin. But if he got close again, Travis would have to strongly consider crossing into Canada. He might be able to lose him in that unknown territory. Maybe that was the only way to be free.

For now, though, he focused on being a blacksmith again. It might not be so bad, working at a forge. This time things were different. This time if he didn't like it he could pack up and move on.

His stomach growled. Now that he was feeling better, his hunger was unrelenting. At least it was if he didn't have to be around Evan Peterson. That man was enough to steal anyone's appetite. He listened a minute for kitchen noises. He'd quickly gotten used to the clank of the coffeepot and skillet as Chloe made breakfast in the mornings. The homey sounds were comforting, but this morning the house was quiet.

Intending to investigate the shop, Travis pulled on his new pants and boots and carefully opened the door separating his room from Chloe's.

She was asleep, her heavy hair tumbled around her. He was crossing the room but stopped for a moment at the foot of her bed. Her high-necked nightgown was partially unbuttoned, revealing the swell of a lush breast. She was a tempting sight, nestled amid lace-edged pillows and pink coverlet, her sharp tongue stilled. A faint pulse throbbed along the side of her smooth white throat.

His long-denied body responded at once to her feminine shape. How long had it been? he found himself wondering as he looked down at her. When had he last lain in a big soft bed with fancy linens and a warm female tucked in his arms? Not since his marriage, he realized.

Well, there was Roxanne, that brassy-haired young barmaid in Canyon City. That had been three months ago, now, but it hardly counted. She'd sold him a half hour of her time and was the first woman he'd had in five years.

She'd taken him to a small, airless storage room that led to an alley and pushed him down on a wobbly cot. The strong smell of beer had risen from dark kegs lining the walls. While cooing over his muscled, rawboned body, she'd emphasized her words by massaging the front of his pants. The intuitive skill with which he'd responded to these practiced ministrations surprised her and their coupling was so fierce, for one semilucid moment Travis had thought the rickety bed would collapse.

Yet when it was over and his body had cooled, he'd felt used and oddly hollow, although he couldn't imagine why. He'd gotten what he'd paid for, physical satisfaction. But the nagging pain that had sent him to the saloon was replaced with an emptiness that felt worse. He'd declined the purring girl's offer to let him have another go, free of charge, and tweaking her chin, let himself out into the alley.

Even the memory of that episode was vaguely depressing and that puzzled him. But gazing at Chloe, he understood the yearning he felt. His desire included physical passion, but a need to belong as well, peace of mind and stability. And for the space of a breath, he imagined taking off his pants and boots and climbing into her bed.

Travis shook his head at the dumb idea. Forget it, McGuire, he told himself and crept out the door leading to the hall. His search for those very qualities—peace of mind, stability—was what had gotten him into trouble to begin with. He didn't need anything or anyone, least of all a woman with a razor-sharp tongue.

This job and this town, they were only temporary. Then he'd be gone from here, and away from the blacksmith's old-maid daughter who was becoming far more attractive than he wanted her to be.

Chloe woke a few minutes later when the sun broke over her windowsill, blasting her in the face.

She rose quietly and took up her hairbrush, thinking Travis still slept in the next room. She would make sure that she kept a businesslike distance between herself and McGuire. Moving him out to the shop would help. Now that he was well the nursery was much too close.

She went to the open window while she brushed her hair. When she looked out, she was startled to see him in the paddock with her horse, Lester.

Travis was bad-mannered and disrespectful, the way he was always challenging her, baiting her, so how could she admire the striking picture he made? The width of his shoulders was a sharp contrast with his narrow hips where his jeans hung low and snug. His leanness accentuated the length of his legs and torso as he advanced in a fluid motion of muscle and bone. Maybe it was like looking at a painting, she decided. She could appreciate a work of art and not like the model. If she thought of him in such abstract terms, his allure was easier to accept.

Again Chloe's imagination combined with her memory of his naked body as she envisioned his bare back, his broad furred chest, his long, straight legs.

Mortified by this mental picture, she forced herself to think of Evan—Evan in his black suit, with his oiled hair and his musty smell.

Her musings were interrupted as a voice, carrying easily on the new day, floated up to her.

"Steady, girl," Travis coaxed the mare, his hands at his sides. "I'm a friend."

The horse eyed him with some suspicion but didn't shy as he drew near. Travis held his palm up to her nose so she could learn his scent. Chloe looked on as he ran soothing, experienced hands over her mare, moderately surprised to discover he really knew something about animals. As if feeling her eyes on him, he glanced up suddenly and looked over Lester's bowed head to her window. She stepped back and closed the neck of her gown.

"Good morning," he called, and she could hear the impudence in his voice. "Can I have some breakfast or will I have to eat with the horse?"

With that attitude he must have spent a lot of time in solitary confinement, she reflected irritably. "Breakfast will be ready in half an hour," she called. "But Lester might teach you some manners."

Travis backed up to confirm the horse's gender, then glanced up at Chloe again. "Maybe, but who's going to break the news to Lester that she's not a boy?"

Chloe flapped a dismissing hand at him and struggled to keep the smile off her face.

When she called Travis for breakfast, she saw he'd put on one of his new shirts.

"Does everything fit?" she asked, trying to ease the funny tension she felt at the sight of him. He'd been disagreeable when he was sick but still she'd felt his illness had given her a slight advantage. After all, it was difficult for a person to be masterful while wearing only a sheet. But it wouldn't be so easy, she suspected, dealing with Travis McGuire now that he was out of his sickbed and dressed.

"Just great," he said, rolling up his sleeves to expose his forearms. "Even the underwear." Chloe felt the heat rise to her face. "You did a good job of guessing the sizes."

Guessing was hardly the term she'd have used. She'd stood in the general store, envisioning his long limbs and wide shoulders while holding the shirts and jeans up to herself to choose the sizes Travis needed. The air in DeGroot's Mercantile positively sizzled with Albert's unasked questions while he hung at her elbow, watching her handle the long, narrow clothing. But her expression and demeanor effectively squelched Albert's desire to pry.

Chair legs scraped on the floor behind her as he settled at the kitchen table. "Tell me about your intended." There was a sarcastic edge in his voice.

She only winced at his choice of words while she pondered the amazing circumstances she found herself in. She knew this lie was going to catch up to her, one way or another. She put bacon and eggs on his plate. "Evan is the schoolmaster."

Travis reached for his fork, waiting for her to continue. For a man who made it a practice to keep his distance, his own curiosity confounded him. But he prodded anyway—there was something about Peterson that put him on his guard. "And?"

Chloe put the frying pan in the sink and pumped water over it. "Well, he, uh, he came to Misfortune a few years ago and he started calling on me after my father died, and uh . . ." There really wasn't much to say about Evan. He wasn't attractive, there were no noble qualities to extol about his character. He was a very plain man.

As she fumbled for a better description, Travis voiced an assumption. "And he doesn't like my being here."

Her gaze locked with his for a moment and then she poured his coffee. "Well, no, but what is there to like? You were very rude to him."

"I suppose you think I was rude to Adam Mitchell, too. But I don't hear you complaining about that," he pointed out.

"What does Reverend Mitchell have to do with this?" she demanded, startled by the reference. She hadn't thanked Travis for his help yesterday, but his manner and station didn't make her feel like she had to. "We were talking about Evan."

Travis shrugged and poured a drip of cream into his coffee. "If my being here is such a problem for your schoolteacher, you should have taken up

Mitchell's offer. But I imagine Peterson would like that even less."

Chloe was livid. She flung her apron on its hook behind the door. "How dare you suggest such a thing? Do you really believe I'm the kind of woman who would let herself be kept by a man?"

He leveled a calm, assessing gaze on her. "Not for a minute."

"Then why would you even bring it up?"

"Because there's not much difference between those two men." He rose from the table, towering and impatient, and thrust his empty cup into her hands. "Look, I don't give a damn about Peterson or his complaints. Just keep him away from me."

"What's going on over at Chloe's house, Evan? She was in the other day buying men's clothes, but I couldn't get her to tell me anything." Albert leaned forward, his elbows on the well-worn counter. The rest of the group pressed a little closer.

This was the very thing that Evan feared, being the subject of the town's speculation. He wanted them to understand that he in no way approved of Miss Chloe's actions. "That drifter actually sat down at the table during our dinner the other night and helped himself. Nobody invited him, he just horned in." Detecting a sympathetic audience, he warmed to the subject. "And last night Miss Chloe told me she's given him a job, after she'd said she wouldn't. She claims not to like him, but she insists on letting him work there."

"Better take her another box of those chocolates,

Evan," Albert advised, adjusting his sleeve garter. The amusement in his voice was thinly concealed. "Looks like you maybe got some competition."

Evan glowered at the flippant remark. That very thought had already occurred to him and he didn't like the idea at all. His palms began to sweat.

Stifled laughter rippled through the group gathered at Albert's counter.

Outrage percolated in Evan. Miss Chloe's involvement with McGuire was entirely inappropriate—tending a strange man who slept in a room he knew adjoined hers, selecting clothes for him, making fools of both herself and Evan. Well, no one was going to laugh at him. A screeching pain lanced through his head.

"Don't you dare laugh at me!" Evan demanded.

A couple of chuckles were suffocated into throat-clearing snorts. Evan was satisfied to see the expressions around him straighten under his reprimand.

Albert's brows rose in surprise and his tone became placating. "Now, Evan, I was just joshing you. It takes a pretty brave man to deal with Chloe—you've proven that yourself. Besides, one of her best qualities is loyalty. Look how she took care of Frank all those years. You don't have anything to worry about."

"Anyway, Chloe doesn't have much choice," Grady Hewitt put in. He took out his watch and compared its time to Albert's wall clock. "Old Frank left her in a real fix with that mortgage, you know. I wish now he'd never asked me for the loan. But if the bank has to take her house, I don't think you two will be very happy living in the Tollivers' attic."

That was true. One of the things Evan looked forward to was getting out of that attic when he and Chloe married. But did that mean he'd now have to put up with the blacksmith?

"I won't tolerate his insubordination." Evan turned to Sheriff Winslow. "I'll be having dinner every night with Miss Chloe as long as that vagrant works there. But I can't be around every minute. I'd keep an eye on him if I were you, Fred. Mark my words, he's trouble."

"Now, Evan," the sheriff reasoned, "the man hasn't done anything. Besides, I trust Miss Chloe to make the right decision. She has good judgment."

Evan had always thought so, too. But suddenly she'd developed a blind spot and Travis McGuire was standing in it.

Late in the afternoon, Chloe went looking for Travis. After their conversation this morning about Adam Mitchell, she began thinking. She was loathe to admit it, but if Travis hadn't come in when he did, that scene with the minister could have been much worse. She supposed some kind of acknowledgment was in order. Perhaps that was why he brought it up. She decided to let Travis have his choice of desserts. That, and a brief thanks, were compensation enough. The town might gossip about her but no one could accuse her of having bad manners.

But the blacksmith was nowhere to be found. The

shop was empty and so was the yard. She even walked around to the front to see if he was sitting on the porch swing.

"Travis!" she called. What was he up to now? she wondered irritably. She didn't have the time or the interest to chase him all over creation. She retraced her steps and there was still no sign of him. She stood by the pump and shaded her eyes while she scanned the property. "Well, for heaven's sake, where—"

From the old shed behind the shop came the clattering racket of things falling, followed by a string of ringing, explicit profanities. Despite having lived in a rough mining town all her life, what she heard made her blush.

Chloe hurried to the weather-bleached shed and found Travis coughing and rubbing the top of his head, surrounded by rusty chunks of iron scrap, old pieces of harness, tin cans with nails spilling out of them, empty bottles and assorted junk. A broken plank that had served as a shelf lay with one end still attached to the wall, the other on the dirt floor. Years of accumulated dust billowed from the doorway.

"Is everything all right?" she asked and jumped back a step while he angrily threw things into piles.

"Damn it, does it look all right?" Travis barked and glanced around the dark shed. Cobwebs crisscrossed his hair and shirt like a lace shawl. Scowling, he aimed a vicious kick at a milk can full of filberts and sent the nuts flying everywhere.

Chloe lingered in the doorway of the musty, windowless room, unsettled by his tantrum. But it seemed to pass as quickly as it erupted because when he looked at her again, she saw only a hint of danger.

He put his hands in his hair, leaned over to shake the dust out, then brushed at the webs on his sleeves. "Well, what do you want?" he muttered.

Oh, that impertinence, she steamed, pursing her lips. Still, no matter how she tried to distract herself, she couldn't help but notice that his shirt was half unbuttoned. And, having noticed, her eyes strayed to his bare skin, the soft hair on his chest, the shadow his collarbone made at the base of his neck . . .

She forced herself to look at his face. "I want to thank you for your help with Reverend Mitchell. I don't think I could have been as—um, persuasive."

Travis jammed his hands into his back pockets, the action pulling his shirt open wider. "Well, I don't have any patience for self-righteous hypocrites like him." He began pacing like a caged wolf.

Chloe had to admit that was a pretty fair assessment of the reverend. When she thought of his sloppy kiss on her hand, her insides clenched.

"Anyway, I was wondering what kind of dessert you'd like. As a reward, I mean."

"Reward?" His face clouded over.

"Well, yes. You earned one," she replied, now vaguely apprehensive as he turned threatening again. "Don't you like to be rewarded when you've done a good deed?"

His eyes on hers became so piercing, she felt trapped like a possum in lantern light, with no will to move. He stopped pacing and took a step toward her and then another. A shine of perspiration suddenly gleamed on his face.

"I don't want a reward," he growled, reaching out to put his hands on her shoulders.

At his firm touch, a thrill of fear, of uncertain expectation, flooded Chloe. Primal strength and power surged from him in waves. What was he going to do? Thrash her? Kiss her?

Instead he pushed her aside and walked out of the shed, kicking up little dust clouds with each step. He stopped a moment and turned to face her, quickened with feral tenseness.

"I didn't do it for a reward," he said, then went out the gate and crossed the road to the yellow grassland beyond the house.

Travis strode through the tall stalks, keeping his gaze leveled on the distant horizon. He sucked in deep breaths as he went, shaken by what had just happened. Five years locked in a jail cell had made him dislike small, enclosed places, but he'd never panicked like that before. When Chloe had put herself between him and the door, he'd felt trapped, claustrophobic, like he couldn't breathe. He'd had to stop himself from running her down to get out of that room.

He saw the tension in her face when he touched her. Apparently that was prohibited—no one was allowed to touch the Vinegar Princess. He sat crosslegged on a low rise that overlooked a wash filled with straggling wildflowers.

And that business about rewarding him, as though he were an obedient dog, he reflected angrily. He pulled up a long blade of grass, its top gone to seed, and tore it into long, thin strips.

He hoped Chloe Maitland had a hard skull because he expected to be butting heads with her a lot while he was here.

Chapter 6

Over the next couple of weeks, Travis unobtrusively assumed his new role. He started slowly, having not regained his full strength. Rest and Chloe's improved cooking were helping.

Without revealing how much money she needed, Chloe had told him he would work there for two months or until they made enough to pay the bank. If, at the end of those two months, she wasn't able to raise the cash, he'd be out of a job and she'd be out of her home. On the other hand, if they made more than she needed, they would split the extra. That part was fair.

First he put the shop in order, repairing stalls and clearing away years' worth of dirt and trash. Chloe felt as though her father's ghost had risen when she looked out and saw Travis in the shop stoking the forge to get it ready for business. After all the months of dark silence, it would seem odd to hear the clang of a maul again. A dozen times she'd asked herself if she was making the right decision in hiring him. But time was slipping away from her and taking some kind of action was better than doing nothing. And after a while the ringing anvil slipped to the back of her mind and became a comforting sound.

They didn't lack for business. Chloe had only to tell Albert DeGroot that the blacksmith shop was open again and word spread like a brushfire. From early morning till Travis came in for his dinner, horses were shod, kettles were repaired, new tires were made for wagon wheels.

Curiosity drew their customers initially—everyone wanted to get a look at the stranger. The quality of Travis's work brought them back. That boy didn't talk much, it was observed, and he could get downright tetchy, one farmer told Chloe, if you asked him about himself, but he knew his iron.

But Chloe didn't like Travis. To think she'd been reduced to hiring an escaped convict to work for her. Oh, she knew he did his job and was good at it. But the sparks still flew whenever they were within speaking distance, and sometimes not even that close.

For the most part, he kept to himself in the shop, either working or in the little room she gave him, coming into the house only for his meals. With Evan over for dinner every night, she set a place for Travis at the kitchen table while she and Evan ate in the dining room.

On the occasional evening, she'd look out the back door or the kitchen window and see Travis sitting in Frank's old spot by the big shop door, a bottle of whiskey resting on his knee. The sight brought back bad memories of her father, too drunk to stand, too tired to care. Once she even stepped out to the back porch and frowned at Travis to express her disapproval. To her intense annoyance, he only raised the bottle in a silent toast and took another drink. He knew she didn't like his drinking, she fumed. He simply chose to ignore it.

But as far as his work was concerned, she was relieved that she'd made the right decision in hiring him. When a little money began to accumulate, she dared to hope she might save her home.

As noon approached one morning, Chloe went down the back steps with a lunch tray for Travis balanced against her hip. It was another sweltering day. The only shade to be had was a two-foot strip running along the east wall of the shop. She crossed the dry yard and set the tray down on the old chair that always stood by the door. That was the chair she saw Travis sitting on some nights, sipping from a whiskey bottle.

Chloe stepped into the shop's gloom. It was brightened only by the glow of the fire, rising and falling like a breathing thing. Travis stood at the forge slowly pumping the bellows. He wore a heavy leather apron and gloves but no shirt. As he maneuvered a pair of tongs in the low flames, Chloe could feel the increasing heat radiating from the forge.

Travis stared at her across the bed of fire, its red embers reflected in his eyes, his hair wet where it rested on the back of his neck.

She paused before the sweating, muscled drifter, fascinated for a moment by the powerful image he projected. Then she remembered why she was there.

"I've brought your lunch," she said, then turned to leave.

"Have you eaten already?" she heard him ask.

"No, my lunch is on the kitchen table."

"Why don't you bring it out here? Unless, of course, you're afraid."

"Of what?" she scoffed.

"Afraid of eating with an outlaw."

She turned back to face him. His eyes connected unwaveringly with hers. "I'm not afraid of *anything*," she said.

Her reply was so matter-of-fact, so casual, he almost believed her. She might even believe it herself, but he knew it wasn't true. He pulled off the heavy gloves. "Well, then, shall we eat?"

Unable to think of an excuse, she nodded and went back to the kitchen to get her sandwich and another chair. When she glanced out the window, she saw him at the pump, sluicing water over his head. It was a simple action but it stopped her, and she watched for a moment as rivulets ran over his shoulders and down his bare back into the waistband on his jeans. His forehead and cheekbone were healing but he still looked like his horse had kicked him instead of thrown him. What did the rest of his face look like, the part that was hidden by that beard? Then she caught herself. If only she could keep her eyes from straying to him. It was embarrassing, it was indecent, the feelings he stirred in her.

He saw her standing on the back porch, trying to

balance her plate and the chair, and came forward to take them from her.

"Let's see if we can squeeze into that shady place over there," he said, indicating the shop wall.

Conversation between them was still strained and she wondered why he'd wanted her to eat with him. Except for a compliment to her cooking, they sat in silence. Chloe fixed him huge meals, knowing the work he did burned a lot of energy.

After two roast beef sandwiches, a pint of potato salad, half a berry pie, and a quart of iced tea, Travis tipped his chair back against the shady wall and closed his eyes, his long legs dangling.

For her part, Chloe only nibbled on her lunch, uncomfortably aware of the strong arms and chest poorly concealed by the leather apron. With decent food, in only three weeks he'd begun to fill out, losing the sickly thinness he'd had when he got there.

As if feeling her eyes on him, he spoke. "You said your father died last spring. Was he sick for a long time?" The shop was in such neglected chaos Travis thought no one had done much work there for several years.

"You might say that," she replied carefully. To Chloe, it was bad enough that Frank had staggered home every night from the Twilight Star for the whole town to see. She didn't want to tell Travis about it. But, yes, she supposed her father had been ill for years. Sick with grief, with whiskey.

Travis noted the lack of emotion in her voice. He'd been unable to talk about his own parents' deaths for many months without his throat constricting. He opened his eyes and kept his gaze trained on the low distant hills far beyond the back fence. "And that's why it bothers you when I take a drink now and then?"

She turned to him sharply, but he was still watching those hills, as if looking for someone. "My father was killed in a wagon accident and that has nothing to do with my objection to your drinking."

"I think it does. I'd say he drank quite a bit for quite a while."

His voice was calm but his words peeved her. "Who told you that?" she demanded, annoyed that this town respected nothing of a person's privacy, not even a dead man's.

"Your father did."

"What?" She grasped the arm of his chair and pulled it forward so hard it landed on its four legs with a crash. "What are you talking about?"

He faced her but waited a moment before answering, debating what to tell her. Finally he settled on the truth. "The first day I came out here to look around, I found a pile of empty whiskey bottles in the back stall. There must have been over a hundred of them."

Over a hundred. Not surprised, but humiliated by his discovery, she tried a feeble denial. "He doctored a lot of horses over the years. They were probably old tonic bottles."

"No they weren't."

His tone left no room for argument, but neither did it judge. She looked into his face and saw a brief flash of sympathy, something she didn't expect. She sighed and then glanced at her lap. "I suppose I'd better get rid of them. I didn't know they were there."

He tipped his chair again and resumed his study of the yellow hills. "I buried them next to the back wall one afternoon when you were out delivering laundry."

She didn't know what to say. He'd done a favor for her and even showed a bit of kindness, but she didn't want to be obligated to this man in any way. In fact, she'd rather that he owed her. And the last time she tried to repay him, after that episode with Adam Mitchell, he'd gotten angry. "Thank you," she finally replied.

He let the chair drop forward, then stood and put the tray in her hands. "That was hard, I bet. It's not easy letting people do for you, is it?"

"I got used to doing for myself," she replied flatly, rising from her chair, "because I had to. I learned I'm the only one I can depend on."

With a mix of respect and exasperation, Travis watched her cross the yard to the house, her back straight, her head up.

"Uh, are you Mister McGuire?"

Travis glanced up from the anvil and saw a tow-headed boy lingering in the shop doorway with a small wooden crate in his arms.

"Yeah, but you can call me Travis," he replied. "What's your name?"

"Cory Hicks. Mister DeGroot said you ordered

this horse liniment. I brung it right away, just like he told me." The youngster advanced only one step.

Travis smiled at him. How old was he? he wondered. Nine, maybe ten years old? He tried to remember being that age, running barefoot and free on summer days, in holey overalls cut off at the knees. But he had no memories like that.

He put down his maul and motioned him forward. "Come on in, Cory. You can set it down over here." He directed him to a stool by the back wall.

The boy obeyed.

Travis walked over, lifted a corner of the box to test its weight and gave a low whistle. "That's a big crate for you to carry. You must be pretty strong."

Cory looked up at him from under snow-blond bangs. He had a bright, engaging face and he nodded in proud agreement. "I got muscles from working with Pa on our farm. That's why Mister DeGroot pays me a dime to deliver stuff sometimes."

"Yeah? Let's see," Travis said. "Hold up your arm and make a fist."

Cory raised his left arm and assumed the stance of a circus strong man, his expression fierce. He had several nasty-looking bruises on his forearm. Some were healing but a couple looked new.

Chuckling with genuine enjoyment, Travis said, "Not bad, not bad. When you get a little more growth, you'd make a good blacksmith's apprentice."

Cory dropped his fist and looked around. His gaze took in the forge and anvil, the tools hanging from the walls, the kettle handles and wheel rims, and came back to rest on Travis. "I guess you gotta be strong to be a blacksmith, huh?"

"You do, and you need to be careful, too," Travis teased, indicating the boy's bruises. "It's easy to get hurt doing this kind of work. Your arm looks like my face." He pointed at his own improving black-and-blue marks. "How did you do that?"

Cory tucked his arm behind him and looked at the hard-packed dirt floor. Travis immediately regretted saying anything about it. He didn't mean to embarrass the boy.

"Aw, it's 'cause I'm left-handed," he muttered, and reached out to finger a sliver on the rough box. " 'Cept I'm not supposed to be. Mister Peterson says it's bad and this is the only way I'll remember to hold my pencil right-handed."

Travis focused sharply on the crown of the child's lowered head, a flame igniting in his belly. He put his finger under Cory's chin and tipped up his face. The disgrace Travis saw there made him feel, for the briefest moment, as though he were looking into a mirror. He reached for the boy's wrist to get a better look at his arm. "Evan Peterson did that to you? Because you're left-handed?"

Cory nodded shamefacedly and turned his eyes to the floor again. "He always got mad at me about it and told me I had to stop trying to be different, that writing left-handed is wicked." He looked up at Travis, his expression earnest, contrite. "And I was learning not to, I swear I was! Then I got scarlet fever last spring and I missed a lot of school. When I was better, my ma asked Mister Peterson to give me lessons. I forgot I'm supposed to be right-handed, and that's when he started correcting me. That's what he calls it when he smacks me with the edge of his ruler."

Travis felt the low flame erupt into a blinding fury that momentarily threatened his ability to reason. His hands clenched into fists and he pulled in a deep breath. When Cory took a step back from him, staring at him with huge blue eyes, he knew his rage must be showing. With effort he released his fists and sank to a crouch next to the boy.

"Did you tell your mother or father that Evan Peterson beat you?" he asked quietly, trying to remain calm while he talked to him.

Cory shook his head. "No, but I'm finished with my lessons for the summer, anyway. I won't have to see him again till school starts." A nervous shiver ran through him, as though at the prospect. Then in a small, plaintive voice he asked, "Is it really wicked to be left-handed? Am I gonna go to hell?"

A twinge of pain twisted in Travis's chest at the question. Goddamn that Peterson, Travis smoldered, rising to his feet. If anyone was going to hell, it would be that son of a bitch teacher. Slowly, to avoid startling him, he put his hand on Cory's white-blond hair.

"No, Cory, it's not bad to be left-handed. *Or* different, or short, or a newcomer, or anything like that. The people who are wrong are the ones who'd tell you those things are bad. Do you know what I mean?"

Cory looked at him a moment, then apparently

satisfied with what he'd heard, nodded. "Can I watch you give a horse new shoes?"

Travis shrugged regretfully. "I don't have a horse here today. Right now, I'm patching a big kettle."

Cory brushed his bangs out of his eyes. "That's okay. I got to be getting back to Mister DeGroot, anyways. He wants me to sweep his store." He glanced up hopefully. "Can I come back sometime, maybe?"

Travis put a hand on the boy's shoulder. "Any day you like, Cory."

The quality of the food had definitely improved over the past few weeks, Travis thought later, but the dinner company had not. It was merely in another room. Tonight, as usual, he sat alone at the kitchen table, while Evan and Chloe ate in the dining room. Their conversation was boring, but Travis had begun to notice that Peterson was becoming more vocal in his objections to his presence. Chloe would usually try to divert the man, but more often Peterson doggedly remained with the subject. Now Travis chewed on a chicken leg and listened to Evan's stage whisper.

"Why does he have to eat in the kitchen?" the teacher whispered loudly at Chloe. "The weather is still good. He doesn't need to come in at all."

"Evan, he isn't deaf," Chloe hissed back.

"If he weren't in the house, he wouldn't be able to hear me," he responded, but lowered his voice a bit. "He should be outside. That man is nothing but trouble and I don't like the way he comes and goes around here."

"Evan, please—" Chloe said.

"I hate to think what he could do with you two alone here at the end of town. Someone like that— why, he looks like a defiler of women. And why do we never have tea anymore?" he complained. "I like tea much better than coffee. Is it because *he* likes it?"

"I thought it would be a nice change," Chloe hedged.

Travis pushed his plate away, fury taking his appetite. He stood and walked out the door, slamming it so hard the windows rattled.

After Evan left, Chloe was folding the tablecloth when she heard Travis come up the back stairs. He paused in the doorway and gave her an even stare before walking to the stove.

"I guess we know where Peterson's mind is," Travis said. He helped himself to a cup of coffee, then leaned a hip against the doorjamb. "He thinks I'm here"—and he stopped a moment, searching for the right word—"*defiling* you."

Chloe tried not to be embarrassed, but she was. Evan's indefensible rudeness put her in an awkward position. The entire topic was one she would rather not think about. She looked at his strong hand gripping the coffee cup and ventured a quick glance at his eyes before turning her gaze.

"He's just protecting me, that's all," she replied, keeping her face carefully averted. Surely that accounted for the almost frantic translucent glimmer in Evan's eyes whenever he complained about Travis.

He snorted. "Protecting you. Don't flatter yourself. The only people Peterson will stand up to are those who are weaker or smaller."

"What's that supposed to mean?" she demanded, her voice rising. "I wish you'd remember that he is my fiancé."

He astounded her with a grim prediction.

"Lady," his voice was low, "if you marry that man, your life will be so miserable you'll wish you were dead."

"What?! What in the world would make you say something like that?" she said, shaken by his words.

"There's something not right about Evan Peterson." He told her about Cory Hicks and the bruises on his left arm.

Chloe frowned. "Surely you don't believe that. Children tend to exaggerate things—everything is larger than life to them."

"You bet I believe it," he insisted angrily. "You didn't see that kid's face while he was talking about it." Then he paused a moment before continuing in a quiet voice. "I guess I owe you my life, but the best repayment I can give you is a piece of advice. If you're half as smart as I think, you'll listen to me."

"But, why—what—" she spluttered.

"It isn't only that Peterson is a mama's boy," Travis went on between sips from his blue enameled cup. "If that was all there was to it, I'd only think the two of you are mismatched. There's something more I can't put my finger on, a weakness of character, a selfishness, a basic *meanness*." He pushed himself away from the doorjamb and poured another half cup of coffee.

Chloe found her voice. "Just because he's worried about me while a strange man is living on my property? Worried that some harm might come to me?"

She heard a mirthless chuckle. "He's not worried about you. He's scared to death for himself."

"I don't wonder. When you invited yourself to dinner that night, you stared at him throughout the entire meal and purposely intimidated him," she snapped.

"No." He shook his head. "I didn't do it on purpose. But he ran out of here as fast as his legs could carry him. If the woman I loved took some drifter into her house, no matter why, I'd be mad as hell. I'd kick his ass all the way to the edge of town."

Stopped by his words, Chloe looked up into his face. She was arrested by a flicker of emotion she saw there.

"And if he thinks I'm that dangerous," his voice was still soft, "how could he leave you here alone with me, the woman he loves? I sure as hell couldn't do that."

Chloe couldn't answer this. How, indeed, she thought to herself. Evan was supposed to protect her from "the stranger," but that mostly amounted to complaining about him. Evan had, in a way, failed her.

"But Evan isn't like you at all," she replied, almost to herself. "And besides, he doesn't love me."

He stepped closer. "No? And do you love him?"

The situation was becoming confusing and the kitchen suddenly hot. He was standing too close and yet not close enough. She tried to look away from his intense gaze but he put his finger under her chin and lifted it.

"Why do you want to know?"

"Do you?"

"No." It was as if he willed the word from her mouth.

He stepped back, the spell broken. What was this man's secret? Why was he able to make her reveal so much more of herself than she intended? She felt exposed and vulnerable. And how could he so confidently size up Evan in such a brief meeting?

As though reading her mind, he said, "You meet a lot of different types in prison. After a while, you become a pretty good judge of character."

Travis was sitting on the porch swing when Chloe went up to bed that night. She took her customary place in front of her pier glass to brush out her hair. Surely she couldn't have told Travis those secrets she had trouble admitting even to herself. Her face burned at the memory.

How had he pried such personal thoughts from her? She'd told him she didn't love Evan. She'd told him Evan didn't love her.

Well, so what if they didn't have the romance of the century? She wanted tranquil companionship, a dependable partner to share the years with. People married for far less noble reasons, and love was certainly not one of them.

What a dark, enigmatic man Travis McGuire was. Although she and Doc guessed him to be about her age—it was hard to tell with the beard and the bruises—there was a world-weariness about him that made him seem far older.

His assessment of Evan had been startling and, now she fretted, perhaps true, although she refused to believe that part about Cory. Evan was strict with his pupils, everyone knew that. But certainly he wouldn't punish a child for being left-handed. Would he?

Travis had been so positive about it, she had the impression he'd felt some empathy with Cory that went deeper than indignation.

Losing count of her brush strokes, she wondered again what Travis was running from, what crime he'd committed. Funny, but she wasn't as afraid of him as she had been.

She no longer worried that he might hurt her. Now she feared him in another way entirely.

One evening two weeks later, Chloe looked out the kitchen window as she washed dishes and saw Travis asleep in the chair against the shop wall. There he was again, with that whiskey bottle of his. It was the second time in a week and she felt her annoyance rise. True, she'd never seen him take more than a swallow or two, but this was just another example of his disregard for her authority and her feelings. Well, she'd been unable to do anything about her father's drinking, but she didn't have to put up with it from a man who worked for her.

Flinging the dish towel on the table, she went outside.

She stood in front of him a moment, watching him. His head was tipped back against the wall, his eyes closed, his feet propped up on an old nail keg. The whiskey bottle sat on the arm of the chair with his hand closed around it. Not wanting to wake him, she carefully began to pull it from his grip, meaning to pour it out.

"I'm not finished with that, Chloe," he said. His eyes snapped open to fix on her.

She jumped and pulled back her hand, as surprised as if a tailor's dummy had started talking to her. Gathering her wits and armed with self-righteousness, she continued. "Oh, yes, you are. This drinking business is going to stop."

Travis put his hand to his forehead to shade the glare of the low-hanging sun. "What bee have you got in your bonnet now?" he demanded.

She pointed at the offending bottle. "I am not going to have you sitting out here swilling whiskey."

He rose to his feet and stood over her. Damn the woman. Whenever he started believing she was bearable, she changed directions on him and turned into a harpy again. "This is the same bottle I brought with me. Got a complaint about my work?"

"Not yet, but if I let you keep this up, it'll only be a matter of time," she prophesied.

His jaw tightened. It wasn't any of her business to know why he sometimes sipped at that bottle and he wasn't going to tell her. "Lady, I had five years of being told what to do and say and think. I'm not about to take it from you. Go order your schoolteacher around—he seems to like it. I don't."

He leaned his face toward hers until his breath fanned her cheek, his gray eyes boring into hers. He smelled of leather, fresh air and faintly, of bourbon.

"At least I can depend on him," she countered, struggling to ignore the enticing combination of scents. Her mind clutched at Evan's vapid image to distract her from the one before her. "Pretty soon you'll start sleeping late and letting work pile up and nothing will get done. That's how my father got me into this pickle and I'm determined to get myself out of it."

He bristled at the implied comparison between himself and the late Frank Maitland. "You'll get out of it with my free labor."

At the mention of this inescapable fact, Chloe felt a faint blush creep up to her hairline, then she rallied. "That was our agreement. I don't need to be reminded of it."

He stared at her unblinkingly for several long seconds until she lowered her eyes. Gripping her chin he forced her to look at him.

"There's one thing you do need to be reminded of," he said, his voice gritty. "I'm not your father."

His gaze fell to her lips and held there. His face was so close her breath caught in her throat; she expected to feel the brush of his mouth on hers.

Instead, he jerked his hand from her chin and stepped back, defiantly tipping up the bottle. Taking a long swallow, he dragged the back of his hand over his mouth, his eyes steady on hers.

With no rebuttal for this insulting dismissal, Chloe glowered at him. Then she turned on her heel and went back into the house, smarting from the defeat.

Travis watched her go, forcing his anger to retreat. The sun was down and that frustrating female had stolen the peace of the mellow summer evening. Goddammit, he chafed. Then feeling he had to say it aloud or bust, he roared, *"Goddammit!"* He stomped to his room in the shop and flopped on the bed.

Nothing was worth having that nagging pain in the ass tell him what to do and tie him up in knots. He was a free man. He could go or stay as he chose. Not for the first time, he was sorely tempted to leave. To think he'd almost kissed her a minute ago while she was looking up at him with those big green eyes, all pushy and demanding and defenseless.

This last thought sat him up again. Chloe Maitland, defenseless? That was a harebrained notion. She was tough and thorny and sometimes talking to her was like jumping into a bag full of wet cats. It was a device, he realized, a means of protection, and that was something he understood.

But he didn't have to like it.

He relaxed against the straw tick. He would wake up in his clothes again but he was too tired to pull them off. His thoughts blurred as sleep overtook him, that last big pull of whiskey doing its job. Maybe it would work, maybe he wouldn't dream tonight. . . .

Chloe heard Travis swear—the whole town probably did. She went back to the sink, seething with humiliation over his contemptuous demonstration. Who did he think he was to treat her like that? Granted, she didn't pay him in cash but she had taken him in, outlaw that he was, saved his sorry hide, put food in his mouth, a roof over his head, and clean clothes on his back.

Taking up the towel again, she wiped the dishes with such furious energy the friction warmed them. She'd risked a lot just by letting him stay—if he were caught, she could even be accused of aiding a criminal. He probably had a price on his head, too.

A big price. . . .

Her hands fell still. Slowly, she sat at the table, jolted by the prospect.

There might be a reward involved in the capture of Travis P. McGuire, escaped convict. Maybe enough to pay off the mortgage and have a nice nest egg left over. It was highly possible that Travis would be worth a lot more to her back in prison than he could earn shoeing horses and mending wagons. She put her elbows on the blue-checkered tablecloth and rested her chin on her hands, envisioning a secure future for herself and Evan as well. She would finally get the last word with Travis and be compensated for his insults and those—those embarrassing, restless feelings he stirred up in her.

But it seemed so weaselly and low, her conscience prodded, to turn him in at this point. He'd been here for weeks now, working hard, and he'd done a couple of nice things for her, like taking care of those whiskey bottles and fixing the chair.

Yes, she reminded herself, but what about his

drinking and that brooding, surly attitude? And the way he managed to pry information from her that she had no intention of revealing? What about his mocking insolence a few moments ago and the fact that he'd almost kissed her out there?

And her sneaking disappointment that he hadn't?

Chloe sat up with a jerk and pulled her thoughts back to the matter at hand. It wasn't wrong to turn in a known criminal, especially one who'd escaped from prison. Wasn't it her *responsibility* to do it?

She sat drumming her fingers, wondering how she could discover whether money had been offered for his return. Sheriff Winslow would be the person to talk to, although these days he didn't do much beyond sit in front of his office and whittle. Since Misfortune's decline he hadn't had anything else to do besides that and mind Morris Caldwell once in a while, and he enjoyed this unofficial retirement. Still, maybe he received wanted posters or information about outlaws. She knew he was afraid of her but that might work to her advantage.

Chloe stood and went back to the sink to finish the dishes, her mind made up. She would talk to Fred Winslow first thing tomorrow morning.

Her conscience reared and shook a finger at her, but she managed to stifle the feeling—sometime late in the night.

Fred Winslow dozed in the mild morning sun, slouching in an old chair outside his office. His hat was angled down over his eyes. Now and then a nice breeze would kick up to keep things from getting too warm. His generous lap and stomach were dusted with curly wood shavings, and a half-finished figure of an owl sat on an upended apple crate next to him. It was a good way to spend a morning, whittling a little, napping a little.

This comfortable limbo evaporated when he felt a shadow fall between himself and the sun.

"Good morning, Fred."

The middle-aged sheriff opened blinking eyes to see Chloe Maitland standing over him, her market basket on her arm. Hastily, he pushed himself back to a sitting position, then lumbered to his feet.

"Uh, Miss Chloe, howdy." Oh, Lordy-Lord, he groaned inwardly. What could she want? Fred made a point of avoiding Chloe. She had a way of making a man feel like his fly was open and everyone in the world knew it except him. In fact, he was one of the only people in town who didn't hire her to do his laundry. He'd rather go naked first. "What brings you by today?"

"Well, actually, I was hoping you could do a favor for me." She smiled briefly at him and Fred relaxed his guard a little. At least she wasn't mad.

"Sure, Miss Chloe, if I can," he replied warily.

She smiled again and went on. "Since *The Observer* stopped printing, I've had trouble getting newspaper to line my shelves and drawers, and now I find I don't have any at all. You know, paper is so hard to come by.":

Fred nodded, mystified.

"So it occurred to me that you might have old wanted posters you don't need. I could use them on

148

the shelves." Her eyes rested on his face a moment, then skittered away. "Of course, the town is so small now, I don't even know if the authorities send them to you anymore."

Fred shifted his considerable weight to one foot and rubbed his jaw. "Yeah, I get 'em once in a while. They come over from Portland, sometimes Montanny and Idaho. But they ain't a proper thing for a lady to line her shelves with. I mean, they ain't about respectable people."

For a moment he worried that he'd made some grave mistake when Chloe's face tightened, but the expression passed so quickly he assumed he'd imagined it.

"I have to make do where I can, Fred. Times are lean. Besides, I can turn over the printed sides of the posters so they don't show. And I suppose the new ones might be cleaner."

He turned and motioned her into his office. "Well, come on inside, then. I'll give you all the ones I have and you can use what you want. Hell, I never bother to look at 'em anymore. 'Cept for that blacksmith you got working for you, we ain't had any strangers here since I can't remember. What desperado would come to Misfortune?" He huffed out a chuckle or two, but Chloe only got that tight-lipped look again. Damn, but she could give a body the yim-yams.

He opened desk drawers and pulled out posters going back at least ten years. The dust and cluttered disorder in his office went back that far, too, although he'd been blind to it until he saw her giving it a disapproving eye. He waited for her to say some-thing, and was surprised when she didn't.

He handed her a sheaf of papers, some yellowed with age. "Here you go, Miss Chloe. I hope they work."

She put them in her basket and he escorted her back to the sidewalk. "I know they will, Fred. I ap-preciate your help."

The grateful smile she turned upon him was so disarming, he forgot his earlier discomfort. "Glad to do it, ma'am, glad to," he replied.

She headed toward home and as he settled back into his chair, he pondered that it might not be so bad to let her do his washing after all.

Chloe avoided the backyard and hurried up the front steps with her cache, guilt and triumph war-ring in her thundering heart. Oh, when Fred made that remark about no desperados coming to Misfor-tune, Chloe felt like she'd swallowed her tongue. But he'd believed her story about lining shelves and hadn't asked any of the questions she'd feared.

She went straight through the parlor upstairs to her room and shut the door. From her open windows she could hear the sound of Travis shaping a wheel rim for the wagon he'd been working on when she left. He hadn't said one word to her at breakfast. Even though apologies seemed to be beyond his scope, she'd expected some kind of repentance for his outrageous rudeness over that bottle of whiskey. Instead, he'd ignored her.

Putting the basket on the dresser, she took out the

posters with shaking hands. A jumble of feelings bumped around inside her: worry that she wouldn't learn anything and fear that she might. Except for meals, Travis never came into the house, but her nerves made her so jumpy she expected to see him burst through her bedroom door any minute.

She sat on the bed and began leafing through the grubby, dog-eared pages, reading around the coffee cup rings. Some of them bore rough illustrations of fierce-looking men, but many had no pictures and only physical descriptions. There were rewards for murderers, bank bandits and train robbers, horse thieves and cattle rustlers. Most of the crimes had been committed in other states like Colorado and Wyoming, although she did find one about the Wallowa National Bank robbery up north in Enterprise three years ago.

But there was no poster about an escaped convict. She let out the breath she'd been holding and pushed a straggling curl back into place. For all she knew, Travis might have broken out of a jail halfway across the country.

She glanced down at the pages again and rose from the mattress. A whole day's worth of laundry waited for her and she'd wasted enough time on this.

In the kitchen she lifted one of the stove lids and shoved the posters inside. A whisper of relief brushed her when their edges ignited.

Chloe pulled a sheet from her laundry basket and secured one corner of it to the clothesline. As soon as she anchored the other end, the wind caught it and it billowed like a full-breasted mainsail. She moved down the line of laundry, touching bed linens she'd hung earlier, checking for dampness. The soap and bluing might be hard on her hands, but she took satisfaction from the clean sheets, gleaming white in the sun. Unable to resist, she opened her arms and hugged one to her, inhaling the fresh, windblown fragrance. No perfume was sweeter.

Travis glanced up from the doubletree he was working on to drag his arm across his sweating forehead. He paused when he saw Chloe embrace the sheet with spontaneous pleasure, her apron ties flapping around her like ribbons. It made it hard to keep his promise to himself.

This morning he'd rolled off the bed, his shirt twisted around him from sleeping in it, certain he'd thought of the best way, the only way, to deal with her: avoid her as much as possible. He wouldn't argue with her anymore, or warn her away from her fiancé, or defend himself against her complaints. He'd simply pretend she didn't exist. He'd managed it through breakfast and lunch, purposely disregarding her silent demands for an apology. He'd freeze in hell before he'd apologize. He didn't have anything to be sorry for. A free man had the right to take a drink—she wasn't his jailer and he wouldn't let her begin to think she was.

But now she stood there, her hair fire-gold against a backdrop of endless blue sky, framed by the doorway he watched her through. Suddenly the wind shifted, molding her skirt to her nicely shaped legs and derriere. He should have kissed her tempting pink mouth when he'd had the chance last night. He imagined the moist softness of her lips, the firm curve of her bottom in his hands as he pulled her up against his hips and—

Travis dropped his gaze back to the doubletree as a suffocating frustration filled him. If he wasn't careful, he warned himself, one of these days he might act on the feelings that were crowding him out of his skin. Then there'd be the devil to pay.

"Howdy, Miss Chloe. I knocked at the front door, then I figured you might be out here."

Chloe turned to find Fred Winslow opening the gate. His polished badge glared like a mirror in the late afternoon sun. She turned a hasty look in the direction of the shop, but couldn't see Travis. The sheriff carried a package tucked under his arm.

"Fred," she hailed nervously. "This is a surprise." She hurried to the fence, hoping to keep him from coming too close to the shop. What had possessed him to come here now? "I didn't expect to see you again so soon."

He cast a lingering, curious look at the smoke rising from the forge chimney. "Is business pretty good?" he asked.

"Pretty good. What can I do for you, Fred?" she prompted.

Her question dragged him back to his subject. "Hmm? Oh, well, after you left his morning I went over to DeGroot's and would you believe it?" he said, giving her the bundle. "These come just this week. I thought maybe you could use them, too. 'Course, Albert was right tickled when I told him what you'd be doing with them."

'Course, Chloe thought. Now the storekeeper knew about this, too. She looked at the wanted posters in her hands, wishing on her soul that she'd never started this. The sound of metal clanking against metal came from the forge. Again, she glanced over her shoulder. "Oh," she answered weakly, "thank you for bringing them by, but really, you shouldn't have bothered."

"Weren't no bother at all, Miss Chloe," he replied expansively. "Looking at these took me back to the old days when I had some really rough customers in my jail. 'Course mostly they was just miners and cowboys sleeping off a Saturday night, but I remember a few times when—"

On he droned down a single-minded track, showing no signs of leaving. She shifted restlessly from one foot to the other. In the span of their conversation this morning he seemed to have lost his wariness of her, a fact she regretted heartily.

After hearing about the time he thought he'd captured Billy the Kid only to find out it was really a dry goods clerk from Albuquerque, Chloe derailed him and led him back toward the gate. It was all she could do to keep herself from pulling on his arm. "Fred, I don't mean to interrupt, but if I don't get back to this washing I'll be out here till after dark."

"Yup, you're right. I do tend to run on, given half a chance," he admitted. He loitered at the open gate, surveying her drying laundry. "You know, I was thinking maybe I should hire you to wash my duds. Looks like you do a mighty nice job of it and it would be a real treat to have shirts done right for a change."

And have him coming by every week? "I'm sorry, Fred, but I've got just about all the work I can handle now." She gestured at the sheets hanging on the line.

"Guess I should've asked sooner," he lamented. "Well, I'll be running along, Miss Chloe."

She thanked Fred again and then, leaning out over the fence to make sure he was gone, she watched as he finally headed back down the street to his whittling.

Just then a sharp gust of wind grabbed the pages from her hands and scattered them across the yard. Chloe chased after them as they whirled in spirals above her and ahead of her. Running and bending, running and bending, she finally cornered the last poster next to the shop wall. She crouched and stretched her hand forward to grab it when suddenly a boot slammed down on the face of the one-eyed cattle rustler named there, scarcely missing her fingers. Her gaze shot up the long, denim-covered leg above the foot, and she saw Travis staring down at her, stone-faced and silver-eyed.

"Let me help you," he offered, his voice deadly quiet.

"Thank you, no," she said, retreating to the safety of her morning haughtiness. She tugged on the page to pull it free. "If you'll move your foot, I can get on with my work."

"And what kind of work might that be?" he asked, his boot still planted on the rustler's face. He tucked his hand under his arm to pull off a glove, then reached down and grabbed the offending poster from the dust. He scanned the page in silence.

"Fred Winslow was kind enough to give me these old posters so I could line my shelves and drawers with them," she answered, taking on an air of injured dignity. "I can't afford anything else."

He snatched the other posters from her hands before she could react, holding them up out of her grasp while he sorted through each one.

"Give me those," she demanded, jumping to reach them. "You—you'll get them dirty."

"All kinds of criminals in here. They're offering nice rewards, too. But there's not one about a runaway state prisoner. Too bad." He jammed the flyers into her hands.

"I don't know what you're talking about," she protested. Again she had the uncomfortable feeling that he read her thoughts as easily as a newspaper.

He locked her wrist in a grip from which she could not wriggle free and pulled her face up to his. His hair was damp with sweat and his face was soot-smudged. "What did you have in mind for me? Were you trying to find out if the law wants your disobedient blacksmith bad enough to pay for him? Since the sheriff didn't try to haul me away, I guess you're still thinking about it."

"No, it's not like that," she squeaked, frightened now. "My shelves—"

He let go of her arm, disgusted. "You're a really bad liar, Chloe. You shouldn't try it."

Her temper rallied then, her moment of fear dissolving. "I didn't know it was a virtue to be a *good* liar. Are rudeness and disrespect talents to be admired? A license to do things someone has told you not to do?"

"Who the hell are you to order me around? I told you I had enough of that to last me *two* lifetimes. You'd better get off my back or you'll be watching it go down the road. And I don't think that's what you really want—you're getting a lot more than you're paying for." He started to walk away, then turned to face her, pointing at her to emphasize his words. "One more thing. I'll kill any man who tries to put me in jail again. You keep that in mind."

He stalked back to the forge and she knew he meant every word he'd said.

Later that evening Chloe was scrubbing the table, trying to justify her original demand for Travis's temperance. After all, that was how he'd started all this, with his whiskey sipping. She'd never have gotten the idea to talk to Fred Winslow if Travis had yielded.

Her conscience was making it a difficult task, harassing her with the inescapable truth that she'd done a conniving, mean-spirited thing. She wished now she'd listened to that conscience when it had spoken before, urging her to abandon the idea of trying to turn Travis in.

"... *you're getting a lot more than you're paying for.*"

That was a fact. He worked hard and his only payment was a roughed-in room in the shop and his meals. She knew that point alone gave her little say over what he did with his spare time.

She moved to the sink and looked out the window. Tonight the chair stood empty in the dark blue twilight. Then as if a ghost had risen from the cemetery, she pictured her father sitting there a hundred nights like this, a thousand. Usually sodden and morose, sometimes he didn't speak for days. Doc had told her she was lucky Frank was a melancholy drunk instead of a mean one.

But she'd never seen Travis drunk, or even tipsy. It was vexing, but she knew she owed him an apology. And if she didn't do it now the problem would keep her awake.

"Oh, *all right!*" she huffed, her better nature winning again. She grabbed a lantern and went down the back steps.

Travis found himself walking through a dim, shadowy country that it seemed the sun had never touched. Trees with black branches rattled like dry bones in the wind. A chilly mist swirled around his knees and hid the spongy ground that pulled at his boots. And everywhere was the smell of dampness and decay.

His heart began to beat heavily in his chest.

Here, in this eternal twilight, grief and loneliness ran like howling wolves, stalking him on a path that twisted deeper into the dark forest of those dead, bare trees.

Fear and despair dried his throat. Something was close behind him—he could hear the pounding footsteps growing nearer. He knew he had to run, but didn't know where to go. He was lost on this black and gray landscape, and the mist around his legs was like molasses, hobbling him. Sweat-soaked and breathless, he struggled to get away from his pursuer, but he could barely move. His heart felt as though it might explode from the effort.

Then suddenly, the one who chased him was now in the path ahead, waiting for him, beckoning him. Man or woman, Travis couldn't tell—a white cowl covered the figure's face. The paralysis that had slowed him fell away and he was propelled inexorably forward.

Who was it waiting for him, who? He wrenched the cowl away and saw Celia, her face blue, his belt around her neck. She held out her arms to pull him into her lifeless embrace.

No—God, no.

When Chloe walked in and saw Travis, she was reminded of the first day he spent upstairs, weak and delirious, thrashing around on the mattress. She wondered briefly if he'd suffered some kind of relapse. No, she decided, he was dreaming.

"Travis," she called, approaching his bed. "Wake up. I want to talk to you." She reached out to shake him from his nightmare.

He plucked her hand from his shoulder and held

it in a viselike grip, apparently intent on snapping the bones. "Goddamn you, Celia," he growled. "Go back to hell where you belong."

"Travis, let go of my hand," Chloe said, alarmed. "You're going to break it!"

Travis instantly relaxed his grip and sat up with a start, the old bed screeching. He saw Chloe standing next to him, her eyes huge in the lantern light as she massaged her wrist. He recognized his surroundings and realized he'd had another nightmare, this time about his wife. The quarrel with Chloe must have triggered it.

"Did I hurt you?" he muttered, embarrassed.

"No, I'm all right." Who was Celia, she wondered, that he would curse her with such fury? The strength of his grip and his venomous words had been terrifying, but he looked even more frightened than she was. Sweat drenched him and his face was pale as death. "What about you?" she asked quietly.

He waved his hand, anxious to change the subject. "I'm fine, fine." His bad dreams were not open for discussion. Feeling foolish and yet still shaken, he tried to make a joke of the incident. "Was I yelling loud enough to bring you out here?"

Now Chloe looked self-conscious as she shrugged and ducked her head. "No, it wasn't that. It's just, well, I wanted to apologize for what I said yesterday. I had no right to tell you what to do and to compare you to my father."

He sat up on the edge of the bed and motioned her to a stool next to the old chest of drawers. She perched on the seat, her hands folded in her lap. He could see this was difficult for her. Chloe was proud, not the type to enjoy admitting she was wrong.

"I saw you on that chair, the same place he sat most of the time. It brought back memories, I guess."

"It made you miss him," Travis ventured.

She shook her head emphatically as she watched a moth bumping against the lantern's glass chimney. "I don't miss him. After my mother was gone he never drew a sober breath, or a happy one. When he died, it was for the best."

Again Travis wondered about the lack of emotion she claimed. It wasn't that she didn't care, he suspected. For some reason, she chose not to let herself care, or forgive. But that was like clamping down the lid on a boiling pot. One of these days the lid was going to blow off. That fool Peterson was not going to be much help when it happened. She deserved better.

When he spoke, he drew the words from a part of himself he rarely bothered to consult anymore. "Chloe, you should try to get over that grudge you're carrying. You've got a long time to live and you don't want that weight dragging you down."

"I don't know what you're talking about," she retorted, frowning. "I'm not carrying a grudge. I told you, that accident my father had was for the best."

Travis abandoned the thought. It wasn't his business. Besides, he was probably the last person on earth to give advice about letting go of bitterness. Then he remembered Fred Winslow.

"What about the sheriff," his tone now demanding and distrustful. "Am I going to have to kill him?"

Chloe felt her cheeks grow hot but his question brought a chill to her stomach. She looked away from his accusing eyes into her lap.

"I told you the truth. I asked for the posters to line the shelves. At least that's what Fred believes I wanted with them." She met his gaze then. "He has no reason to think otherwise."

"None?"

Chloe maintained her connection with his eyes. "None. I told him nothing."

For several silent moments he watched her unflinching gaze. They weren't friends. He only worked for Chloe. But he'd come close to admiring her for her directness and gumption. She was stubborn, but at least she was honest about it. He nodded, satisfied.

"Does my drinking bother you that much?" he asked.

She thought a moment before answering. After the fuss she'd made, his whiskey bottle didn't seem as important as it originally had. He was nothing like Frank Maitland. It wasn't the drinking so much as his muleheaded defiance that made her fry.

"No," she finally admitted. "It doesn't bother me that much."

"Good, because I'm not about to change."

No, she imagined not, but somewhere inside her, a tiny voice cheered. He was rude, angry, and dangerous. But there was something about him, a heat, an energy . . . something.

162

"It's getting late," he said abruptly. "You'd better go back in."

She started to rise, then paused and sat again. "I'll just stay for a little while," she replied, reaching out to lower the lantern flame. "Why don't you see if you can go back to sleep."

He studied her a moment, then nodded, accepting her unspoken offer. It was a simple gesture really, but it was the nicest thing anyone had done for him in years. He lay back against the mattress, one hand resting on his chest.

Just as he was dropping off, he thought he felt her hand cover his.

Chapter 7

The next morning was overcast, a rare occurrence at this time of year. Chloe decided to take advantage of the cooler day and make soap. It was a hot, messy job so she wore her oldest clothes to stand over the kettle in the sun-faded yard, stirring fat and lye water while it boiled.

The sound of Travis's maul striking iron intruded on her thoughts, reminding her of last night. How he'd looked while held in the arms of his nightmare: terrorized yet enraged as some unseen wraith named Celia appeared in his sleep.

Later, after he was asleep again, a wave of tenderness had engulfed her while she watched him. Awake, he was often rebellious and independent, harboring a cold, inexplicable anger. But asleep, his face still bruised, he looked like an exhausted teenage boy who'd been in a fight. The impulse to hold his hand after he'd dozed off had been so compelling, she'd been helpless to stop herself. It was a very forward thing to do, but she'd sat with him for a half hour, just watching over him.

For the thousandth time Chloe wondered about

the man working in the shop. She knew little about him beyond the fact that he was running from the law. She still didn't even know why he'd been sent to prison, and she frequently regretted her pretended lack of curiosity the day he would have told her the reason.

In fact, he knew far more about her than she did him. For the most part he appeared to be carefully controlled, but she sensed frightening, turbulent emotions churning just beneath that surface. She'd glimpsed them when he first arrived. She also detected a strength of character. The few things she had learned about him only served to make him even more puzzling than before.

She swished her paddle through the bubbling mixture in the kettle. Steam and the smell of wood smoke drifted over her. One thing was certain. It was becoming very difficult to ignore him. His powerful physical presence alone ensured that. Time and again Chloe had caught herself following his shape with her eyes. Or during some boring job like this one, her transgressing thoughts would stray to him. No amount of scolding herself made any difference. And now she'd held his hand.

Evan—he was the right one for her, she reminded herself anxiously, pushing the paddle with more determination. Not the outlaw blacksmith.

The anvil rang again. Anyway, he didn't remember what she'd done, she was certain of that.

She ladled the harsh soap into pans to harden, then stopped. At least she *hoped* he didn't.

* * *

But Travis did remember. He had Doc's mare in the shop and as he tucked the horse's foreleg between his knees to nail on her shoe, the memory of Chloe's hand on his stirred up more feelings than he wanted it to. Now and then he glanced at her standing over her black iron pot, wearing a blue dress bleached by time and washed to the color of a morning sky. Her rolled-up sleeves revealed slender pale arms. Damp strands of reddish hair, loose from her hairpins, twisted into curls at her neck and on her forehead. He tried to ignore the way her hips swayed as she stirred the concoction she brewed, but he wasn't having much luck.

Lately, he had to admit, he was discovering there was more to her than orders and opinions. Life was much easier when Chloe was bossy and irritating. Her occasional gestures of kindness only complicated what he wanted to remain as very simple. When the time came to leave, he wanted to walk away without one backward glance or a single regret.

She would make that hard, he realized. He'd never known a woman with so many sides to her. Faces, yes. Several women he'd known had owned lots of faces, each with a different, self-serving purpose. But Chloe had just the one. Her unpredictability was frustrating but at the same time, intriguing.

The smell of homemade soap floated to him and as he snipped the last shoe nail in the horse's hoof, Travis wondered how many of those sides he'd get to glimpse before he left.

* * *

Late that afternoon, Chloe sat in the oak swivel chair at her father's desk and unlocked it. Lifting the rolltop, she took out her pen and ink pot, and a scuffed leather-bound box. When she opened the box and looked inside, she was buoyed by the sight of silver and gold coins jumbled together. She added the ones Travis had given her today, then reached in and ran her fingers through the money like a miser, enjoying the weight of it in her hands.

Each day, her blacksmith shop made more money to add to the cache, and every night before dinner she counted it, marking her progress on a piece of paper. She was going to make it. Her father had left her in this mess, but she'd picked herself up and found a way out of it. She still had three weeks till the mortgage payment was due and she finally dared to believe she would meet that deadline.

Three more weeks and she could breathe easier.

Three more weeks and Travis McGuire would be gone.

Her head came up at the thought. That was their agreement, that he'd stay till the payment was made. Yes, of course, he'd be leaving. It certainly would be for the best, she told herself sensibly. She could then move ahead and have a life with Evan.

Odd, but that wasn't as comforting a thought as it had once been and she struggled to understand why.

Chloe sat up abruptly, straightened her papers and closed the box with a thud. Three more weeks—

She put down her pen and gazed out the open door at the emptiness of the prairie just beyond the yard. It was just that, well, she'd sort of gotten used to Travis being out there, working. To seeing him flood water over his dark hair at the pump at the end of the day, to hearing his footfalls on the back steps at dinner time. She was beginning to expect to find his eyes leveled on her if she turned suddenly, to look out at night to see yellow lantern light in his window and know he was just across the yard. . . .

Her hands were poised on the handles of the roll-top to close it when she glanced down at one of the pigeonholes and noticed her father's old mining claim. She sat back in the chair and stared at the yellowing paper. It made her smile to think about it, the commotion that claim had stirred up. She'd been a very little girl at the time. Her father didn't drink back then. He'd wanted to give gold mining a try, close the shop for a while. Everyone he knew was getting rich, he'd said, and he wanted his share. Although it sounded like a wonderful adventure, Chloe hadn't wanted him to go. She knew she'd miss him too much. Emma was adamantly opposed to the idea, and her parents went round and round until Frank finally gave up and stuffed the claim into an old cigar box and put it in the desk.

She stood again and closed the desk. Then far off and dreamlike, she heard music. On summer evenings when the wind was right, Chloe could hear old Zeke Lomax playing the piano at the Twilight Star Saloon and she'd stop what she was doing to listen a moment. Tonight as she sat at the desk, a cool breeze lifting the curtains, the sweet melody of "Annie Laurie" floated to her. She left her chair and went to stand at the door. A bittersweet smile pulled at the corners of her mouth. She hadn't thought of that song in years.

Her memory traveled back to a long-ago harvest dance held in Misfortune. She must have been, oh, let's see, she pondered. It had been before her mother died. She was about sixteen then. She'd worn a beautiful pale pink gown with a daring neckline that so irked her father he threatened to lock her in the house. As a compromise, she'd draped Emma's best cream lace shawl over her shoulders. Her hair she'd tortured into foot-long sausage curls that trailed down her back and bounced like springs with each step.

Doyle Higley, on furlough from the Apache wars in New Mexico, had called for her in his lieutenant's uniform. She'd felt like a princess that evening, dancing under the big autumn moon with a handsome young knight.

The song ended and Chloe moved away from the door. Ah, well, she reflected, that was all long ago. Doyle had been killed in battle three months later and her own life had changed a lot since that night.

But now as Zeke took up "My Darlin' Clementine," Chloe lifted her skirts a couple of inches and pirouetted around the room, remembering a time when her worries had been as light as thistledown.

Travis found her thus. He'd come in looking for his dinner and tracked her down to the parlor. At first he wasn't sure what she was doing, then he heard the faint music. He had to smile to himself as he watched her twirl and swish her skirts like a

child, completely absorbed. Dancing! He didn't
think the fussbudget was interested in much else
besides riding roughshod over everyone. On impulse,
he stepped into her path when she reached his side
of the room and let her dance right into his arms.

Chloe bumped into his chest, then pulled up
short, startled and feeling foolish. A blush burned
her face. "Good heavens, what are you doing?"

"Dancing with a lady," he said, and grasped her
waist. "And don't tell me 'no'." Zeke was now playing
a waltz and Travis swept her away, navigating them
around the furniture.

Flabbergasted not only by his actions, but as she
floated within the circle of his arms Chloe was also
surprised to find that Travis danced so well. Sometimes she forgot he hadn't been *born* in jail, that he'd
had a life before, even if she didn't know anything
about it.

His combed hair was slicked down with water,
still wet from its dousing at the pump. His clean
chambray shirt smelled of her soap and his own
scent. Where her hand rested on his shoulder she
felt warm, firm muscle moving beneath the fabric.
Chancing a look at his eyes, she saw a smile there,
though it didn't reach his lips. She really wished she
could see the rest of his face, the part hidden by his
beard.

She knew she should stop; it didn't seem right to
be twirling around the parlor like this. But before
she could protest, he'd maneuvered them out the
screen door and Chloe found herself waltzing on the

wide wraparound porch. The dry lawn whizzed past in a yellow blur.

"Travis, this is crazy. Stop it right now," she demanded, but the bubble of laughter in her words completely diluted their impact. "What if someone sees us?"

She was right, it *was* crazy. And he was enjoying himself. He heard the amusement in her voice that she tried to stifle and knew she was enjoying it, too. The muted fragrance that was so much a part of her drifted to him now, and he pulled her a little closer. To hold a woman again was a sweet luxury, with her breasts brushing against his chest. She was softer than he'd imagined; she was so angular and unyielding in other ways.

They whisked around the corner, past the side windows, his boot heels thumping on the flooring. Her sparkling eyes and flushed cheeks made her look like a girl and made him feel his true age. It was good to do something just for the pleasure of it, in a life that had been so serious and difficult. "No one comes down here this late in the day. Who's going to see?"

"Evan, for one," she replied.

"Aw, the hell with Evan. He's as much fun as having your bowels purged," Travis said, as he turned her to make the trip back along the porch.

"*Travis,* what a horrible thing to say!" Despite the crude analogy, she choked on a laugh. "He'll be here anytime. What would he think if he found us like this?"

"I would wonder what's going on," a voice pronounced.

Chloe peered over Travis's shoulder and saw Evan standing on the front steps, a coolly righteous expression on his face. She jumped out of her partner's arms, feeling vaguely guilty for having a good time.

Travis turned and frowned at Evan, then grabbed Chloe's hand back in his. For a moment he thought of pulling her into his arms and planting a full-lipped, moist kiss on her, to touch her tongue with his, to really get Peterson riled. But just when he turned to do it, he caught sight of her long-lashed eyes staring back at him and the red-gold wisps of hair curling around her face. He knew Evan Peterson had nothing to do with it. What he desired of Chloe was too potent to act on, too personal to share with a witness.

With difficulty he checked the impulse and said, "It's considered good manners to return a lady to her chair after the dance." He tucked her hand in the crook of his arm and opened the screen door for them both.

Chloe glanced back at Evan where he stood on the porch, his jaw hanging.

In the kitchen, Chloe felt as though she'd developed ten thumbs. Aware of Travis now in a way she'd never been before, she dropped his knife and fork before she could get them into his hand. When she tried to put a boiled potato on his plate, it rolled off back into the steaming pot, splashing her with hot water.

"Need any help?" she heard him ask.

Her forehead damp, she was acutely conscious of him behind her, watching her while she fumbled clumsily with a slab of roast.

"I don't imagine cooking is one of your specialties," she replied, desperately trying to sound unaffected by his presence. Finally she handed him the dish, piled awkwardly with two servings of everything, and a biscuit perched on top of it all.

He looked at the mountain of food. "I must be hungrier than I thought," he said, nonplused.

"Oh, I'm sorry," she replied, realizing what she'd done. She held her hand out for the plate. "Here, give it to me and I'll take part of it off."

He pulled back. "No, I'll keep it. That dancing gave me a big appetite."

Their eyes met for a long moment, gray and green. For the first time he looked away before she did. Then he turned from her and went out the back door.

Chloe took a deep breath and smoothed her hands over her apron, then carried the platter of meat and vegetables to the dining room.

As she expected, Evan was waiting for her at the table, fired up over what he'd seen. At least, as fired up as Evan could get.

"The man obviously thinks nothing of your reputation." He helped himself to the pot roast. "Dancing on the porch! What if someone had seen you? Someone besides me?"

"It was pretty harmless, Evan. Anyway, no one did see us," she responded lamely. She picked at her food, not hungry. She couldn't deny what he'd ob-

174

served, and she couldn't pretend that Travis had held a gun to her head to make her dance.

"But someone could have," he insisted. "It's not you I blame, Miss Chloe. I know it's all that blacksmith's fault. This is just another reason why we should set a date for our wedding. When we're married and I'm living here, McGuire won't dare take such liberties with you."

This was not the first time Evan had mentioned their wedding. He appeared to have forgotten that she'd never accepted his proposal, acting as though they needed only to choose a day and time.

"He was very insulting to me, too," he went on, reaching for the butter. "Comparing me to—to, well, I won't repeat it now, especially at the table." The glare he turned on her was brief, but so malevolent she was instantly chilled. "I didn't hear you object much, either."

"I most certainly did object!" Chloe replied, stung by the truth of his words. "I told him it was an awful thing to say. I'm not his mother, Evan."

"No, you are his employer and he's becoming too bold," Evan harped relentlessly. "You should tell him he's not welcome in the house."

Chloe sighed. This was one of Evan's favorite complaints, that she should banish Travis to the shop. Actually, since Travis had arrived, Evan had become a chronic complainer.

"I'm not going to do that. It would be rude." This triggered a discussion during which Evan again declared his concern for her safety. But Chloe was beginning to get the very uncomfortable feeling that Evan's chief objective was to control her.

She could only remember what Travis had told her, that Evan was less worried about her than himself.

After the meal, as she carried the dishes to the kitchen, she imagined doing this every night for the rest of her life while Evan sat in the parlor.

While Evan lived in her house.

While Evan slept in her bed.

At this last thought, she nearly dropped the plate she carried. The idea of a loveless marriage based only on tolerability was becoming less attractive to her every day. Originally, it had seemed like the practical thing to do.

Now she wasn't so sure.

That night she tossed and turned for hours. For the first time in her life, indecision plagued her. Even at the most desperate moments in her past, she'd known exactly what to do. She simply hadn't always had the means.

Long after midnight, she finally got up and pulled a chair over to the window. It was a moonless night and stars were scattered like a million diamonds across the sky. A low wind lifted her hair from her shoulders. She put her elbows on the sill and turned her face into the breeze to catch its coolness. Looking down, she saw a light in Travis's window. It was so late, she wondered if he was having nightmares again.

Or maybe he was thinking about a dance he'd shared with a woman on her front porch.

"Have either of you gotten a look at Chloe lately?" Mildred DeGroot asked. She addressed the question to Albert and her best friend, Bertha Preston.

Albert was checking the latest shipment of yard goods against a bill of lading. Now and then he'd wet the point of his pencil on his tongue and make notes.

"Not since last week," he replied distractedly, squinting at a bolt of gingham on the shelf. "Why? What's wrong with her?"

"That's just it," Mildred said. "Nothing is wrong. No, not the gingham, Albert. We're on the bleached muslin now," she interrupted herself, pointing to a white bolt. "Chloe came in just after lunch to buy coffee again. For a while she was buying so much tea a body would have thought Queen Victoria herself was living over there. Anyway, she smiled a time or two and she wasn't so prickly." Mildred stretched for a good description. "I guess you might say she nearly *glowed*. And her hair, she's still wearing it that new way."

Albert looked up over the rims of his spectacles. "Maybe she and Evan are finally getting married. He's been in a real dither since that McGuire feller got here."

Mildred leapt on this exciting possibility. "Oh, I'll bet you're right, Albert! Those two probably *are* getting married."

Albert went to the storeroom and Bertha nodded in agreement. "And high time, too, if you ask me. She's not getting any younger and it's not as though

177

they're strangers. A husband is what the woman needs to dull that sharp tongue of hers." She glanced at the storeroom door, then lowered her voice. "Of course, he's not much to look at, but neither is Chloe anymore. A man in her bed ought to put some color in that pale face of hers."

Mildred and Bertha cackled viciously over this and then a wicked sparkle lit Mildred's eyes as she added, "Maybe his, too."

An hour later Evan Peterson walked over to DeGroot's to buy a bag of candy. He was on his way to Chloe's house for dinner and hoped the gift might close the distance he'd felt growing between them from the minute McGuire had arrived in Misfortune.

Chloe had always commanded their courtship and now she had abandoned that role, which was not at all in keeping with her usually determined personality. Evan knew candy or flowers weren't much but he was helpless to do more.

He waved to Albert as he crossed the scarred wooden floor to the counter. He stood there a moment, studying the rows of jars containing hard candies in drops and sticks that gleamed like jewels in the five o'clock sun pouring through the front window.

"Afternoon, Evan," Albert said. "What can we get you today?"

"I guess I'll have a few of those butterscotch drops," he replied.

Albert reached for the jar and Mildred came out

of the storeroom. After a brief greeting, she tact-lessly plunged in. "You know, I'd forgotten what a beauty Chloe used to be. But when she came in to-day for coffee, she was glowing like a firefly, Evan." Mildred paused dramatically before adding, "She sure looked like a woman in love."

Evan felt the blood drain from his face.

She prattled on obliviously. "I'll bet you two love-birds thought you were keeping it a secret, didn't you? You can't fool me. I can spot romance like a horse can sniff out clover."

Albert handed the butterscotch to Evan, who re-plied hastily, "I'll give Miss Chloe your regards, Mrs. DeGroot." He backed out nervously and was on the sidewalk before either of the DeGroots realized he hadn't paid for the candy.

Evan gripped the paper bag holding the candy as he dragged through Misfortune to its west end. At first, Chloe's dislike for the drifter had been obvious, and the reason for him being there, a loathsome ne-cessity. But his very presence had changed Evan's re-lationship with Chloe—just how, he wasn't sure. She used to fuss over him a bit. Now she always seemed preoccupied, disinterested. She'd even stopped brewing tea for him.

A sudden, sharp pain lanced through his skull, a pain so acute it made a buzzing noise in his ears that sounded like a voice. What were the words? He stopped in the road a moment, listening intently, but it left as quickly as it came.

Evan had perceived a current that passed between

Chloe and McGuire when he caught them dancing together. For a moment he'd felt like a voyeur, observing an intimate scene in which he had no part.

He made up his mind he would have to act. He would deal with McGuire first.

When he got there, Evan loitered at Chloe's gate, looking at the thin plume of smoke that rose from the forge's chimney. She was in the house, he supposed. That was good. She didn't need to know about this. Again in his mind rose the memory of his Chloe in McGuire's arms, and worse, the vulgar comment the man made about him, which was probably only a sample of more. The gnawing doubts that now plagued him night and day rose again. What were they doing when he wasn't there? What were they saying about him?

His hand pushing open the gate, he made his decision. With each stride he took to the shop, his determination grew. He detested McGuire and the familiar ease with which he moved through Chloe's house, as though he actually belonged there, a house Evan had come to think of as his own. If she didn't see fit to put him in his place, Evan was prepared to do so.

He stopped in the doorway of the dim shop. He saw McGuire at the glowing forge, pumping the bellows like one of hell's gatekeepers. The acrid smell of burning metal in the air seemed fitting. The blacksmith's back was turned to the door so Evan nearly jumped out of his skin when he heard, "Something I can do for you, Peterson?"

McGuire turned to stare at him over his shoulder.

The man said nothing more and his face was devoid of expression. But his feral danger was as perceptible as the heat.

Evan quailed before approaching, then swallowed hard, drawing on his resentment for courage.

"Miss Chloe and I want you to know you're doing a good job here," Evan began, anxiously noting that McGuire's grip tightened on the long iron bar he held in the low flames. Determined to speak before his nerve abandoned him, he continued hurriedly. "But Miss Chloe asks that you remember your position here and keep to this shop. While you were sick, of course, you had to be in the house. But that isn't necessary now. Since it's summer, you can eat your meals out here. And Miss Chloe's reputation must be protected. Dancing on the porch last evening could have been very damaging to her, especially with a hired hand. You understand, don't you?"

Evan immediately regretted coming out here; as McGuire's eyes narrowed, they also appeared to turn silver in the low gloom. He pulled the iron bar out of the coals, the end of it white-hot. The shop suddenly grew close and stuffy.

"You didn't hire me, Peterson. Chloe did," McGuire growled, "and she's the *only* person I'll discuss this with. You go back and tell her that."

"Uh—she sent me to handle this—" Evan floundered in his lie. He desperately wished he'd never begun this. McGuire advanced on him, the iron bar held at his side. Evan could see the muscles in the blacksmith's arm flex convulsively as he clenched his fist around the metal. He could feel its heat even while he backed up, trying to keep his distance. Fear and hatred filled him as McGuire again emasculated him with only a look.

"She wants me to stay away from the house? Well, here's something for *you* to think about, Peterson." McGuire's gaze was as white-hot as the iron. "I want you to stay out of this shop. If you come back again while I'm here, I'll rip your throat out. You tell Chloe I said so. *You understand, don't you?*"

With a shaking voice that cracked, Evan tried to sound composed. "How dare you th-threaten me? He continued backing away until he felt the door frame between his shoulder blades. One of the few brave moments Evan had known in his life evaporated and was replaced by absolute, nauseating terror. Sweat beaded on his forehead and crept down his temples in itchy rivulets.

"No threats, Peterson." McGuire leaned forward until his face was only inches from Evan's. "I swear it."

Evan slid around the doorjamb and crossed the yard swiftly, grateful that no one saw his disgrace. His first impulse was to run to Chloe and tell her the savage threats her precious blacksmith had made. Then he realized he'd only be hiding behind her skirts. And while there was nothing he desired more at this moment, to have her defend him against this tormentor, his slim pride wouldn't let him do that.

He sat heavily on the bottom step at the back porch and waited for his breathing and heart to slow. A silence surrounded him, broken only by the jeering call of a blue jay perched on the clothesline post. His undiluted hatred of Mcguire stirred again as he looked down at his shaking hands where they rested uselessly on his lap.

Somehow, he'd find the opportunity to get even with McGuire. To make him sorry. Suddenly the buzzing pain in his head was back. He pressed his hands to his skull until it left.

When he raised his head, his gaze fell upon the shop door where McGuire stood leaning against the jamb, his arms folded across his chest, his silver eyes boring into Evan. His heart began thundering again and sweat stuck his clothes to him.

Evan heard a wordless sound of terror from his own throat, then he scrambled up the stairs to the back door, seeking protection. The pain in his head was back, the buzzing louder, taking shape, forming nearly discernible words.

Chloe answered Evan's urgent knocking. "Evan! I'm surprised to see you at the back."

She pushed the door open for him, but he stayed on the porch, saying nothing. His eyes were wide and his nostrils flared with each breath. "What's the matter? You look like the devil himself is chasing you. Don't you want to come in?"

"N-no," he stammered, then thrust the bag of candy into her hand. The top of the bag was crumpled and damp with sweat. "Th-this is for you, but I won't stay for dinner." He backed away from the door. "I will not come back as long as McGuire is here." He looked over his shoulder then, as if someone really were chasing him.

Alexis Harrington

She scanned the yard but saw nothing. "What has he done? Evan, wait a minute," she called. But he practically ran to the gate, glancing back at the shop a couple of times.

In frustration, Travis threw the cooled iron bar across the shop to dispel some of the rage churning in his belly. He paced with heavy steps back and forth over the hard-packed dirt floor. It had taken all his willpower to keep from smashing Peterson's nose with his fist. That miserable little pee-pants, Travis seethed, telling him not to come into the house. It wasn't an angry challenge, one man telling another man to stay away from his woman. Travis could have respected that. No, it was a watery, patronizing speech designed to reduce Travis to the status of a servant.

From Peterson he expected it. But disappointment over Chloe's involvement weighed like a stone in his chest. He thought they'd reached a level of mutual, if wary, respect. He was surprised and furious that she'd sent Peterson to talk to him.

His past rose to scorn him again. Yeah, he thought bitterly, it was probably galling her that she'd actually danced with an ex-convict. He kicked a saddle soap can into the wall. He'd almost begun to feel better about himself, despite the circumstances.

Though he'd vowed he'd never go near a forge again, working as a free man, even without pay, had given him back some of his self-respect. He felt good about the quality of his work and the compliments the customers gave him. Why wasn't that good enough? Why had Chloe's opinion come to matter so much more than anyone else's?

"Travis!"

He heard the wrath in her voice. Oh, hell, he moaned to himself. Now he had to deal with *her*. Damn it, he wasn't going to apologize for anything he'd said. He imagined her dragging Peterson out here and making them shake hands. No, by God, he wouldn't do it. Why couldn't she see what kind of man Peterson was?

"Travis," Chloe repeated as she came through the doorway. She stood uncertainly for a moment, letting her eyes adjust to the low light. At least she was alone.

"What did you do to Evan?" she demanded, finding him over by one of the stalls. "He left like he'd seen Death and said he won't be back as long as you're here."

Travis almost laughed. "Sounds like I've done both of us a favor." He stooped over to pick up the iron he'd thrown.

She rose to her full height, her chin out slightly. "What did you do?" she repeated. "And how dare you? You have no right to meddle in my personal affairs!"

His patience was exhausted. He yanked at the ties of his leather apron and ripped it off, throwing it down with all the strength his anger gave him. "Then do your own dirty work instead of sending your piss-ant *beau*!" he snapped, his voice rising with a sharp sarcasm. "What did you expect? Was I supposed to drop to my knees and say, 'Yes, Mister Peterson, I'll stay away from the house and the Missy'? Lincoln freed the slaves, Chloe, although you'd hardly know it around here!"

Chloe's brow furrowed in bafflement. "What are you talking about?"

Travis took long, rapid strides past the stalls to his room, with Chloe on his heels. He lifted his saddle-bags from the foot of the old iron bed, and pulled open the dresser drawers.

"You know, you told me you aren't afraid of anything. I didn't believe you then, and now I know why. If you wanted me to stay away from the house, to eat my meals out here, you should have had the guts to tell me yourself."

He pulled his few belongings from the drawers and jammed them into the leather bag, then turned to her. "I really expected better of you." His eyes lingered on her a moment, then he picked up a shirt and put it on. "I'm going. Now."

Chloe had no definite idea of what he was talking about but this last statement was glaringly clear. She didn't think of payments or having no place to live. No, through her mind ran a jumbled picture of the shop without Travis in it—silent, abandoned. "Going! You can't go!"

"Wrong, Chloe." He lifted the pillow on the bed and pulled out his whiskey bottle. He held it up in the low light to see how much was left, then put it in the bag. "When are you going to get passed the notion that you ride point for the whole world?"

It no longer mattered that she didn't know what

this was about. His accusations, his very tone, were as effective as holding a match to her fuse.

"When it honors its responsibilities!" she fired, pounding her fist into her palm. "If you will recall, McGuire, you practically insisted that I give you this job—I wasn't very excited about the idea. You said you'd work here until I make the mortgage payment. Now you're telling me you won't."

Travis had the saddlebags on his shoulder and had begun to push past her, but that stopped him. He turned back to her slowly, his frown black. "Are you saying my word is no good?" he demanded.

"No, Travis. You're saying it."

She wore a self-satisfied expression that goaded him. Oh, hell! He knew he couldn't leave. He'd salvaged little of the man he once was but, for good or bad, he had to see this through. He'd made an agreement with her. Otherwise he'd be gone so fast her head would spin. He flung the saddlebags back to the bed.

"I told you before, Chloe. You can't order me around." He forced himself to keep his hands at his sides for fear he'd throw something. "You think you're so tough, lady." He stepped closer to her, capturing her shoulders in his hands. She looked up at him, her eyes snapping green flames, and he thought a man could get lost in such eyes. "Well, I'm tougher."

For that instant, before she could say anything more, his control slipped.

When his mouth came down to cover hers, the kiss was not gentle. She could feel his beard against her chin, his lips briefly pressed hard to hers. He didn't hurt her, but it was a reprimand.

She struggled against his grip, finally able to free herself. She backed away, staring at him. Anger and something else, a low, throbbing current within her, made her breath short.

"Now you go back to the house and do your job," he ordered gruffly. "I'll do mine." His shirt was hanging open and he took it off again, throwing it over the stool.

How could she be so furious with him, yet long to touch curious fingers to that muscled chest he was showing her? Evan was right. She had to stay away from Travis. Not for Evan's reasons, but to save her own sanity.

"I'll leave your dinner tray on the back porch," she said with a voice that shook, then turned swiftly and fled to the house.

Chapter 8

Over the next couple of days, the two combatants took great pains to avoid each other, retreating to their respective corners.

At first, Travis hadn't believed Chloe would go as far as to leave his meals on the back porch. Apparently he'd underestimated the level of her contempt. When he came up the steps to get his dinner that first evening, he found it cooling on the tray in front of the closed door.

Furious, he left it there, barely resisting the urge to hurl the plate at the screen. Now he knew where he stood, as if he'd needed more proof. He went back to the shop, trying hard to ignore the racket his empty stomach made.

He sat down hard on a small keg in the corner, leaning his back against the rough wall. His arms hanging at his sides, he stretched his legs out in front of him and let a long, weary breath escape him.

Damn fool! He berated himself a dozen times over for giving in to his urge to dance with the Vinegar Princess and hold her in his arms. Because it had

been a hard lesson to learn, he'd easily begun to forget that others, once they learned about his past,
saw him as nothing more than a saddle bum with a
prison record. Although now he didn't even have the
saddle or a horse to put it on. He shook his head in
irony as a humorless chuckle escaped him.

The itch to leave, to save the shredded remains of
his self-respect, flamed so high in him he could feel
the wind at his back and the earth under his boots
as they carried him down the road.

But he'd promised to stay, and so he would, exiled
to this side of the yard. From the paddock, he heard
Lester nickering. He slowly got back to his feet to
give the horse her dinner. At least *she'd* get to eat.

After he fed Lester, Travis put on a clean shirt
and combed his hair in the scrap of mirror Chloe
had given him. This town had a saloon and saloons
could always put a meal together. He took five dollars out of his saddlebag.

He was in a foul mood as he walked toward the
gate, feeling rather than seeing a pair of green eyes
following him from the kitchen window. Let her
wonder, he thought.

He cast long shadows on the dusty street as he
headed east toward the Twilight Star. When he got
closer, he could hear the jangling sound of a piano
and the combined scents of beer and tobacco smoke
reached him. There was a certain comfort to be had
in the rough, unstarched atmosphere of such an es-
tablishment, where the presence of women was the
exception rather than the rule.

There was only one horse tied at the hitching post

in front. Things were pretty slow inside and Travis found a table in the corner. After he ordered his dinner and a beer from the bar, he noticed a woman sitting against the wall over by the piano languidly waving a fan. She wore a tired-looking blue satin dress with a low neckline. A cameo hovered above her ample cleavage, suspended on a wrinkled length of black velvet ribbon. In the low light, he couldn't guess her age, but her hair was too red to be real.

She caught his gaze, then rose from her seat to saunter over. She leaned her hip against his table and gave him a long, appraising look from the top of his head, pausing at his fly buttons, down to his spurs.

"Hi, sugar," she breathed. Her smile was hard and bright. "I haven't seen you around here before. What's your name?"

Travis chuckled. Prostitutes always spotted him as soon as he walked into a place, whether it was crowded or not. He must look like he had a lot of money. He didn't want what she had to sell, but it would be interesting to talk to her.

"My name is Travis."

"Mmm, I like that. I'm Dove Lassiter. You got a last name?"

"Travis is enough." He pushed the chair out for her with his foot. "Sit down, Dove. I'll get you a beer."

She sat eagerly, arranging her skirts with great care. Now that she was closer he could see the lines in her face, put there by more than age.

The barkeep brought his dinner, a big steak and fried potatoes, and gave Dove her beer.

"Are you a cowboy?" she asked, looking down at his spurs again. "I'm partial to cowboys."

"No, a blacksmith," he replied, wondering why her questions didn't bother him. Usually he clammed up when people got curious. He cut into the steak while she talked.

"You must be the one working for Chloe Maitland. I heard she was running her daddy's shop again."

"Do you know Chloe?"

Dove ran her finger around the rim of the beer mug. "I've never talked to her, if that's what you mean. But this is a small town. I know who she is, and her daddy used to come to see me regular before he got killed last spring." Her face clouded over for a moment. "He was a real lonely man. Shoot, most of the men who come to see me are lonely. But he was good to me, used to bring me nice presents, new dresses and such."

Travis nodded, thinking that Chloe didn't need to know she was paying back a loan that had helped to support Dove Lassiter. "Are you from around here, Dove?"

She shook her head. "I got left here by a cowboy on his way to a cattle drive in John Day. He said he'd be back in four months to marry me. That was two years ago." She shrugged, her hard smile slipping a bit. "I'm a littler smarter than I was then."

He watched her, faded and brittle in her blue satin, then thought back to Adam Mitchell's proposition to Chloe. This was what sometimes happened to women who had no money and no one to turn to. The world was a hard place for them, sucking the hope and beauty right out of them.

Travis finished his dinner and stood. "It was nice meeting you, Dove."

She looked up at him, disappointment plain on her face. "Don't you want to come upstairs? I'll take real good care of you."

"Not tonight, darlin'," he replied. "Maybe some other time."

She studied him, then shook her head. "Nope, I don't think so. Some other woman's got you good. I can feel it. I don't like it when a man falls that hard. Doesn't leave anything for the rest of us gals."

He gave her a short laugh. "No, there's no other woman." Then he leaned over and asked in a low voice, "What's your time worth to you?"

"Three dollars," she said, preparing to take him upstairs.

Travis took the money out of his pocket and pressed it into her hand, then pinched her chin. "Goodbye, Dove," he said.

This time her smile was genuine. " 'Bye, sugar," she called and dropped the dollars into her bodice.

Chloe had peeked at Travis from behind the kitchen curtains and watched him stalk away on long legs, empty-handed. When she was sure he wasn't looking, she opened the door and brought in the cold food. He couldn't hold out forever, she told herself, trying to slip out of the blame. He was obstinate but he had to eat. Hunger usually won out over stubbornness.

But then she saw him leave, all slicked down and clean-shirted. She followed his progress, going from window to window, and knew he was headed to town.

She still couldn't put her finger on what had started this battle. Evan was involved somehow, she knew. But that kiss Travis had forced on her, she fumed, that had finished it. She remembered the feel of his mouth hard on hers, reproving . . . dominating.

In the morning, the breakfast tray she set out for him remained untouched, too. The bread dried out, the eggs and sausage turned cold and unappetizing. This was ridiculous. If he wanted to starve himself to spite her, then fine! It made no difference to her.

She went on about her business, but the disharmony hung over her in a black gloom and nothing went right. She burned herself with the iron while trying to press the minuscule tucks on a camisole. She looked everywhere for her box of starch and had to open a new one when she couldn't find it. She'd even misplaced some of the bread she'd baked the day before, and began to wonder if she was losing her mind as well.

Chloe made a special effort to avoid the shop. When she had to stand over the washtub, she kept her back turned to the shop door. She hoped that by staying away from Travis, she'd be able to stop thinking about him. The effect was just the opposite.

Travis, withdrawn into the reclusion of his work,

wondered how she could keep her back so stiff and still reach the scrub board.

Miserable, she even made a trip out to the Tollivers' farm to see Evan, certain she could change his mind about coming to the house. It was just so much silliness for him to be this stubborn, and not at all like him.

But when she got to the farm, he wouldn't tell her anything about what had happened between himself and Travis. He only reiterated his refusal to return while the blacksmith remained, although the oddly sly, baleful looks he gave her made her feel very ill at ease. His headaches were worse, he said, and implied that she was solely to blame. The unsatisfactory meeting left her more irritable than before.

By the end of the third day of hostilities with Travis, Chloe found herself returning to the open kitchen door again and again to look across the yard at her father's old chair. And every time she looked, she found it empty.

What in the world was McGuire eating? He worked hard and he was a big man. He couldn't go without food. Maybe he was buying his meals at the Twilight Star Saloon. Oh, that would really cause a stir. She could hear it now. *What's the matter, McGuire? Ain't Miss Chloe feeding you? . . . Say, maybe she and Evan sent you down here so's they could do a little spoonin', privatelike. . . .*

Oh, God, Chloe agonized. Travis wasn't a man who encouraged prying, but he might be angry enough to answer such nosy questions. Her imagination galloped onward, then suddenly reared when she remembered that Dove Lassiter still sold her favors in a room above the saloon.

Not that she cared, Chloe tried to tell herself as she put on the kettle to heat water for her bath. That drifter's rough embrace, his mouth on hers, they weren't what stole her sleep at night. And those confused, edgy dreams about bare chests and straight, broad-shouldered backs, they were just a lot of nonsense produced by an anxious mind. And she'd had good reason to be anxious lately, with the mortgage and Evan's absurd ultimatum.

But she'd promised Travis meals in payment for his work and she meant to keep her part of the bargain, even if she had to force him to accept it.

Travis headed across the yard toward the back steps, his dirty clothes wadded under his arm. He wasn't even sure if Chloe would still do his washing. He'd just dump the bundle inside the kitchen door and go back to the shop.

It was a mild dusk, clear and fragrant, with a sliver of a new moon rising in the eastern sky. He went up the stairs slowly, reaching for the handle on the screen door while he studied the progress of Chloe's kitchen garden next to the porch.

He looked at her potatoes and decided to bake two or three in the forge again for dinner. It had worked last night. It wasn't that Chloe didn't provide him with food—she did. And sometimes it was hard to ignore when the aroma of her cooking floated from the kitchen. But it was left for him on the back porch with less ceremony than he used when he fed the horse. He wasn't about to give in to that kind of treatment, especially not for the simple crime of dancing with Her Highness. And he knew he couldn't go back to the Twilight Star again after that dinner a couple of days earlier. Dove would begin to expect him and he didn't need that kind of entanglement. Besides, he wasn't starving.

Hell, when his parents were children, living on poor tenant farms in Ireland, they'd *survived* on nothing more than potatoes. They would certainly keep him going for a few days, along with the bread he'd taken two nights ago. If Chloe wasn't in the kitchen right now, he'd try to grab some more butter, too.

But when he raised his eyes and looked through the screen, his hand froze on the pull and a hush fell on his spirit at what he saw.

Her back to him, Chloe sat in her bathtub pouring water over her hair with an enameled pan. The lamp above the kitchen table reflected on the water falling through the long strands in crystal sheets.

Travis had seen too much in his life, both obscene and immaculate—neither struck a deep chord in him anymore. But the beauty of the sight before him now, that of the rosy, softly curved woman in her bath, humbled him. He was surprised to feel a flush creep up his neck and face.

He'd sat with Celia many times while she bathed. In fact, she'd made quite a flashy production of it, using it as a powerful means to arouse him when it suited her. It had rarely failed to reduce him to a sweating, desperate agony of desire.

This was far different. This was just a woman in an old galvanized tub, washing with a chunk of that harsh lye soap she made. There was nothing flirtatious or romantic about it. But there was an intense intimacy to it that flustered him in a way that Celia's practiced pouting never did.

He stood at the door watching Chloe wash her arm with an old piece of toweling, feeling like a Peeping Tom but not quite able to back away. Why did this woman so capture his interest? She often had a tongue as harsh as a rusty saw blade. She was tough and pushy, with strong opinions about the right and wrong way of things, and she sometimes made him so mad he'd pack to leave.

But some undefinable pull she had always stopped him. He knew there was a soft side to her because he'd glimpsed it once or twice.

He turned and quietly went back down the steps, his clothes still tucked under his arm, wondering what new torment his dreams would bring him after seeing this.

The following morning, Chloe brought in the last tray she was going to leave for Travis. It was foolish to continue this way. If his bad manners kept him from coming forward first, she'd just show him who the bigger person was, in spite of that kiss and—and everything.

Toward noon, she fixed the kind of lunch she'd been serving him before all this began: big sandwiches, blueberry pie, lemonade. She would have made potato salad, too, but Morris Caldwell must have gotten into her garden again because the potatoes were mostly picked over.

She carried everything outside, and with a quick nervous smoothing of her blouse and skirt, she walked into the shop.

"Travis?"

He was so surprised to hear her voice, he almost swallowed the nails he held in his mouth. A big draft gelding stood behind him, patiently waiting for his last shoe. Travis glanced up and saw Chloe standing by the scrap bin.

His heart lightened at the sight of her, his defenses jostled. His memory of her soapy and sleek in her bath raced from his mind through his heart to his crotch. "Chloe," he said. He wasn't willing to let her see the effect she was having on him. He returned his attention to his work but not without noticing every detail about her.

Her hair was pulled to a loose twist on the crown of her head. She was dressed in a lavender skirt and creamy muslin blouse, clothes she'd often worn in the evenings when Peterson came for dinner. But it was the middle of the day so he was probably in the kitchen at this very moment. They must have reached a compromise: she'd ordered him to come back. Great. Peterson could have her.

At the thought, a funny twinge coiled in him that felt a little like jealousy. He swiftly crushed the feeling.

Chloe could only see the top of his dark head as he bent over the gelding's huge hoof. She'd felt his glance as his eyes swept over her, giving her a brief, oddly intimate look from her hair to her hem, as though he'd long ago claimed her as his own. She shook off the frivolous notion when he spoke.

"What brings you out to the wrong side of the yard?" he inquired curtly, nailing the shoe on.

Chloe hadn't thought of what she would say, then suddenly the words popped out. "I have forgiven you, even though I don't know why you started this disagreement, and I've brought your lunch."

He shook his head and there was a hint of incredulous, taunting laughter in his voice when he spoke. "Hot damn, isn't this my lucky day," he said, not bothering to favor her with a glance. "Mercy from the woman who sent her fiancé to order me to stay out of the house just because I danced with her." He dropped the horse's hoof and straightened to look at her. "Yessir and yes ma'am, this sure is my lucky day."

His clear gray eyes were so piercing Chloe almost backed up a pace, but when he mentioned Evan again she stopped and held up her hand. "What did Evan tell you?" she demanded.

"Exactly what you wanted him to. That dancing on the porch with someone like me would ruin your reputation and from now on, I'm to remember my place, and that place is out here." He gestured broadly at the low ceiling of the shop. "As if you don't remember."

Those were the very words Evan had used when he carped about that evening he'd found them. All the pieces fell into place and Chloe realized what had happened.

"Evan said that I asked him to talk to you? And you believed him?"

"Why shouldn't I?" he asked, raking his hair back off his forehead. "After all, you've reminded me how fortunate I am to have this job, griped about what I do with my free time, tried to sell me to the sheriff—" He shrugged. "I had no reason not to believe it."

Chloe was chagrinned. She turned away, glancing for a moment at a joint in the rafters where sparrows had found a nesting place. Everything he said was true and she had no defense. Absently she ran her hand over the smooth, cold surface of the anvil, then turned back to him. "I apologize for Evan. He shouldn't have done what he did. He feels insecure with you here, I guess."

"Don't make excuses for Peterson."

"Well, then, he was wrong," she conceded softly. "I didn't send him out here to talk to you. I didn't want you to stay away . . ." She trailed off, embarrassed at how that sounded, then straightened to her full height. "I promised you board and room for your work, and I insist that you accept them."

His brows rose. "You insist?"

Damn him, he was thinking she was being bossy again. She relented. "Please."

Travis thought it over and then nodded. She noticed how a shaft of sun falling from the loft window revealed mahogany-colored strands in his dark hair. He held out his arm as though he would put a guiding hand on her back to escort her through the door, but didn't touch her.

Outside he found she'd brought a little table to their picnic spot in the shade of the shop.

"It looks a lot better than plain bread," he said, lowering himself to his chair.

She looked at him sharply and realized where her baking had disappeared to. "Did you take my bread?" she asked.

He nodded. "Butter, too, when you were asleep upstairs, and potatoes from the garden."

There was a barely concealed touch of humor in his voice and she imagined him sneaking into the house in the dead of night to steal bread and butter.

She started laughing then and the sound of it reminded Travis of music.

"I thought I was losing my mind when I couldn't find those loaves," she said, glad to have back their unpredictable truce. He had a full-blooded vitality, even when he was sullen and angry, that she enjoyed and had missed. She shouldn't, she knew. No matter what she might think of him, he was still an escaped convict, maybe a thief or a murderer. But she had a hard time remembering that.

He watched her profile and the way the sun caught the shine and fire in her hair. A breeze came up and ruffled the wispy curls framing her face and blew a long strand across her eyes. She reached up to pull it aside.

What did a woman like Chloe see in Peterson? he wondered, not for the first time. She was smart, strong, brave—why did she want a worthless do-nothing like him dragging her down? When he thought of her trapped in marriage to Peterson, a familiar uneasiness nagged at him.

Travis considered this while devouring two sandwiches. As she was pouring his lemonade, he said, "So you're still going to marry the teacher, huh?"

Chloe was handing him the glass and she faltered for an instant. "I know you don't like him, Travis."

"No, that's a fact. I'm just wondering why you do. We've established that you don't love him and he doesn't love you. Doesn't sound like a grand passion."

"All that passion business is for young people. It's just a lot of fuss and bother about nothing," Chloe scoffed, trying harder than ever to convince herself it was true.

"Where did you get an idea like that?" Travis demanded with a frown and leaned toward her, his elbows on his knees. "It's one of the best things about being alive. To hold a person in your arms and feel their heart beating against your own. To become one with someone you love and join bodies and souls. To wake up in the night next to that person, knowing if the world ended at that moment, your life would be complete." He leaned back and shook his head, as though at her thoughtless ignorance. "God, girl, no one is too old for that."

Chloe sat wide-eyed and hot-faced at the vehement intimacy of his words. She had no firsthand experience of what he was talking about. She'd sometimes tried to imagine what married people did and mostly had come up with an embarrassed blank. But life's ancient rhythms—the ones that turned the seasons and tides, that made earth's creatures yearn to pair off—were strong within her. She'd been most aware of their power since the day Travis McGuire arrived.

What if he was right? Oh, she hoped he wasn't because she feared that a life with Evan would never bring her any of those things Travis mentioned.

He put his plate on the table next to him and slouched down in his chair. He stretched his long legs out and crossed them at the ankles, lacing his fingers over his full stomach. With his head resting against the wall behind him he thought of the spark of response he'd felt shoot through her when he'd kissed her. And that had been more a battle of wills than anything else, he knew. How would she react to the kind of kiss he sometimes imagined giving her when the night was getting long and sleep wouldn't come to him?

"Peterson isn't the man you need. You need a man with some guts to stand up to you and the strength to think of you before himself." He caught her green eyes with his own. "You need a man who loves you."

The certainty in his remark shook her. "But Evan cares about me," she protested, clinging to the threadbare illusion. "He's told me so."

He heard the shadow of desperation in her voice and it irked him. He was fed up with her blind defense of the schoolteacher. "Oh sure. By trying to drive me off, the only other person besides you who can help put a roof over his head when he marries you. If you ask me, he's nothing but an opportunist—and not a very smart one."

"I *didn't* ask you," she snapped, furious that inexplicable tears began to gather behind her eyelids. She turned her head until she forced them back. "Why do you care about this, anyway? It's none of your business."

This truth sliced through him, steadying him. "You're right, Chloe, it isn't. I don't mean to meddle in your personal affairs, as you put it the other day. But if Evan Peterson comes back to this shop while I'm here, I'll beat the living hell out of him." He gave her a long, even look. "I'd get a lot of pleasure out of smashing his face."

Travis stood and held out his hand to help her to her feet.

Chloe looked up at the storm-gray eyes, beguiled. Despite his violent promise, the lulling tone of his voice, warm and familiar, made his words sound like a hypnotic endearment that pulled her to him. She put her hand in his and stood.

His grip was sure and gentle when it closed around her fingers. She studied the lines beginning to fan out from his eyes and the strong mouth that was overshadowed by his dark beard. It would be good to rest against him, to depend on him.

As though an unseen force controlled her, she found herself leaning toward him and then he toward her. The tip of her tongue wet the center of her upper lip as she looked at him.

He put his free hand to the base of her neck, resting his thumb on her jaw. His other hand, the one that held hers, he tucked against his chest. She felt the leather of his apron and his bare skin above it, warm and smooth. Her eyes closed of their own accord, without her help. Somewhere a magpie twittered. . . .

The scent of her hair and skin and soap blended together to fan the low blue flame she'd kindled in him weeks ago. When he heard a little moan deep in her throat, his hand slid from her head and down her back to her waist to press her softness to his torso. He looked at her closed eyes and saw for the first time the delicate scattering of pale freckles across her nose. Her long lashes threw crescent-shaped shadows on her cheeks. His gaze drifted to the soft, tempting lips. This was what he wanted to taste, what he'd struggled to resist, but now she was here, yielding and sweet.

He lowered his head to touch his mouth to hers, first to the place where her tongue had licked it and—

"Say, young feller, where are you? Old Gus and me got to be gettin' back to the farm," Elmo Sturgis called from the dooryard.

"Shit," Travis muttered in Chloe's ear just before she jumped out of his embrace. Then in a louder voice, "Out here, Mister Sturgis. We just stopped for lunch." He kept his eyes on her lips.

The weathered old farmer came through the shop to the door. Chloe was certain her face must look sunburned it felt so red. Elmo would take one look at it and know exactly what they'd been doing. But he only stopped to greet her, "Oh, how do, Chloe," then turned to Travis. "Old Gus and me got to be going. I hope he's ready."

While Travis concluded his business with Elmo, Chloe, glad for a distracting task, escaped to collect their lunch dishes with hands that trembled ever so slightly.

Still, she couldn't stop her eyes from straying back to Travis. Standing in the low-lit shop, he controlled the powerful broad-chested draft horse with just a light touch on his bridle and a stroke of the animal's nose while he talked to the farmer.

Travis must have felt her gaze on him because he turned to her for an instant and sent her a brief look of such raw yearning she hurried to the kitchen, overwhelmed by the desire he kindled in her.

That evening after dinner, Travis lingered at the kitchen table while Chloe washed the dishes. God knew he shouldn't. A voice in his head cautioned him again and again to keep his distance, to go outside. Especially after that near-kiss in the shop at lunch. But there were so many things here that enticed him—the comfortable kitchen, the homey surroundings, the simple pleasure of her company. So he ignored the warning and remained.

Chloe was very aware of Travis sitting behind her. Her senses seemed to expand with his presence. From the corner of her eye she saw him, leaning back in his chair, his ankle crossed over his knee, his steepled fingers resting idly on the rim of his coffee cup. An evening breeze lifted the curtains and carried his clean smell to her nose. She heard the chair creak when he shifted in it. She remembered the heat of his palm on her waist earlier today, pulling her close; her mind had let her think of nothing else for the rest of the afternoon.

She rinsed the last dish, then wincing, carefully blotted her chapped hands with the flour sack towel. They felt like she'd held them over an open flame.

"You should put something on that raw skin," Travis said, unhooking his ankle and rising from his chair.

Startled to realize he'd been watching, Chloe faced him, clenching her dish towel. She let her hands drop to her sides, hiding them in the folds of her skirt. She knew they looked as bad as they felt and an unusual twinge of self-consciousness flashed through her. "Nothing I've tried works for this."

Travis took the towel from her, hanging it over the edge of the sink. Then he reached for her fingers and examined them in his own, his dark head bent in concentration. A slight frown creased his forehead at what he saw. "Do you have a pair of gloves?"

She nodded.

"Go get them and the petroleum jelly you put on my face," he said.

"Why?"

"If you coat your hands with the petroleum jelly and wear gloves all night, this will be better tomorrow," he said, tapping her knuckle.

Chloe closed her hand and withdrew it, uncomfortable with the scrutiny, and gave a jittery little laugh. "Like a lady of leisure? I'm too busy for that."

"At night you're only busy sleeping. It'll work." A shadow darkened his expression for an instant and he glanced out the window at the soft, violet dusk, muttering, "I used to know someone who did it."

"But the gloves will be ruined," she protested.

"So? When did you last wear them in this town?" he asked, bringing his eyes back to hers and holding them there.

"Well, I can't remember exactly. But I only have one pair." She supposed there wasn't much logic in that statement. True, she couldn't recall the last time she'd put them on. But she had only a few dressy things in her chest of drawers. Most of her clothes, even her underwear and nightgowns, were so plain. Those gloves, a few lace hankies, and her new wrapper were the only really feminine things she had. "Nice things are hard to come by."

Was that empathy she saw in his eyes? She searched their gray depths, but the mask to which she was so accustomed was firmly in place, and she chided herself for the wishful thought. She must have imagined it.

"Go on now and get them," he repeated, nudging her elbow. "I'll show you what I mean."

Skeptical, she turned and went after the ointment and gloves. When she returned with them, he pointed to a chair at the kitchen table.

"Sit down," he said and took the chair next to her.

She sat, somewhat gingerly, filled with a tension that she couldn't name. "What are you going to do?" she asked warily.

Travis scooped two fingers of ointment from its tin and reached for her right wrist.

"Really, Travis, I can take care of this myself. I'm

not helpless." Chloe moved to free her arm. It wasn't that she didn't like his hand around hers. That wasn't the case at all. The rare circumstance of being touched, with him so close, so fiercely vital—she worried she would tremble and betray her nervousness.

"Stop fidgeting and sit back," he ordered, tightening his grip. "This will help."

He began smoothing the petroleum jelly over the back of her inflamed hand.

A delicious, soothing languor settled over her. It felt dangerous, almost wicked. The approaching dusk filled the kitchen with soft lavender light and it was all she could do to keep her eyes open.

"Hmm," she breathed, the involuntary sigh wrested from her.

"Does that hurt?" he asked, rubbing in the ointment with his fingertips in long, slow strokes. He looked up from the task, waiting for her reply.

This intense contact—eyes, fingers—robbed her speech and she could only shake her head.

No, she didn't feel pain. She was confounded by the opposing sensations building within her— comfort and craving, respite and restlessness. She glanced at his hands, strong and dexterous, hands she'd seen control a high-strung horse, swing a maul, and lift an iron bar as though it were a willow stick. With the same firm but gentle skill, he calmed the fire in her skin and started another deep within her.

When he put her hand, warm and slippery with ointment, between both of his and massaged it, Chloe suppressed a moan. His fingers enclosed hers, threaded with hers. If this wasn't utter heaven, it was as close as she'd ever been.

He repeated the intoxicating treatment of her left hand, then encased them both in her good white gloves.

"Leave these on until tomorrow morning," he instructed, and stood abruptly. He wiped his hands on the towel he'd hung earlier.

She sat with her own hands drooping over the ends of her chair arms. From beneath heavy lids she gazed up at him and wondered why he looked vaguely annoyed, as though she had done something wrong. But before she could ask, she heard his boots thundering down the back stairs.

Be careful, Travis warned himself again as he paced in restless irritation around the darkened yard. It had begun innocently enough. He'd only meant to do a good deed, helping Chloe with her hands. He knew what a beating they took every day, and they really looked painful.

But the minute he'd held her fingers in his, slick and supple, a heat sprang up between himself and her. This time he knew she'd felt it, too. There was no mistaking it. Those sighs she'd breathed—she hadn't done that just because her skin stopped hurting. Though he knew she had an ember of desire slumbering within her, up until now she'd rigidly denied such feelings. Even in the shop today, he hadn't been sure she'd respond to his interrupted kiss.

Tonight, though, he'd felt her passion stirring, stretching like a cat after a long sleep, and it scared him. He should have ended it right then, but no, like a dimwit he'd kept her fingers entwined with his much longer than he needed to.

He stopped at the pump and glanced up at the kitchen. It was dark now, but a faint candle glow came from the window on the floor above. Her bedroom window.

His jaw tight, he turned and strode to the shop, his spurs ringing like chimes on the wind.

Be careful. . . .

Chapter 9

After that Chloe set a place for Travis at the table every morning and evening, and he appeared for the meals. Although he didn't try to kiss her again, remembering the preliminary brush of his lips, and later, the feel of her hands tucked in his, often kept her awake and staring at the ceiling over her bed.

He'd been right about the petroleum jelly and gloves—her hands were much better. They weren't those of an idle, pampered woman, but at least she could flex them again.

When she finally thought of Evan one day, she realized she hadn't missed him a single minute since she'd last seen him. What would happen when Travis was gone and she was left with only the desiccated teacher?

Early one morning Travis was finishing his coffee and Chloe was rolling out pie dough when young Andy Duykstrom delivered a towel-covered apple crate to the back door.

"The Missies told me to bring this straight to you, ma'am, with no dillydallying," Andy said, eyeing Travis. It was the first chance he'd had to get a look at the stranger up close and he lingered in the kitchen.

Travis stared back at the slow-witted boy, trapping him in his gaze.

"Was there anything else, Andy?" Chloe asked.

Dragging his eyes away, he fished an envelope out of his pocket and handed it to Chloe. "Yes,'m, they told me to give you this, too." She gave the youth a peanut butter cookie for his trouble and sent him on his way.

She opened the envelope and found a note from the Grover sisters expressing sympathy for Frank's accident, and apologizing for being so late in writing to her. They asked that she accept this small gift from them. Lifting the towel, she found the crate contained twelve quart jars of their elixir. Travis glanced at the note when she dropped it on the table.

Chloe stared at the jars while she gripped the edges of the box. A wave of an emotion rolled through her, one she'd felt a long time ago when her mother died. But there was nothing about twelve quarts of whiskey that should make her think of her mother, she puzzled.

"Who are 'the Missies'?" Travis asked.

"What?" Chloe asked absently.

He repeated the question, watching her closely.

"Oh, they make moonshine about ten miles from here. Except they think they're making medicine, elixir. Everybody buys the stuff from them. Albert even sells it sometimes at the Mercantile. My father was on his way back from their place when his wagon overturned and he was killed."

Travis watched as she lifted the jars out, dusted each one and carefully put them on the pantry shelf, taking great care to ensure they were precisely aligned with each other. Then she took them all down and began the process again.

His brows drew together, her behavior worrying him. Finally he rose from the table and went into the pantry. "That's enough, Chloe," he ordered gently, taking the dust cloth from her.

Detached, she glanced up at him for a moment and saw concern in his eyes. Then she looked at the perfectly ordered row of jars on the shelf, their contents the color of clover honey. "I guess I'll go find something else to do," she said.

He started to touch her cheek but stopped himself. He nodded and handed the cloth back to her.

She wandered aimlessly to the parlor, sat at the desk to count her money and discovered she finally had enough to pay the mortgage, with a little extra besides. She wouldn't lose her home. She knew she should feel joy, but instead she just sat and stared at the pigeonholes, the bubble of that nameless emotion still growing in her chest. Her father's mining claim caught her eye again and she pulled it out to look at Frank's faded blue signature.

Suddenly, her mind showed her a series of images, like pictures in her mother's old stereoscope, of a laughing, kind, leathery-faced man lifting a blond little girl to his shoulder, helping her to build a birdhouse, taking a sliver from her foot.

That man had been her father, not the silent, drunken stranger who had been killed last spring. A seed of understanding began to take root in Chloe's heart.

Her father had really died with her mother.

That afternoon Travis was sitting by the open shop door repairing a saddle when Chloe abruptly left the washtub and walked across the yard to the gate. He glanced up in time to see that her face was pale but her expression was determined.

"I'll try to be back by dinner," she said over her shoulder, her hand on the latch. She still wore her apron, damp from dipping into the tub.

"Taking a walk?" he asked, carefully casual, as he stitched a stirrup with a big curved needle.

But she didn't reply. She only pulled open the gate and set out across the open prairie.

Troubled, he put his work down and followed her, staying far behind but keeping his eyes on her lavender skirt as she strode over the dry grass. After they'd walked about two miles, Chloe disappeared behind a low rise. When he topped the hill, he saw her approach a wild, overgrown graveyard below, its picket fence sagging in and out.

Travis paused under the limbs of an old lone oak, anchored like a sentinel on the side of the hill. He saw Chloe pacing next to a head marker. It was new and not yet weathered much. She waved her arms as she carried on a fierce monologue, railing at the man buried under it. Travis couldn't hear her words, but he heard her anger. Finally she dropped to her knees and began to rock, her head bowed. Hot winds tugged at her hair and skirt as she knelt at the grave.

For the first time in many years he felt the reluctant stirrings of empathy. He'd learned to shut out nearly every emotion save bitterness and anger. But grief he could understand, that awful sense of loss and of being lost.

When the sound of her sobs floated to him he took several steps forward, intending to go to her. Then he stopped and leaned against the oak. She needed to work this out, to make peace with Frank Maitland's ghost and put it to rest.

Struggling to maintain the distance between their hearts, Travis stood there keeping watch over her for the rest of the afternoon.

Roxanne's customer rolled over and looked at her. "Smells like they're boiling old buffalo hides down there," he complained.

The brassy-haired saloon girl had brought him up to this second-story room. It wasn't fancy—located directly over the kitchen, all the cooking odors drifted through the floorboards. The old bed sagged beneath their combined weight, and the sound of squawking chickens in the alley floated through the window.

Offhandedly, he asked, "What did you say your name was, honey?"

"Roxanne," the girl replied. "What's yours?" She didn't usually ask, but he was different from the typical cowboys who came to her from the trail drives.

"Jace."

"Well, Jace, this is a sight better than the store-room I used to work in. That one smelled from the beer kegs." She stretched out a languid hand to brush his dark hair off his shoulder, then let her fingertips trail down to his bare hip. Hmm, he was a handsome one, with his boyish face, and, well, skill to please her. She didn't get many who bothered. And she'd never met a bounty hunter before.

"The beer would be an improvement," he said. Then, like a conjurer, he produced a silver dollar from behind her ear and held it tantalizingly before her. "Want to buy something nice for yourself, Roxanne? A pretty girl like you should have pretty things."

She pulled her hand away, miffed. "It'll cost you more than a dollar if you want to go again. I ain't giving no discounts."

"I only want to talk."

The words were whispered, a seduction of their own. She looked into his ice-blue eyes and at the cool smile curving his mouth. He was nothing but trouble and good looks and, she gathered, accustomed to getting his own way. That element of danger only made him more attractive. She grabbed for the coin but he was faster and he snatched it back with a low chuckle.

"Not yet. First you have to tell me what I want to know."

"What?"

He flipped the dollar with his thumb and sent it spinning into the air. "You meet a lot of men in your line of work. I'm looking for one in particular."

Roxanne didn't often remember the men who sought her out. They passed through her life in twenty minutes and then were gone. But the man whose description she was listening to was one who'd stayed in her memory. He'd been another handsome one, and had come to her with an intense ache and carefully leashed emotions. He, too, had seemed dangerous.

"Yeah, I remember him," she said, still watching the dollar. "He was here about three months ago, but I don't know where he went."

After a moment, Rankin nodded. Satisfied with the information, he tossed the coin into her waiting hands. "You're lucky to be alive," he said. "The man's a killer."

She tried to read his face but it was as blank as any gambler's with a winning poker hand. Then she shrugged. "Ain't they all?"

Again he gave her that cool smile and smacked her backside. "Okay, you just made some easy money. Now back to work."

"Five dollars, same as last time."

"No, this one's free."

"You're dreaming, mister," she huffed and sat up, reaching for a faded wrapper. "Why, I can't be giving my favors away."

He pulled her back down to the mattress and tucked her beneath him, silencing her protests with a long, slow kiss.

The next evening Travis came up the back stairs, gripping his whiskey bottle by its neck. He saw

Chloe was sitting at the kitchen table and he paused for a moment, taking in the scene. She'd dealt with the grief of her father's death and now, he hoped, she could put the bitterness behind her.

It was a rare opportunity, the chance to look at her when her guard was down. The planes of her face were mellowed by the golden edge of the summer evening and he watched her while she absently ran her finger around the rim of her coffee cup.

That haggard look she'd had when he first met her was gone. He knew her life hadn't been easy these past few years, but she'd held up. There was a spirit and strength in her that he admired and those qualities, for reasons that eluded him, made him feel reluctantly protective of her. And in spite of her plain dress and shawl, he saw the beauty and grace in her tall form he'd done his best to ignore since he got here.

Her breasts were full and softly rounded. Her long waist flared to trim but generously curved hips, and she walked, he remembered, with graceful allure.

At the sound of her sigh, he pulled open the door.

Chloe glanced up. For the briefest moment, she didn't recognize him. All she saw was an attractive, lean-jawed man. Then she realized Travis had shaved.

She had counted the hours of his recovery and the dollars in her strongbox with impatience, so anxious had she been to get rid of him. Though she'd eventually lost her fear of him, she'd considered him a cold-blooded scoundrel with no soul, no conscience, no heart. After all, who got sent to jail, choir boys? No, indeed. Prisons housed thieves and murderers, depraved maniacs. That she'd felt unwillingly attracted to him had been a source of great annoyance. But over the weeks her opinion of him changed. He'd helped her save her home and her initial assessment of his character no longer fit him.

"Mind if I sit down?" he asked. Without waiting for an answer he pulled out a chair to settle next to her, resting the bottle on his knee.

Grateful now for his company, she shook her head and tightened her shawl. It was a warm evening but she was cold. Then she said into her cup, "I have enough money now to make the mortgage payment. I'd like to thank you for everything you've done."

She thought a shadow crossed his face. He leaned back and hooked a boot heel on the rung of his chair, stretching the other long leg out in front of him. "You needed a blacksmith. I needed a job."

"I think my father would have liked you, at least the man he once was."

"I doubt it." Travis knew she was unaware he'd followed her to the graveyard and he left it that way. It was too complicated otherwise, too many feelings and questions would be raised. He uncorked the bottle in his hand and held it over her empty tea cup. "Here, have a little."

"Oh—I probably shouldn't," she said and self-consciously smoothed the skirt over her lap. She was very aware of his nearness, the clean male scent of him, of his strong, lean hand around the bottle.

Her fluttery hesitation, so unlike her, amused and touched him. "It's okay, Chloe. Whiskey isn't the evil you think it is. Some people think money is evil, too. But they're just—*things*. The harm lies in the way they're used."

"Well, maybe," she replied, partially convinced.

"Come on, just a sip. It won't kill you. Nobody will know." He smiled slightly, his face kind, sympathetic.

"I suppose it might be all right . . ." and he poured a small shot into her cup, then tipped his head back and took a long pull from the bottle. She watched the muscles in his throat work as he swallowed and imitating him, forced the fiery liquid down in one gulp. It burned a path to her stomach like boiling oil. She gasped and coughed and pressed her handkerchief to her mouth.

He chuckled, thumping her on the back. "You're not supposed to slug it down like that. Sip it."

She took a deep breath and let it out. "Whooh! How can you drink this stuff?"

He splashed another dollop into her cup. "It serves its purpose now and then." He clinked her cup with the bottle. "Sip this time."

So she did and it wasn't as bad. A false but welcome warmth spread through her limbs and loosened her tight muscles. "What purpose?"

He waved his hand casually. "It's a cheap painkiller. You feel better, don't you?"

Yes, she did. For the first time since she'd let herself accept her father's death, she stopped shivering. Somehow the horror of the past couple of days was blunted a little. The sharper edges were rounded off. She nodded.

"Uh-huh," he agreed knowingly. He drank deeply again and poured one last drop for her. "A little more. You'll sleep better."

She swallowed again. Travis crossed his ankle over his knee and cradled the bottle against his crotch. He slouched low, sitting on his spine, and she felt her gaze pulled to the bottle's resting place. And maybe it was a trick of the light or the whiskey—she wasn't sure—but Chloe suddenly realized that his shaved, healed face was very attractive.

Now that the bruises and beard were gone, it was easy to see that thick dark lashes, as long as a woman's, framed his gray eyes, which could range in color from deepest slate to silver. His features were smooth and well-defined. His mouth, now she could see, was full and sensuous. Maybe that was why it felt so good when he kissed her.

"You know, you're really handsome," she announced in a burst of alcohol-induced frankness, and then blushed at her own forward remark.

He turned to look at her, a sheepish, full-toothed grin lighting his face, the first she'd ever seen on him. The total effect nearly took her breath as the whiskey had. Why, he was more than handsome. He was beautiful!

"Not a mess anymore?" he teased.

"Dimples!" she fairly shouted with uninhibited delight, forgetting to worry about how it sounded. "You even have dimples!" She leaned forward to put her fingertip to one.

He grasped her pointing finger and held it, laughing openly now at her giddiness. He wouldn't have expected the Vinegar Princess to be so charming. "No more whiskey for you, you tenderfoot."

She wished he would keep holding her hand but he let go. How boyish and appealing he looked when he smiled! She'd never have guessed such a face lurked under the frowning, bearded mask she'd grown used to. Laugh lines crinkled around his eyes, making him look as young as he really was, and his straight white teeth were positively dazzling. And, she marveled, how much more at ease she felt sitting with him than she ever had with Evan.

They talked for a while about things both important and trivial, each feeling almost relaxed in the other's presence. Chloe even gave Travis a brief outline of Misfortune's history and the bonanza of gold that had been reaped from the placer mines surrounding the town.

As her voice trailed off, she drained the last few drops from her cup. "This is a painkiller, of sorts," she agreed, abruptly changing subjects, her tongue and curiosity loosened. "But what pain is it you're trying to kill? Don't you think it's time you told me about yourself?"

Travis gave her a sharp look and folded his arms over his chest, retreating into himself, every muscle tight. This was the first time she'd questioned him about his past. They'd been getting along so well, just sitting here in this comfortable kitchen. Why did she have to ask? If I tell her, he thought, she'll probably throw me out into the road right now. But the whiskey had brought roses to her cheeks and softened the expression in her eyes, and he sensed her genuine interest.

He breathed a long sigh. He'd kept all the bitterness bottled up for what seemed like an eternity while it ate away at him. He wanted to tell her, tell someone, but fear of her reaction coiled him up as tight as a new spring.

"Maybe I can help," she urged and put her hand on his tense arm.

Maybe, he thought, and was just light-headed enough to risk losing whatever respect she'd developed for him.

"You know I was in prison," he began.

She nodded.

"You probably think I deserved to be there, even though you don't know why I was sent."

She glanced at her lap.

"And you think I escaped."

"Well, didn't you?" she asked, looking up at him.

"No." Shifting in his chair, he searched his back pocket and produced a piece of grimy paper, folded many times, and handed it to her.

Hesitating a moment, she reached out and took it from him. She opened it and found a document decorated with seals and ribbons, authorizing the release of one Travis P. McGuire from the Oregon State Penitentiary. It was dated February 5, 1894 but offered no details.

Surprise was plain on her face. "Why didn't you tell me? Why did you let me go on believing you'd run away?"

His smile was wintry. He'd let her believe it because it had been one more way to keep a barrier between them. The reasons for that barrier had once been so very clear to him. "It doesn't matter."

He began talking but putting feelings into words was a struggle for a man who'd learned to choke back his emotions. He glossed over the pain of his lonely childhood, his feelings of insecurity and rootlessness, of his desire to settle in one place, of the cholera epidemic that took his family.

Chloe listened carefully as his story washed over her, lulled by the sound of a voice she'd become accustomed to.

"So, Lyle Upton agreed to let me apprentice in his blacksmith shop," he continued, "and Lyle had a daughter name Celia." He paused here, recalling the first time he'd seen Celia, and the ghost of a long-dead passion crept into his voice.

"She was beautiful. A tiny little thing with a waist no bigger than this." He made a circle with his hands. "Sky blue eyes and hair the color of ripe wheat."

A faint smile curved his mouth and he stared at the tabletop for a moment, lost in a memory.

Chloe caught the name she'd heard him say during his nightmare. He may have cursed Celia then, but now Chloe felt an unfamiliar pang of jealousy nag at her over a woman who brought such a rapturous look to him, and worse, who was small and dainty. It made Chloe very conscious of her height and the fact that she didn't have a waist "no bigger than this."

Suddenly Travis roused himself and lifted the bottle stowed between his legs to take another drink. Then he left his chair and began pacing the kitchen. His face was animated with an angry hurt that would no longer remain silent. His words poured out in a torrent.

"I was crazy about her. A year after we met, we got married. Huh. What a heartless, selfish woman."

Chloe blanched at his words. He was married?

"I was happy with my wife and my work, glad to have a real home, an ordinary life. But not Celia. From the first day we tied the knot, she started nagging. She wanted to see bright lights, new things—she wanted to move to San Francisco, for chrissakes." His voice was full of exasperation and growing louder by the minute. He didn't seem to be aware of Chloe's presence anymore. He thundered at the walls, the stove, the floor.

"I didn't want to move. I'd been on the road all my life. I was born in a damned covered wagon." In frustration, he kicked the leg of the stove as he passed it.

"When I got home at night, all we did was argue. After a year or so, she pretty much admitted that her main reason for marrying me was to get out of Salem. Like an idiot I kept trying to make her happy. To make her love me. But she was telling her father I made her miserable."

He whirled toward Chloe with such fierceness that she shrank back in her chair and gripped its arms.

"But the worst part . . . the hardest thing . . . I was hearing rumors, dirty little stories. Rumors that my wife was being promiscuous and bringing men home to our bed when I was gone. I realized she wasn't a virgin on our wedding night, but hell, I sure wasn't either and I figured, those things happen. It didn't much matter to me. As bad as things got between us, though, I didn't believe she was cheating on me. Not then, anyway. Later I found out how wrong I was."

Travis stopped then and flopped back into his chair, pinching the bridge of his nose in an effort to regain some control. He set the whiskey bottle on the table and folded his arms over his chest again. His words took on a tortured, quiet tone.

"One night in February, Lyle and I stayed late at the shop to catch up on some work." He shook his head in wonderment. "I still remember it just like it happened yesterday. The details are so clear.

"I didn't get home until about nine. It was raining to beat hell and I even remember my horse nearly trampling a man on my street who was running to get out of the weather. The house was quiet and I looked everywhere for Celia. I found her naked in our bed." He paused and faced her. "She'd been strangled with a belt."

Chloe, who'd sat listening to his bleak story, gasped. "Oh, God! Travis, how horrible!"

His eyes were as dark as thunderheads. "I rode for the sheriff right away and he investigated but weeks went by and he couldn't find the killer. Lyle was furious, like a mad dog. Someone had to pay for the death of his daughter." His mouth twisted into a hideous grin. "He accused me."

"But, Travis—he was with you the night it happened!"

"Yes, but he sent me on an errand at seven and he claimed it gave me plenty of time to kill Celia. Actually, I was only gone for a half hour and he knew I never could have done his errand, gone home, and come back in under an hour. But Lyle also knew Celia and I weren't getting along and he believed the stories she told him about our marriage. And it didn't help that it was my belt she was strangled with. It was all circumstantial evidence but he had a lot of influence in Salem. And I think in his own mind he believed it was true. The verdict was in before the trial ever started."

He mercilessly recounted to Chloe his arrest and the years of degradation and brutality he experienced in prison. His candor made her blush uncomfortably but he didn't notice.

"I guess I was luckier than most of the others locked away in that place. I had a real job." His words were heavy with sarcasm. "When one of the trustees learned I was a blacksmith I was set to work making iron manacles."

The cruel irony of this squeezed her heart and she remembered the angry scar on his ankle. "But how were you released? For that matter, why weren't you, uh . . ."

"Hanged?" he supplied, and was out of his chair again, restlessly pacing from the table to the window to the door in a continuous circuit. "The jury found me guilty but the judge was never satisfied that I was. He sentenced me to life. As for how I got out, six months ago Lyle Upton took to his deathbed and decided he wouldn't get to heaven with such a black lie on his soul. He finally admitted that it was impossible for me to have killed Celia. But he said I was *responsible* for her murder, the same as if I'd cinched that belt around her neck. Because I failed to make her happy, she was driven to other men and one of them killed her." As he passed the table, he grabbed the whiskey bottle again and held it up to his mouth. Then, as if thinking better of it, he slowly set it down without taking a drink. "I was released with five dollars and an apology from the warden. He said Lyle asked that I go see him after I got out. Why? So he could ease his conscience? I was afraid of what I'd do to him if I ever laid eyes on him again, so I headed east."

"But if you were legally set free, why do those manacles look like they were broken off? Why do you even keep them?"

Again, that awful smile. "Oh, one of the guards took a serious dislike to me after I turned down an offer for his—company." His eyes riveted on her face, as if he suddenly remembered who he was talking to.

"Company?" Chloe asked, mystified.

"Well, never mind," he mumbled awkwardly, then continued. "The day I was let go, he was supposed to unlock the leg irons but, wouldn't you know it, he just couldn't find the key. So he shot the locks off. I keep those chains as a testament of human kindness. Besides, I made them." He raked a hand through his hair. "Anyway, I've drifted from town to

town ever since, always worried that someone
will . . ."

Here he faltered for the first time since he'd begun his story, then looked away.

"Someone will what?" she prompted quietly.

He paused for a moment at the window and
turned to stare at the yard, leaning both hands on
the counter, shoulders hunched.

"That Jace Rankin will hunt me down like an animal, saying it was all a mistake. That I was never
supposed to be released. And that'll be my last day
on this earth because he'll have to shoot me before
I'll go back."

"Who's Jace Rankin?" she asked.

"He's a bounty hunter who started chasing me
about three months ago. I don't know why he's after
me, but I've never let him get close enough to ask,
either."

"But why run from him? Why don't you talk to
him and find out what he wants?"

"Were you born in this house?" he asked.

"Yes," she replied, puzzled by the question.

"And every night since you were a baby, you've
gone to sleep under this roof." He paused and
glanced at the ceiling. "Warm quilts in the winter.
Cool, clean sheets in the summer."

"Yes, I guess that's true," she responded, still not
sure what this had to do with the bounty hunter.

"So you don't know what it's like to be locked up
in a dark cell that leaked like a rotten canteen when
it rained. To freeze in the winter under moth-eaten
blankets and try to see the sky from a window that

was one-foot square." His voice was rough with weariness. He looked over his shoulder at her. "Well, I do know what it's like and I'd rather be dead than go back to it. I can't take the chance to find out why Rankin is looking for me."

Chloe thought back to that first day he spent upstairs. "When you woke up here that's what you thought, wasn't it. That you were in prison again."

He nodded, his back still to her.

"Did you ever learn who killed your wife?"

Travis continued to stare out the window. "No. I used to lie awake nights imagining what I'd do to that man if I ever found him. Celia was a blue-ribbon bitch but she didn't deserve to die, especially like that. And thanks to that swine, whoever he was, I lost almost five years of my life, too."

Chloe was heartsick. It was difficult for her to comprehend a woman as self-serving and uncaring as Celia. It was impossible for her to imagine a father so vengeful and crazy with grief that he would send his own son-in-law to jail, fully aware of his innocence.

"Why didn't you tell me all this sooner?" she asked. "You knew what I was thinking and you let me go right on thinking it. You aren't guilty but you act guilty."

He pushed his hands into the tight pockets on his denims. He took so long to answer she thought he wouldn't.

Finally he murmured, "I don't really have anything to be ashamed of, either, but I *am* ashamed. You can't begin to imagine what it's like to be thought of as a con, a jailbird. The first time someone called me a jailbird, I wanted to die." He turned toward her then and said to the floor, "The reason I take a drink sometimes is because of the nightmares. Now and then it helps me sleep, but not always." He raised his eyes to look at her. "Now you know what pain I'm trying to kill. Since you've got enough to make the payment on the house, you don't need me anymore. I've got to be leaving town in the morning."

She realized then that he was far more sensitive than he'd allowed her to know. She was so positive she'd been right about him but now she regretted her harsh assumptions. She rose a bit unsteadily and came to him. Several seconds passed before he looked up at her. The evening was quiet except for the crickets outside.

"Thank you for telling me," she said. "I'll never repeat it. But you don't have to leave. You're innocent. Stay awhile longer." What could she say to ease the hurt? Unable to think of something better, she opened her arms.

He stood uncertainly, considering her offer of basic human comfort and contact. Oh, he wanted to go to her, to feel a hug again. She opened her arms wider, reinforcing her invitation, and with a low groan he leaned into her embrace. She enfolded him and his throat closed with emotion.

She felt a silent sob wrack his body, once, twice, and her heart ached for him. He drew a deep, shaky breath and then he was still, his arms tight around her. It felt good and right to be in his embrace and to have him in hers.

As impatient as she had been to see him go, she now could not tolerate the idea of it. She wasn't sure if she loved him but knew she stood on the edge of it, feeling closer to the emotion than she ever had with Evan.

Bah, Evan! There was no thrill of fire and ice water rushing through her when she looked at Evan. She didn't long to have his lips on hers as she did Travis's. The only feelings she could summon for Evan were impatience and mild revulsion, the same ones she'd always had for him and had been unable to really admit. If Travis would stay he might even come to care about her, too. She did not examine her motives too closely or ask herself what she expected of him. She only knew that if he left, she'd never see him again and the thought was unbearable.

Finally he stood away from her, drained and exhausted, but not sorry he'd confided in her. As he looked into her face, he saw vulnerability, trust, and desire. Before he realized what he was doing, his mouth was covering hers.

Except for their interrupted kiss the other day, the sensation compared to nothing Chloe had experienced before. Evan's awkward attempts had not felt like this. Those uncomfortable encounters had left her feeling like she should wash. This was far different and with a sigh she gave herself up to the moist softness of his lips moving slowly over her own.

The urgency of the kiss increased and Travis parted her lips with his tongue. Panic grew in her to mingle with emerging passion. She could feel one hand low on her backside pulling her against his hips. His other hand cradled her jaw.

In the dim corners of his reasoning mind, Travis knew he was overstepping his bounds, that he might be frightening Chloe. This wasn't what she'd offered when she took him into her arms. But her soft mouth, the scent of her hair, and the feel of her body against his fanned the desire he'd had to deny for so long. He wanted this woman, this blacksmith's old-maid daughter.

She tried to pull away and discovered that the muscled arms she admired were every bit as powerful as they looked. When his hand left her head and slid down her shoulder to cover a breast, she struggled in earnest.

Suddenly he released her and they backed away from each other, neither certain what might happen next.

Chloe was tempted to prolong the scene, lured by the physical sensations Travis ignited with his kiss. Propriety dragged at her and held her back, but with just a look, a touch, he had the power to make her forget propriety.

Travis knew it was up to him to stop this before it went too far. It would be so easy to escape his bitter memories for a while in her soft body. It would be easy, but not right. They were both vulnerable. And he was afraid that once he'd tasted that rich sweetness, he'd never be able to leave. Taking control of the moment, Travis leaned forward and kissed her flushed cheek.

"Good night, Chloe."

Before she could respond, he was out the back door and down the steps, lost in the darkness.

Maybe telling Chloe about his past triggered the image that came to him as he lay on the cot in the shop. He unbuttoned his shirt and pulled its tails out of his pants. The evening was silent, the air hot and still. Somewhere a dog barked, then was quiet.

Travis closed his eyes and Celia appeared before him again as she sometimes did when his memory forced him to relive her death.

He remembered the moment he'd walked into their bedroom and found Celia—her face blue, her horrible look of surprise.

His wife had been murdered, that beautiful blossom, the deceitful bitch.

For weeks he had slept with the lamp burning. Only he couldn't sleep. Stunned and grieving her death, and confronted with her faithlessness, he'd stare at the ceiling and get that ache in his chest from trying not to cry. It was dumb, he supposed. What did it matter if he cried? Nobody was there to see him during those black winter nights.

Sometimes when the wind had rushed down the valley and moaned around the corners of the house, it almost sounded like Celia was calling him. The voice was a lot kinder than hers had been when she was alive.

Or, when he'd finally found sleep, she would come to him in dreams as she had in life: sweet-scented, with skin so creamy and pure that a man was afraid to touch it. Always the dreams would dissolve into grisly nightmares as she turned from bride to corpse.

Then the sheriff had come and arrested him. That was the day Travis had stopped loving his wife and promised himself he'd never risk his heart again. He'd loved Celia more than he wanted to care about another person ever again.

But that was before he met Chloe, who pulled him in directions he didn't want to go.

Chapter 10

Chloe stood in the kitchen, dazed by the warm tenderness of Travis's touch. She pressed the back of her hand to her mouth, remembering the feel of his lips on hers. She hadn't expected this rush of sensation, filling her with a longing she had never known before and couldn't identify. She glanced at the front of her dress, envisioning his hands where he'd caressed her.

She put out the lamp over the kitchen table and went upstairs to begin her nighttime ritual. Her bed loomed before her, now seeming a place of empty loneliness rather than rest. Stepping out of her dress, she went to the open window in her camisole and petticoat, every nerve in her body sensitized. A full August moon, heavy and yellow, hung low in the eastern sky. In the remaining twilight, she looked across the sun-baked plains and saw green-black clouds gathering on the horizon. The wind came up, cool and rain-scented, blowing the curtains against her body. Then glancing down at the shop, she saw Travis standing in the doorway, looking up at her. Startled, she almost jumped back, but the sight of him leaning against the doorjamb, ankles crossed, his shirt open, made her want to loose her hair and let it hang down her back. A restlessness filled her. Instead of pulling away, she stayed at the window, her gaze steady on his face.

He read her naive invitation, and his hands itched to pull the pins from the red-gold length of her hair. He straightened and crossed the yard to stand beneath her window. He'd tried to be gallant, to make her save her virginity, but self-sacrifice was not one of his virtues and his resistance was worn down.

She watched his approach, the wind catching his shirttails and blowing them back to reveal his torso. Again she admired his natural grace, the long, slim waist and strong chest, and the way his pants hung so low on his hips.

"You're leaving tomorrow?" Maybe he hadn't meant it.

He sighed but didn't look away. "Yes, I am. Nothing will change that," he warned, his voice husky. "But there's a storm coming tonight. Can you feel it?" A rumble of distant thunder followed his words.

She nodded and left the window then to put on her wrapper. Ignoring the woman in her mirror who might have tried to stop her, she went downstairs to meet him at the back door. He was on the porch, looking at her through the screen. She pushed it open to let him in and he stepped inside.

"What do you want, Chloe?"

She knew what he meant, even in her innocence. "We're practically strangers. I don't know you," she responded, wanting him to convince her to take this step.

"Yes you do." Travis moved a pace closer. His voice was low, intimate. He grasped her with a look, held her without touching her. His eyes darkened with a passion she felt emanate from him like static electricity. "I'm the one you can't get off your mind. When you wake up deep in the night from dreams that leave you edgy and restless, I'm the one you're reaching for."

Again, his perceptiveness astounded and embarrassed Chloe. There were too many nights when she woke from fragmented dreams of him, hugging her pillow, or stretching a hand across the sheets in search of him. What he said was true and he read that truth on her face.

Thunder sounded again, nearer this time.

He moved closer until his breath stirred fine strands of her hair. Mesmerized, she remained rooted to the spot as he continued.

"You know me. And I know you. I know every curve of your body, the silky feel of your hair when its brushed out." He reached out and removed her hairpins, combing the long strands with his fingers as they fell to her waist. "The sweet spot behind your ear that gives you goose bumps when its kissed." God knew he'd imagined it all often enough.

"That's not true," Chloe replied, her voice found. "You've never touched me. You don't know anything about me."

"Let's find out." He leaned forward and she felt soft lips just behind her ear that made her shiver as every hair stood on end. To assure his success, Travis also ran his tongue around the opening of her ear. Then he grasped her wrist and pushed up her sleeve. Chloe saw the goose bumps on her arm and her life took the final, unalterable turn toward a destination she'd been approaching since Travis had appeared in her yard.

Shyly, she put a hand on his muscled chest, looked into his eyes, and looked away again. His heart turned over at the apprehension and trust he saw on her face. He covered her hand with his own and lowered his mouth to hers, gently sucking first her upper lip, then the lower. The wind blew through the door, lifting her hair and winding it around them. His hand tightened on hers as he enveloped her mouth in a full, lush kiss.

When the contact ended she buried her face against his neck and he wrapped his arms around her, resting his chin against her temple. He didn't want to startle her by moving too quickly. He forced his hands to his sides and took a deep breath. The pressure in his groin was becoming unbearable but he had to give her one last chance to change her mind. "Chloe, are you sure this is what you want to do? I can go back outside and that will be the end of it. But if I don't stop now, I won't be able to."

She realized she was in love with him as soon as he spoke those words. Maybe she couldn't change his mind about leaving but if he was going away forever, she wanted him to share this night and its secrets with her. Then she would have the memory to savor after he was gone.

Timidly, she reached for his hand and raised his palm to her lips. "Don't stop, then."

Travis put his hands on her shoulders. He couldn't remember the last time anyone had accepted him for what he was. Now this woman, who had taken him in and patched him up, who'd bawled him out and then listened to the story of his past with compassion instead of contempt, wanted to give him her body as well.

"God, Chloe, I don't want you to end up hating me."

He tried to read her face in the dim light. All he could see was what looked like a very young girl, wearing only a flimsy dressing gown and her long thick hair.

"I won't hate you. I promise."

At this last, so solemnly childlike, the feeble scraps of his self-restraint dissolved. Flames ignited within him, licking through every part of him.

"I hope not," he muttered under his breath and pulled her back into his arms.

"What happens . . . shall we go . . . ?" she asked, her words muffled. Oh, this was difficult. She was so ignorant about what happened between men and women.

"Don't worry, it'll be all right," he whispered to her. "I'll take care of everything." He tried to encourage her as much as himself, worried at that moment about only one thing. He'd never taken a virgin before and had only a vague notion of what it might be like. He'd have to take things easy, move slowly. He didn't want to hurt her and knew he would. "It'll be all right," he repeated to her.

The kitchen momentarily glowed with a faint blue flash as lightning moved toward Misfortune. Travis took her hand and led her through the darkening parlor upstairs to the rooms he first saw in this house.

Her curtains alternately blew into the room, then were sucked out the windows. He went into the nursery and she heard a match strike as he lit the candle on the nightstand, giving her room the barest glimmer of yellow light.

She stood in the middle of her bedroom, twenty-eight years old and about to become a woman at the hands of this handsome, enigmatic man who'd wandered into her yard.

Nothing had ever seemed more right in her life.

He returned and deliberately steering her away from the bed, he bent his head toward hers and kissed her again. He wanted to give her time to get used to her escalating desire before he carried her to the feather mattress.

The pressure of his lips on hers seemed to intensify with the approaching tempest outside. His fingers searched for the fastenings on her wrapper, his touch feather-light on her breast. He caught and held her gaze while he opened the plain gown and pushed it from her shoulders. Beginning at her collarbone he laid a line of soft kisses up the side of her throat. When he reached her ear, this time she felt his tongue slip inside the opening and a tremor shook her.

She stood before him now in her thin undergarments, weak moonlight outlining both of them in silver. She felt awkward and insecure but he smiled at her then, a sweet, reassuring smile. His hands on her hips, he covered her face with more slow kisses.

Arousal and the chill wind hardened her nipples. Seeing them strain against the fabric of her camisole, he reached out and brushed the backs of his fingers against a nipple, then filled his hand with her breast. She sucked in her breath, and putting her arms around his neck, leaned into his palm. Each caress, every new sensation, burned hotter than the last, making her arch against him, to feel her body against his.

Then he opened the row of tiny buttons on her camisole and carefully folded back each side of the garment, revealing her soft full breasts. She heard him swallow.

"You're a beautiful woman." He skimmed the side of her breast with his palm. "Even more beautiful than I imagined all those nights when I couldn't sleep."

He'd imagined her this way? Undressed before him? She suddenly felt too naked under his examination. She self-consciously closed the edges of the fabric but he moved her hands to his waist.

"Don't hide, Chloe. This is part of making love. You get to take your clothes off."

"But you haven't taken anything off," she pointed out.

Another flash of lightning and its faint buzz filled the room, and she saw the broad grin he'd first shown her earlier. "Well, that's not fair, is it," he asked and kicked off his boots and socks.

"Not that you have to," she replied hastily, panic in her voice. She clutched her camisole again, wishing the wind would blow out the candle in the other room. She wasn't ready for so much maleness, so much strength.

He threw his shirt into a chair by the mirror. "Yes I do. That's how it's done." He opened his belt and skinned out of his pants, the buckle clanking on the floor.

In spite of her reticence, she couldn't tear her gaze away from him. She'd seen him without clothes when he was sick, but it hadn't prepared her for this. His back to the mirror, she could see the reflection of his tall straight form, from his wide shoulders and muscled arms down his torso and long legs. Facing him, the low light showed her only his silhouette, but at that moment she was positive she'd never seen anything more magnificent.

When he crossed through the candlelight she was confronted with his hardness, full and threatening. But her concerns were forgotten when he took her into his arms again and dipped his head to her breast. His warm lips closed on her nipple, gently sucking, and a low moan escaped her. The sensation went deep inside, down where a heavy ache began to grow, and she twined her fingers in his dark hair. When he released her, the cool air tightened the sensitive bud even more. Her heart beat like a hammer and her skin burned under his touch. She felt like a leaf on a swift-moving river, being swept along by primal rhythms too elemental to control.

Her response shot through Travis like wildfire. His muscles rigid with tension, his pulse pounding in his head, he craved release in her body. The smoothness of her skin, her satiny hair, the soft lushness of her breasts—he wanted to prolong the feverish torment, he wanted to end it.

Outside the wind thrashed the maple tree in the yard as the storm gathered strength and another blue flash lit the room. Thunder quickly followed.

Travis nuzzled Chloe's soft flesh, savoring the fragrance of her skin, his senses electrified. "You feel like silk, like velvet," he murmured. He struggled to pace himself, to resist tearing away her remaining underwear and taking her right now. He wanted to be gentle with this flower, to make certain he gave her every part of the experience he could.

His mouth moved to her other breast as his hands searched for the closures on her petticoat and pantaloons. Finding them, he slowly pushed these last coverings down her legs. His palms flat to her thighs, a trail of soft, moist kisses followed the path of his hands over her skin. In the near-darkness, his fingers grazed her nakedness as a blind man might study a Braille text, exploring her shoulders, stomach, and back. His feathery inspection filled her with delicious shivers and raised goose bumps once more. Then he hugged her to him, chest to breast, hip to hip. She could feel the silky hair on his belly, but his swollen hot length grinding against her was intimidating. How would this ever work?

She pulled away and he knew the reason for her fear, positive she'd never encountered a fully aroused male before. He tried to think of some way to soothe her. "Sometimes things seem a lot scarier than they really are. I know what that's like." The urgency of his need battled his wish to be patient.

"Travis, I don't think you've ever been faced with this," she responded dryly.

"I'll be careful, Chloe, I swear." Then he did a curious thing. He lifted her hand, put her little finger in his mouth, and slowly moved his tongue around it.

This simple action scorched her senses in a way she'd never have believed. The heat of his mouth combined with the slickness and texture of his tongue to increase the strange heaviness she felt in her belly. How did he know these things? How could something as ordinary as sucking on her little finger make her want his touch on the rest of her? Longing to feel him, she stepped back against him and boldly put her mouth to his. He buried his hands in her hair when she tentatively ran her tongue over his lips. Then he took her hand, still wet with his saliva, and moved it across his chest and hard-muscled stomach, encouraging her to investigate his body.

Imitating what she'd learned from him, she put kisses on his throat and across the breadth of his chest. When her lips found his nipple, she took it in her mouth as he had hers. He flinched in surprise and she heard a pained noise deep in his throat.

"What is it?" she asked, full of concern. "Did it hurt?"

"No, no. Oh, God," came his ragged whisper. "Chloe, please. Touch me."

Wasn't she touching him? She wondered what he was talking about, but not for long. When she didn't move he grasped her hand and held it firmly around his throbbing erection. The shock of the contact would have made her pull back but he held her fast. He was hot and hard and velvety.

He moaned and dropped his forehead to her shoulder as his hips moved in automatic reflex to this exquisite torture, relishing the sparks coursing through him.

His reaction made her feel like a magician, able to conjure the same exciting response from him that he raised in her.

"I want to touch you, too."

"Touch me like—like that?" she asked, uncertain.

"Yeah, sort of. You'll like the way it feels, I guarantee it, honey."

The simple endearment, which came from him so naturally, tugged at her heart. This was how other men addressed their wives and sweethearts, but she'd never heard it applied to her.

Her breath caught when she felt his hand quickly whisper over the tender flesh between her legs, just once, before moving to the softness of her thigh. She sagged against him, feeling she could no longer support her own weight.

Swinging her up into strong arms, he carried her to the bed.

The cool white sheets smelled of fresh prairie sun and wind. Chloe lay against the pillows, her hair fanned around her. Travis stretched out on his side so close to her she could feel his warm breath on her cheek. He put his arm under her pillow to cradle her head and gazed into her face.

"You know, one morning before I moved out to the shop I got up earlier than you," he said, lightly brushing her hip, "and when I saw you asleep in here, I wanted to get into bed with you, just to hold you in my arms. I wanted it a lot." He tucked her leg between his own.

She knew what he meant. She'd wondered what it would feel like if he held her. From far away came the intoxicating thought that this was how it should be. She wanted to share her bed with this man, safe from storms in this haven. Safe in each other's arms. "I'm glad you're here with me now."

He reached beneath her other knee and pulled it up. His lips were on her lips, on her body, in her hair, and sensuous words filled her ear as he sought to put her at ease.

"You feel so good, Chloe, soft, so soft." He pressed a kiss to the tender place under her breast. He continued down the center of her stomach and was below her navel when he felt her tense. "It's okay, Chloe, it's okay. I won't do anything you don't like."

She wasn't sure what he meant but when he began lightly massaging the inside of her thigh she didn't think about it anymore. The demanding want deep within her continued to grow, making her need to move her hips, reaching for something. She didn't understand it but she couldn't stop, either. She'd never felt anything like this before, this yearning, and didn't even know what she craved.

But Travis knew. With gentle skill he delved his fingertips into that most sensitive part of her. Startled by this intrusion, she instinctively tried to close her legs.

"Chloe, just relax," he urged. His hand rested on her thigh.

She felt like an idiot, not knowing what to expect. No one had ever explained these intimate details to her. People just didn't talk about such things. "I'm sorry, I just don't know how . . ."

"I know. Don't be afraid, honey. Let me love you." His voice was patient but his breathing was getting ragged. He put a trail of kisses straight down her throat and rubbed the inside of her leg until he felt her relax. When her hips lifted again under the onslaught of his ministrations he reached for the wet, aching want of her. This time she didn't resist.

His knowing fingers caressed the dewy tenderness, slowly at first, and then more quickly, like the beats of butterfly wings.

She squirmed against his hand. God, what was he doing to her? she wondered. What was in those slick, rapid strokes that made her feel like her body was going to explode?

"Travis," was all she could whimper, her ability to speak dimmed by the boiling frenzy he was creating within her. Frantically she gripped his hand resting near her head, needing to hold onto him.

"Just let it happen, honey," he encouraged, closing his fingers around hers. Her passion thrilled him, but the furious heat of her response only heightened his need and made minutes seem like hours.

When she was certain she could take this no longer, that the fire surging through her would kill her in a spectacular conflagration, the intensity increased and forceful spasms hurled her into a dark place where only she and Travis existed. She heard herself sobbing his name and rolled toward him, unable to contain the emotional and physical forces swamping her.

Travis himself felt like he was going to explode and if she'd been like the other women he'd had, he would have simply buried himself in her without having to worry about hurting her. But he couldn't do that with Chloe. She being a virgin almost made him feel like one, too.

He put a knee between her legs. His shadow loomed over her and his hand went to her cheek.

"I guess this is going to hurt, since it's your first time, but just this once. Do you trust me?" he asked.

She turned her face against his palm. "I have almost from the beginning."

Her simple words pulled at his emotions just as her body, open and ripe before him, made him ache to join her. He tucked his arms under her pillow, raising her head closer to his as he covered her. Turgid and throbbing, his body demanded relief and he probed her flesh, finding the opening of that warm comfort.

Slowly, gently, he pushed against the seal of her femininity. Her body beneath him tensed. Finally, with one piercing thrust he broke through, sinking into her tight warmth. A low moan of comfort sounded in his throat. He was still for a moment, savoring the perfection of being surrounded by her.

At the first sharp twinge her breath stopped on a gasp in her chest. Then she felt his length fill her, complete her. She forced herself to relax and discovered that he really did fit. His hips began to move, driving him into her with powerful strokes. Instinctively, she matched her movements to compliment his and found the same yearning ache beginning to grow in her again.

Faster he moved, pushing with a frantic rhythm, as he sought to quench the blaze burning through him. With each stroke he thrust her closer and closer to the edge of their existence until she felt all her muscles close in on themselves in tight powerful contractions. She knew she called his name but heard her own voice uttering other incoherent words.

For another endless moment his hard smooth strokes continued. Then from deep in his chest an animal groan rose as pain and pleasure mingled in hot, pulsating jets, giving him the release he sought.

Watching his face, she thought he looked as though he were in agony.

Spent and panting he relaxed against her and rested his damp forehead in the soft curve of her neck. Chloe welcomed his weight pressing her into the mattress and a wave of tenderness washed through her. As she rubbed his back, unexpected tears ran from the outer corners of her eyes and across her temples. She took a deep, shuddering breath to stop them.

One tear fell on Travis's forehead. Still within her, he immediately braced himself up on the full length of his arms to search her face in the low light. "Chloe," he questioned anxiously, "are you all right? Did I hurt you much?"

She quickly reached up and dried her face, not wanting him to see the depth of his effect on her. "No, it was good. Just like you said it would be, Travis."

He hovered over her a moment. Then he kissed her eyelids and closed his arms around her.

When the gray eye of dawn opened on the lovers in their feather bed, it found Travis awake with Chloe nestled against him, her long hair spilling over his chest. In her sleep she looked so innocent. Her hands were not soft and white as Celia's had been, and he wished they were. Not because he yearned for any quality his wife had possessed. He only wished Chloe hadn't had to work so hard. He smiled when he thought of the many sides he'd seen of this female—the tough-talking harpy, brave when threatened with losing her home, the shy virgin, and now the generous lover.

Now he understood why the saloon girl in Canyon City had left him feeling unsatisfied. Having Chloe's softness in his arms felt like the best thing that had ever happened to him and made leaving ten times harder.

He looked around the room, felt the clean sheets

against his skin and the soft mattress beneath him and thought of the hundreds of nights he'd stared at a moon through a barred window. He'd never expected to see anything like this again, much less be part of it, even briefly. He'd been just a kid when he went to prison, scared and angry, convicted of murdering the woman he had loved, a woman who'd used and betrayed him. Facing a life sentence at twenty had sucked the hope right out of him. But there was something about Chloe with her sassy tongue and gentle touch that made him begin to believe all the old wounds could be healed, made him think of the future. Last night his sleep had been dreamless and unbroken for the first time in over five years.

It didn't matter, he thought, abruptly capturing his wandering imagination. He couldn't stay. As much as he wanted to fulfill that long-ago dream of home, he wouldn't, couldn't take that chance again. Life had left him with nothing but a fragile shell of himself that he guarded carefully. Now it was time to leave.

He began to disengage himself from Chloe's arms and legs. She rolled over and presented her smooth white back to him.

Still, it wasn't daylight yet and he didn't need to be gone this instant. There was no telling when he'd have this kind of luxury again. He tucked the sheet around them and pulled her close. Feeling safe and comfortable, he slept again.

Chloe woke to a strange sensation, the new but very pleasant experience of feeling Travis's warm body pressed against her back. She'd once heard of sleeping spoon-style but couldn't imagine what it meant. Now she knew. His arm was wrapped around her middle, hugging her to his long torso, and she fit perfectly in his sheltering embrace.

He stirred behind her and she felt his lips on the back of her neck.

"I have to leave."

His whispered words fell on her like rocks. She'd known he would be going today but knowing didn't make it easier. She thought of the night before and marveled at the fury that had raged through her. Along with her clothes Travis had also lifted away her inhibitions and tapped into a primitive part of her she hadn't known existed. He seemed to sense just where to touch her and when, before she even knew, and aroused in her a craving to fuse with his spirit as well as his body. She had never guessed it was possible to feel so close to another human being, to share something so powerful. For that brief time, it was almost as though they'd exchanged souls.

She turned and looked into his handsome slumberous face, now shadowed by a one-day beard. "Why not stay? No one here knows what happened to you." She reached up to touch the bristles on his jaw. "Besides, Misfortune is about as dead as a town can be and still have people living in it. Nobody comes here. That bounty hunter probably won't even be able to find us."

He pulled himself up to one elbow. He didn't have the nerve to tell her the confused truth, that he was dying to stay and frantic to leave. He shrugged carelessly. "I've caused you enough trouble. People here will start talking."

She scowled. "Hah! When haven't they talked about me? It's been going on for years!" Already hating the emptiness he left, she watched as he rose from her bed, his back a pattern of sheet wrinkles. "Anyway," she continued softly from her pillow, "if you go there'll be no blacksmith in Misfortune."

Travis studied her for a moment before turning to the washstand. "It's not that simple, Chloe." It would be hard for anyone to grasp how relentless Rankin was. "I've got Jace Rankin looking for me and he's not going to give up." He washed and dried himself.

"But where are you going? Do you have something to do?"

"I heard they're looking for hands at the Silver Creek Ranch. I was headed there before I had that sunstroke. If that doesn't work out, I'll keep looking till I find something. I just need to buy a horse." He reached for his pants, not bothering with underwear.

She glanced up at him as he buttoned his shirt and tucked it in. "Stay here. You can have a new life. A new start. The town needs you." To hell with the town, she thought. I need you.

He sat on the edge of the bed, his back to her, and pulled on his boots. "I don't want to be needed. I have to keep moving."

How could he make her understand his need for self-protection? She kept trying to scale the wall he'd built around himself. Not that she was pushy or coy—it wasn't that at all. Her devices were guileless: the way the sun sparkled on her hair, her unexpected moments of shyness, the way she'd cried when he made love to her. . . .

He turned to her and took her chapped hand. He didn't want her to think he had heartlessly used her and was now rejecting her, but he knew nothing he said would help much. "Last night meant a lot to me, Chloe. But I told you before we started that I had to be leaving today."

He really meant it, he was going. In spite of last night. Or maybe because of it, she agonized. Maybe she'd given herself too easily, too completely, and the bounty hunter was just an excuse he was using to get away. In any case, she certainly wasn't going to beg him to change his mind and her pride wouldn't let him see how much this was hurting her.

"And I won't keep you one minute longer," she replied and sat up, her voice now crisp and businesslike. She wound the sheet around herself and rose to pull an old wrapper from the wardrobe.

He winced at her tone, the one she'd used on him when he met her, and stepped over to touch her elbow. It had been a very long time since he'd had to worry about anyone's feelings except his own. "Chloe, I don't want to leave with bad feelings between us. We shared a very special thing." The sight of her with the sheet twisted around her and that sleep-tangled sunset hair falling to her waist made him think of a Grecian statue he'd once seen in a book.

Her expression was stony. "And now I'm supposed

to smile and wave farewell with my handkerchief and throw rose petals at you. Well, let's get on with it."

He sighed. She pointedly turned her back and put the wrapper on, shutting him out.

"Goddammit, Chloe! I didn't force you into that bed. I asked you if you were sure you wanted to make love with me." His face was hot and he was feeling more like a heel every minute, though he wasn't sure why. His defense sounded weak and self-ish to his own ears. Distracted, he stood at her mirror and tried to comb his dark hair with his fingers. When he turned, she was screwing her own hair down into the ugly knot that hid its beauty.

"You asked and I said yes, so I don't see why you feel like you have to justify yourself now." She tightened the tie on her wrapper and stood by the door. He wasn't even leaving her for a worthwhile purpose. He had no place to go, no task requiring his attention. He'd rather do nothing than be with her. Rejection weighed like a millstone on her heart, but sheer brass kept her head high. "You'd better be going or you'll be late."

"Late for what?" he asked and then wanted to kick himself for walking face-first into her barb.

She followed him downstairs to the kitchen, watching helplessly as he went out the back door to the shop to gather his belongings. It was the last time she'd hear his boots on the stairs, the last time she'd see him in the yard.

She found her good wrapper on the floor where they'd dropped it, remembering a Travis McGuire who held her in his arms in the dark and awakened her unused emotions and feelings. But as she picked up the discarded dressing gown, last night seemed like a million years ago. The spell that had enveloped them was broken by the sunrise and Chloe had to face the reality of her future.

Automatically, she went to the sink and pumped water into the coffeepot, just as she'd done hundreds of times. With Evan gone and Travis going, the house would be so empty. The prospect of her coming loneliness was almost more than she could bear.

He came back up the stairs, the whole blue denim length of him, and laid his saddlebag on the kitchen table. Chloe looked at it and her heart ached.

"Can I have my gun back?" he asked.

She went to the pantry and retrieved the box of bullets and the loose shells wrapped in her handkerchief. He put them all in the saddlebag, where she'd originally found them.

"Your revolver is in my father's desk." They went to the parlor and she rolled back the top and removed his big Colt from a pigeonhole. "Here," she said, holding it out to him.

Then she opened her strongbox and counted out all the money they'd made over and above what she'd need to pay the bank, and handed it to him. "You earned some extra money."

Travis hesitated. He could always get by, but her position was more chancy by far. Besides, it didn't sit well with him to take money from a woman, especially under the circumstances. "No, Chloe." He shook his head. "You keep it."

"It was part of our agreement. You worked for it, it's yours."

He took it, the coins clinking in his hand, but he didn't like it.

Then her eyes lighted on her father's old mining claim. She pulled it out and found her pen and bottle of ink. She scratched a paragraph relinquishing her ownership as Frank's heir and transferring it to Travis. She held the document out to him. "Take this, too."

"What is it?"

"Just take it," she repeated, trying to control her quavering voice. When he didn't, she threw it at his feet. "If you're so anxious to be alone and have no one need you, go dig in the hills. It's the most solitary life there is. You could go for months without seeing another human."

Travis picked up the claim where it fell and read what she'd written. "Why are you giving this to me?"

"I told you why. You can go sit up in the hills and never have to talk to another person or be responsible for anyone except yourself. You won't get bored because there's backbreaking work to do all day long, every day. You'll love it." And maybe if you have that, you'll keep my memory with you, too, she thought.

All the sweetness, all the loving affection he'd discovered in her were once again sealed away behind a stout wall of defense, riveted in place with hairpins. "I can't accept this, Chloe. It's part of your in-heritance," he said, trying to hand it back to her.

Determined not to cry in front of him, she fought a sensation of mounting hysteria. "Then pay me for it. Do I look like the type to go prospecting? If you don't take it, I'm going to burn it."

There was an edge in her voice he hadn't heard before and it worried him. "All right, all right," he said and tucked it into the saddlebag. Then he reached into his pocket and pulled out a five-dollar gold piece.

"I don't want your money," she contradicted herself.

"Then I won't take that claim," he retorted.

She stood with her arms crossed over her chest, stubbornly refusing to hold out her hand. He put the coin on the desk.

He stood before her and dropped the bag on the floor, his hands hanging at his sides. "Well, I guess this is it."

She nodded. She hated him in that instant for being so handsome, for making her love him, hated him for everything about him that was wonderful. But she hated herself even more for letting him get so close.

"Honey, I'm sorry—"

She frowned at the endearment, the sound of it knifing through her heart. "Don't call me that. And you don't have anything to be sorry for."

He stumbled to an uncomfortable halt in his apology. "Anyway, I appreciate everything you did for me. I probably wouldn't be alive if it weren't for you."

And I wouldn't wish I was dead if it weren't for you, she thought. But she was gracious enough to acknowledge his thanks. "You're welcome, Travis."

He suddenly pulled her into his arms for a last, brief embrace. They held tight to each other and she tried to absorb every sensation, the scent of him, the feel of him, lean and tall, the texture of his shirt under her fingers.

Releasing her, he put a kiss on her forehead and chin. "My mother called these cross-kisses," he murmured, pressing his lips to her left cheek and then right. "When I was a kid and I was scared, she'd do this. Then, she said, the angels would watch out for me."

The muscles in Chloe's throat clamped down and she lowered her head for a moment so he wouldn't see her chin tremble.

The saddlebag over his shoulder, he crossed the parlor to the door. His hand was on the doorknob when her pride slipped and she tried one final, desperate time. In a low, choking voice she said, "Travis, don't leave."

He gazed at her for a long moment, his faint smile shaky, his eyes welling up. She looked defenseless and the sight wrung his heart. He didn't trust himself to speak, to ask her to understand something he barely understood himself. He only knew if he stayed one minute more, he'd be on his knees before her, burying his face in her wrapper like a frightened child. "Goodbye, Chloe."

His boot heels thumped down the porch stairs, over the walk, and out the gate, taking him away from her life. Her throat tight with despair and regret for things that would not be, on bare feet she ran to the end of the fence and watched as his image became smaller with each step he took down the road. The hem of her gown dragged over the yellow rain-soaked grass but she could think of nothing except the excruciating pain she felt and at that moment, wanted him to feel it, too.

"Go ahead and leave, then!" she shouted. "I'd—I'd rather be married to Evan for a hundred years than spend another minute with you."

In her anguish she seized upon the worst thing she could say to him. At his retreating form Chloe shrieked the one word she'd never be able to take back, though in the long sleepless nights to come she'd pray again and again for the chance.

"Jailbird!"

Chapter 11

Tarpaper Bolen's jaw dropped. "You mean that stranger is goin' prospectin'?"

It was another Saturday afternoon at DeGroot's Mercantile and today's assemblage lounging at the counter was made up of Tar, Albert DeGroot, and Ned Langford, who lived three miles outside of Misfortune. It was nearly closing time and Albert draped the merchandise with dustcovers.

Albert nodded with some amazement, pleased with the effect of his news. "Looks like. He came in here this morning, big as you please, and asked me if I had any mining equipment. Have I got mining equipment! 'Yessir', says I, 'I can outfit you with whatever you need.'"

That was certainly true. When the boom ended in Misfortune, Albert hadn't been able to give the stuff away. He neglected to add that McGuire had seemed to be aware of that and when all was said and done, Albert had let the merchandise go for next to nothing.

He flapped a drape over a display case. "He bought a whole load of things—pans, picks, shovels, blankets, food, Grovers' elixir—I don't recollect what all. Then he said he was going out to your place, Ned, to buy a couple of horses."

Ned helped himself to a peppermint stick from the jar on the counter. He was a pumpkin of a man, round and short, with faded orange hair and silver bristles in his three-day beard. He was also given to cutting the front end off his sentences. "Sold him that gelding what belonged to my wife afore she passed last year. Took that piebald, too. Paid me twenty dollars. Didn't tell me what he was up to, though."

"Getting information from McGuire is like pulling hen's teeth, and that's a fact," Albert agreed, putting the lid on the cracker barrel. "Why, it might have been days before we knew his name if Evan hadn't told us." He paused here as another thought occurred to him. "I guess Evan doesn't have competition for Chloe after all if McGuire's gone off to the hills."

Tar was apoplectic. "You mean that stranger is goin' prospectin' around *here*? Just let's see him get within five miles of my claim, I'll—"

"Damnation, Tar!" Albert snapped. "To hear you carry on so, a body would think you were worried about losing a woman, or maybe even a horse, instead of that miserable patch of ground you have."

Ned removed the peppermint stick from his mouth, bit off a chaw of tobacco, and replaced the candy. "Reckon McGuire's going to file a claim?"

"Now that's the funny part," Albert replied, pleased to be able to provide new information. "He says he's already got a claim. You s'pose he bought Frank's parcel from Chloe?"

Tar made a strangled noise. "By Jasper! That stranger *is* goin' prospectin' around me. Frank's claim is only half a mile from mine!"

Chloe stood in the doorway separating her bedroom from the nursery. The last of the day's sun brightened the rooms with low golden light, as though the thunderstorm last night had never taken place.

She had dragged through the long day with a tight knot in her stomach that made her feel sick and guilty. Why should she feel guilty? she demanded of herself. She hadn't left Travis, he'd left her. Finally, she'd forced herself to eat a little dinner and then wandered up here.

She went into the nursery and sat on the rocker, holding her rag doll on her lap. Gently rocking, her eyes closed and she remembered sitting here before, while Travis was sick. It was easier to think of him as angry and hostile, the way he'd been when she met him. But her mind was not going to allow her an easy way out and instead showed her pictures of him achingly handsome without his beard, smiling at her, kissing her, loving her. . . .

Her eyes snapped open and she impatiently rose from the rocker and went back to her own room. She'd banish him to a little-used corner of her memory, she told herself. It would just take a little time. She flopped on the bed, burying her face in the pillow, and the unmistakable scent of him rose from the linens.

Oh, God, she mourned, her guilt rising to assail her again. How would she ever forget? How could she forget the way he looked when she screamed that word at him this morning? He stiffened like she'd shot him in the back, but he kept walking. And now added to her sense of loss was the miserable certainty that Travis McGuire would hate her for the rest of his life.

Early the next morning Chloe put on her good skirt and blouse, then paced in the kitchen for an hour until it was time for the bank to open.

Her sleep had been fitful. Sometimes she'd been awakened from her half-consciousness by the ringing anvil, only to realize it was the tinny chimes of the parlor clock striking every hour. Just before dawn, she had flung back the sheet and got up. Her hand mirror had shown her eyes with faint purple smudges under them and two frown lines on her forehead that looked like an angry quotation mark. At least one good thing had come of this heartache and it had been her original goal: the mortgage would be paid.

Now, finally at the bank, she lifted the leather-bound box from her lap and placed it on Grady Hewitt's desk. "I think we have a little business to conduct," she said with a smile. She'd actually worn a hat for her walk down here, feeling the occasion warranted the formality.

The bank was one of Misfortune's more august

structures. Built thirty years earlier to transact hundreds of thousands of dollars in gold, it still maintained an air of faded dignity even though only Grady and an ancient clerk still worked there.

Grady leaned forward in his chair, looking even more relieved than she was. "I can't tell you how glad I am to see you here today, Chloe, and two weeks early at that," he said with obvious sincerity. "I'd hate like the very devil to foreclose on you, but it's not up to me. You know if it was, I'd tear up that mortgage right now."

"I know, and I appreciate that," she replied, smiling again. She pushed the box across the desk to him. "I believe you'll find it's all here. But I had some sleepless nights, I can tell you."

Chloe was surprised to hear herself admit that. It wasn't like her to be so open.

She watched as he counted the gold and silver coins, counting with him in her head. When he handed her the receipt, she looked at the paper that gave her the right to live in her home for one more year and carefully placed it in the box. A year was a long time and she'd find a way to make the payment again.

"What became of your shop? I hear your blacksmith left," Grady said while walking her to the door.

She saw the apprehensive look on his face, as though he realized he may have asked a question she felt was nosy. She tipped her head, hoping her wistfulness didn't show.

"We agreed that he would stay long enough to help me make this payment. There were reasons—

other things that—he had to move on." Her words trailed off into silence, then she roused herself and put out her hand. "Well, Mister Hewitt, I'll be back next year."

He shook hands with her. With the leather-bound box tucked under her arm, she turned for the home she'd saved. When she got to the backyard she paused at the shop's side door, her hand on the knob, debating whether to go in. Resolutely, she turned it and stepped inside.

It was dark, with the big door closed, and it seemed crowded with the spirits of the men who'd worked there. Slowly she walked to the forge and felt the low heat radiating from it. Travis had banked the fire before he left, probably out of habit. That it was still warm after two days was evidence of his skill.

Tears threatened her again and she pushed them back. She hadn't cried since he left and she wasn't going to break down now. She'd get over him, she told herself yet again. It would just take a little time. She turned swiftly and crossed the dry yard to change her clothes to begin work.

That evening, she fixed a special dinner to celebrate her victory. From her place at the table, where she sat alone, she glanced around the room remembering how frightened she'd been that night she was forced to hire Travis. She'd worried that all her belongings and furniture would be sold out from under her if she couldn't raise the money she needed.

She'd succeeded, with his help. But while relieved beyond measure that she still had her home, somehow the triumph wasn't as thrilling as she'd imagined it would be.

She looked at the chair opposite her that he'd occupied for a short while, then lifted her coffee cup in a kind of toast.

"Congratulations to me."

Swayback Blevins interrupted his singing to jovially curse the mule team he drove. "Heyup there, you sorry bastards, keep a'movin'. We gotta get this load of bacon and sugar to them fellers at the Lady Belle Mine and the day is about gone." He really didn't intend for the animals to increase their speed—he just swore at them now and then for good measure.

The big wagon they pulled rocked down a narrow dusty road in the shadow of the Blue Mountains. Lazy and shallow under the late summer sky, the Burnt River drifted alongside. To the clatter of hooves and jingling bit and harness, Swayback resumed his off-key bawling.

Presently, he rounded a curve in the road and spotted a youngster at the river's edge watering his horse. While the horse drank, Swayback saw the youth wiping the dust from a long rifle with a square of cloth, then check the rounds in his revolver.

Alerted by the noisy wagon, the boy glanced up as he holstered his pistol. His eyes shaded by his broad-brimmed hat, he never looked away from Swayback's hands where they held the reins. He gripped the rifle, the barrel leaning back against his shoulder, his finger on the trigger.

Swayback pulled on the lines and the team came to a halt some yards distant. It was odd to see a boy that young with so much ammunition. Still, this could be rough country at times and it wasn't impossible to have a scrape with a rowdy miner or an insulted Indian. A body ought to be prepared, he supposed.

"Howdy," Swayback called. "You got trouble?" He leaned over and aimed a hefty stream of tobacco juice at the dirt.

"Not yet," the youth replied. His voice was low and resonant, like an adult's. "Unless you're bringing some."

"No, no, not me. I'm Swayback Blevins," he offered. "Swayback on account of a mule what fell on me when I was 'bout your age. Now I just drive 'em, I don't try to ride 'em. I have the route from here to La Grande. What's your name, son?"

"Jace Rankin."

Swayback repeated the name in his mind, wondering why it sounded familiar. Then it came to him. "The bounty hunter?" he asked, incredulous. He nearly swallowed his chaw trying not to laugh at the swaggering pup. In his travels around the state, Swayback had heard of Rankin. Ice-cold, hard, fearless, he could make a man wet his drawers just by looking at him, that's what they said about the bounty hunter. In a pig's eye, this boy was Jace Rankin. It was on the tip of his tongue to say, "Run along now, son. Your mama must be looking for you."

At that moment the stranger left his horse and approached the wagon, leaning the rifle against his leg.

He pulled a silver dollar from the watch pocket in his jeans and sent it spinning into the air. When he tipped his head up to look at Swayback, the old teamster felt a sudden disadvantage in having the low sun in his eyes. And in that instant he knew the critical blunder he'd almost made.

"You say you run this road often?" Rankin asked. The coin flashed as it spun. He caught it on the back of his hand and looked at the side facing up.

Swayback nodded, still trying to grasp the contrast of what he'd supposed Rankin looked like compared to what he saw before him.

"I saw a fork back there a couple of miles. One sign pointed toward Baker City. The other pointed to a place called Misfortune." He glanced back toward that fork, then up at Swayback. "If you wanted to hide, which town would you go to?"

Swayback leaned forward eagerly, his fear set aside. "You lookin' for someone? A bank robber? Or maybe a killer."

Rankin smiled slightly. "Heads, Baker City. Tails, Misfortune. Which would you choose?"

The driver waved his hand. "Hell, there ain't nothin' in Misfortune. It's almost a ghost town and it's easier to hide in a bigger place with more people. Being an outsider is too hard, 'specially for a sociable man like myself. I'd go to Baker City."

Rankin flipped the coin once more and caught it on the back of his hand. When he lifted his palm, he studied it and nodded, as if to himself. Then he tossed the dollar into Swayback's hand.

"Thanks," Rankin said. He picked up his rifle and walked back to his horse.

Travis looked down on Misfortune from his vantage point in the hills. Another long day was nearly over. On the western horizon the sun had dropped behind clouds that wouldn't come close enough to bring more rain.

He sat cross-legged on a boulder, absently tying knots in a dry stalk of grass. He opened his hands and looked at the blisters formed on them from swinging the pick into soil as hard as granite. He'd started in as soon as he found Chloe's claim. She was right. This was backbreaking work, monotonous work. In the week he'd been here, and with water he got from the El Diablo ditch that ran behind the claim, he felt like he'd panned all the dirt in the hillside. But among the sticks, grass, bugs, clay, and mud, all he'd found were a few flakes.

Then that old coot had hobbled over from the other side of the mountain with his mule, asking all kinds of nosy questions and acting as though Travis were trespassing. He smelled so gamy, Travis struggled to stay upwind of him.

He looked down at his jeans that were caked with mud up to his knees. Huh, he might not smell much better himself when he ran out of that hunk of Chloe's soap that he'd brought with him.

He tried to keep his gaze from straying to the blacksmith shop on the west end of town, but time and again he caught himself staring at it. He'd searched out Chloe's roof his first day up here. Her last word to him still rang in his head. When she'd yelled "jailbird" at him, it had been like hearing it again for the first time, compounded a hundredfold.

What did she want from him, anyway? He'd gone to work for her when she couldn't find anyone else, he'd helped her make that payment, and he'd taken nothing.

He'd held her in his arms and taken something she could give only once.

His conscience stirred.

When he'd left Chloe's house, Travis had every intention of going to the Silver Creek Ranch. It would have been best if he left this town and never saw her again. But these hills were a good hiding place. Their height gave him a view of anyone approaching and he could stay up here.

These hills were also close to her.

What the hell, he pondered, he might get lucky and strike it rich. If he did, he'd share with her any gold he found. Maybe giving her a little financial security would get her out of his heart and off his conscience. Then he remembered Evan Peterson. If Peterson was so wonderful, he could take care of her, although he doubted the fool could wipe his own nose without help.

But the thought of her sharing with Peterson what she'd given to him was almost unbearable. And worse than that was the vague sense of worry that plagued him whenever he imagined Chloe legally chained to that man in a loveless, maybe even risky, marriage.

He shouldn't care and wished that he didn't, but

he seemed to have lost his ability to shut off painful thoughts. Disgusted, he tossed away the grass stem.

He got to his feet and took one last look at the house on the edge of town.

"If I can sleep tonight, I guess I'll be dreaming about you again."

The evening was unusually warm, the tail end of a blistering hot day. Nothing moved—not the air, not the birds, not the temperature. Chloe sat on the porch swing with her dinner plate on her lap, her blouse and camisole unbuttoned halfway down her bodice. She'd taken off her shoes and stockings and pulled her skirt up to her knees. With one foot tucked under her she kept the other on the floorboards to nudge the swing.

She picked at her food, telling herself she had no appetite because of the heat. She'd pushed herself hard today, standing over the washtub this morning, ironing this afternoon, certain that she'd be so exhausted she'd get a decent night's sleep.

Travis had been gone six days and by strength of will Chloe was finally able to think about him without getting that squeezing catch in her chest every single time. Even when Albert had given her a detailed account of everything Travis had bought, she'd expressed only mild interest and then steered the shopkeeper off to another topic. The comfort of knowing he'd gone to the claim was mixed. He was close, about ten miles from town, but with the way they'd parted, he might as well be on the moon.

She glanced at the plate on her lap and gave up

the idea of finishing it. A cool bath held far more appeal. She was just about to get up when Evan appeared at the fence.

She was so surprised to see him, she gaped.

He wore the same black suit he'd always worn when he came to call on her, and his horseshoe of hair was slicked down with Macassar oil. He held a small bouquet of drooping wildflowers and stared back at her, his eyes glittering oddly.

When she realized what he was looking at, she hastily pulled her skirt down and buttoned her blouse. There was nothing she could do about her bare feet. She'd left her shoes in the house.

"Hello, Chloe," he said. She was quick to note that he'd dropped the more formal "miss" he'd always used.

"Hello, Evan."

He opened the gate and came up the walk, then stood at the bottom of the stairs. "Well, are you going to invite me to sit down?"

She was immediately aware of a difference in him and she wasn't sure it was for the better.

"Yes, Evan, please do." She scooted over on the swing to make room for him.

He held the flowers out to her and she took them, feeling uneasy. Chloe hadn't seen him since that day a month earlier at the Tollivers', and she herself was forever changed from the woman who'd gone to visit him that afternoon. Travis, and the rapture and the pain he'd brought her, had given her insight that would keep her from looking at things the same way ever again. But when Evan sat next to her, with his faintly musty smell, the same old urge to pull away was stronger than ever.

"I would have been here sooner," he began, "but I've been helping at the farm with the harvest. I just found out this afternoon that McGuire is gone at last."

The wound was still too new for Chloe to hear this without feeling a sharp twinge. She only nodded.

"I'm glad you finally came to your senses and realized how much you risked by keeping him here. Now we can be married with no misunderstandings between us. Just name the day."

Chloe stared at him. Did he really believe that things would simply continue from where they'd left off? And he still seemed to have no grasp of the main reason Travis had worked there.

"Evan, I needed Travis's help to make the mortgage payment. You know that."

"Hmm, yes, well, and I assume you have, so that's behind us now. We'll carry on as though McGuire never existed," he asserted and let his arm rest along the top of the seat.

She *could* marry him, she supposed. She had no future with Travis. It wouldn't be a very satisfying life but she'd have the companionship she had thought she wanted.

Chloe immediately abandoned the idea. Even if she'd never met Travis McGuire, being alone for the rest of her days would be preferable to living with Evan. After what she'd shared with Travis that rainy night last week, the idea of Evan and—and she—oh, God, it was too horrible to even think about.

Travis had been right. Being married to Evan would be a living hell.

She retreated to the corner of the swing, trying to remove herself both from him and his arm, which threatened to drop across her shoulders any moment.

"Evan, when you first proposed to me two months ago, I never gave you my answer." She looked into his pale face and continued gently. "It would be a mistake for us to marry. We don't love each other and we don't have enough in common to overcome that. Our lives would be . . ." She paused, searching for a way to describe what she meant. "Our lives would be *lonely*."

His lashless eyes assessed her with an appraising harshness she'd not seen in them before now. "Did McGuire tell you that?" he demanded. "You are far too practical to have come up with such a notion on your own."

"I beg your pardon," she returned icily.

"You can't live in this house by yourself forever. Women who live alone get talked about."

"Oh? And who's doing most of the talking, Evan?" she inquired. "You?"

He had the grace to look uncomfortable for a moment. "Even though that drifter ruined your reputation, and probably more, I am still willing to make you my wife."

Chloe jumped to her feet and stood over him, no longer finding a need for diplomacy. "As hard as it

may be to believe, I am going to turn down your un-
selfish offer and ask you to leave. Now."

He stood, picked up the flowers he'd brought her
and threw them at her feet. Then he stomped down
the stairs and over the walk. From the fence he
turned one last glare on her.

"You'll die an old maid, Chloe. No other man will
want you," he pronounced, then hurried away.

Now she had one more thing to thank Travis for.
If he hadn't come to Misfortune, she would probably
have married Evan.

"You'll die an old maid . . ."

As if that was the worst thing that could happen
to her, Chloe thought, after being threatened with
the loss of her home.

After all these lonely years.

After grueling heartbreak.

There was only one man she knew who made Evan's assertion a bleak and desolating prospect. She
glanced at the far hills, lambent in the golden sun-
down.

Pushing herself away from the porch railing, she
went back into the house to put the kettle on for her
bath.

"Dad blame it, boy," Tar Bolen snapped. "Quit
swirling that pan like you was gettin' ready to feed
the hogs. No wonder you ain't findin' much gold. Yer
throwin' it all back into the water."

Travis looked on as Tar once again demonstrated
the proper technique to shake the gold to the bottom of the pan instead of sloshing it out. The mo-

tions involved rocking the pan from side to side and tapping the edge of it.

The crusty prospector had gotten used to the idea of having a neighbor once he decided Travis wasn't going to jump his claim.

At first Travis hadn't been too happy to have him nosing around, making a nuisance of himself, but now he was really learning something from him. If he could just get used to the smell.

The early September sun beat down on the back of his neck as he crouched on one knee next to a gently flowing spot in the El Diablo. The icy water had soaked him up to his thighs and his hands were freezing, but at least it numbed the blisters.

"There now," Tar announced proudly, giving the pan a final swish. "Now that's a fine mess of flakes." Travis was fascinated by what the old man had collected, a pea-sized mound of gold winking up from the bottom of the black pan. Still, it didn't seem like much.

"Thanks, Tar," Travis said.

"Nothin' to it," he replied. He stood stiffly and untied his mule, turning her to head back down the hill to his own camp. "Come on, Hannah, ol gal. Let's let this young feller get on with his work."

Travis watched him go, then looked back down at the gold and at the pile of wet sand he still had to go through. Right now that sand looked as big as a mountain. Resolutely, he sank his shovel into the pile. There might be another mortgage payment hidden in it.

Chloe pulled out a kitchen chair and sat down to read Evan's letter in hands that trembled ever so slightly. The morning sun streamed over her checkered tablecloth and the page containing Evan's cramped, rigidly precise handwriting. She'd opened the back door to carry two buckets of hot water outside to the laundry tub and found his envelope. She hadn't known what to expect in his words.

> ". . . I see everything differently now and I realize how wrong I have been. My behavior at our last meeting was unforgiveable, still I implore you to find mercy in your generous heart. . . ."
>
> "I would like to call this evening after dinner to offer my apology in person. I miss the pleasure of your company and our evenings together. Perhaps we cannot be partners in life, but I will be honored if I can call you a friend. . . ."

She sighed and pushed the refolded letter back into the envelope. Evan was right, his behavior had been unpardonably rude. Yet what was to be gained by holding a grudge?

Chloe was more alone now than at any other time in her life and she felt it very keenly. Isolation crowded her even as it cast her adrift. She hadn't seen Evan in weeks. In fact, he had been the last person to visit, if she could call it that. Adam Mitchell had made it impossible for her to attend church anymore. Not that she'd enjoyed it very much before that morning he'd come here with his insulting proposal. Her days were filled with work. Her evenings were spent doing mending, or reading in the parlor. Except for the ticking of the clock and the wind in the grass, silence was her only companion. Sometimes it seemed like she was the last person in this town.

She lifted her gaze to the blacksmith shop beyond the window. No, she didn't want Evan for a husband, or even a beau, but it might be good to have a friend.

All right, she told herself, and put the letter in her apron pocket. She'd give him a chance, just one, to make amends.

Chloe was sitting on the porch swing when she saw Evan's dark figure coming down the road. He carried none of the trappings of courtship—no flowers or candy—and she was relieved. As he neared she saw that even his clothes were less dressy; he wore a work shirt and dungarees. Apparently he'd dropped all pretense of the ardent suitor.

Still, her better judgment had made her decide to hold this meeting on the front porch instead of in the house. If the situation became unpleasant again, it might be easier to sweep into the parlor and close the door than to try to make him leave.

When Evan reached the far end of the fence, he followed it slowly, watching her with eyes that held the same peculiar, feverish glimmer she'd seen before. Vague apprehension ruffled Chloe like a chill breeze while he stared at her and then at the house, letting his hand drag along each weathered picket. Feeling a little tense, she smoothed her plum broadcloth skirt.

"You found my letter?" he asked, standing at the gate.

"Yes, Evan, and I appreciated it." After a second's

hesitation, she gestured at the empty seat next to her on the swing. "Please—come and sit down."

He crossed the walk and came up the stairs. "You're looking well, Chloe," he said, lowering himself to the swing. "A bit thinner, perhaps, but I suppose that's due to . . ." He let the sentence hang unfinished, as if having reconsidered the remark.

"But I'm here to make amends for my rude conduct the last time I was here," he went on, fidgeting next to her. "I didn't understand then that even if we don't marry, our association needn't end. I've missed this." He gestured broadly at their surroundings. His knee began bouncing up and down.

She sighed and pushed a loose pin back into her hair. "Friends are hard to come by, along with everything else," she reflected, almost to herself. "It's not good to have no one in the world, no one to talk to, to share things with." She was so acutely aware of that now.

A knowing, satisfied expression crossed his face. "Then you accept my apology and forgive my bad manners?"

She wasn't going to let him off that easily. She brushed a speck of lint from her skirt as she considered his question. "I don't know, Evan. You said some pretty hard things to me."

He hung his head in regret, then looked up at her, eyes glinting. "It was wrong of me. I was just disappointed."

The confession surprised her and it occurred to her how much he'd changed in the last few months. He certainly was very different from the man who'd originally come calling on her. Then he'd been hesitant, timid and respectful, afraid of offending her, unable to look her in the face. Now he was edgy and more direct and Chloe again was struck with the odd feeling that she was looking at a stranger's eyes through a mask of Evan's face. She couldn't shake the feeling, no matter how silly she told herself it was.

But maybe he *had* been disappointed, she thought, jumping to his defense again. All these months she'd excused his rudeness and tried to understand that he'd been threatened by Travis's presence. The two men were nothing alike and Evan must have sensed that he was lacking in so many ways when compared to Travis. Perhaps that was why he'd lashed out at her. "I do forgive you, Evan. Life is too short to bear grudges."

He smiled, looking pleased. "Good." He leaned back against the swing, his knee still bouncing nervously. His gaze drifted over the pleated bodice of her blouse, then lifted to her eyes.

Chloe read what she saw there and suddenly felt very uncomfortable. All her niggling qualms about Evan, which she usually ignored, clamored in her mind. He edged closer to her on the swing, his pale eyes lingering on her, his thigh brushing hers. She shifted slightly, instinct moving her closer to the other end of the swing.

"You don't have to feign false virtue anymore, Chloe. Not when we're finally beginning to understand each other."

False virtue? A horrible suspicion began to dawn on her that Evan's idea of friendship didn't match

hers. "I don't think I understand you," Chloe retorted, her shoulders drawing away from his out-
stretched hand.

She realized then that she didn't like Evan
Peterson. She wasn't sure she ever had. And she suspected that he *despised* her. He'd failed her at every
turn—when she'd needed his help, his protection,
his resourcefulness, his loyalty, he'd simply sat back
and left her to find her own way. Now he'd failed
her as a friend. His selfishness and weakness were
finally clear to her.

"Your blacksmith is gone, your virginity is gone—
the town is nearly gone. Why can't we make the best
of our lives?"

Disbelief threw her into stunned silence. Apparently assuming that she agreed, Evan took her arm
in a rough grip and pulled her against his thin chest.
His words came to her in an obscene whisper, as he
pressed wet, repulsive kisses on her neck. "McGuire
did me a favor, actually. Now I don't need to play the
attentive admirer, trying to win your favor."

Fear and revulsion gave her back her voice but her
words were muffled under his assault. She tried to
bring her hands up to his shoulders to push him
away but he possessed a strength she would not
have suspected. Her squirming served only to
heighten his arousal and she was flooded by the fear
that he was going to rape her.

His face looming bare inches from hers, his expression frenzied, he snapped, "You probably let that
uneducated savage kiss you but with me you're always so puritanical." Again he tried to connect his

lips to hers, this time his sweaty hand grabbing her breast. "Did you like what he did all those nights you two were here alone? Did you suppose I didn't know what was going on?"

"Evan!" she shrieked. Finally working her arm free and twisting away from him, she pulled back her hand and slapped him with every ounce of strength that terror and anger had given her. The blow sounded a sharp crack, like a dry barrel stave snapping, and Chloe's palm stung like fire. But it gave her enough time to roll off the swing and she landed on the porch flooring, immediately scrambling to her feet. Hoping her fury covered her fear, she glared at him, her breath coming in short gasps. "Did you think you would come here and—and—Get off my porch and off my land! Don't you ever, ever come back here!"

Evan covered her red palm print with his own hand, then gripped his temples between his thumb and second finger, as he did during one of his headaches. He looked up at her from lowered brows. His voice came from a dark, hateful soul—Chloe hardly recognized the sound as his own. "Why did you invite me over here and lead me on if you had no intention of following through with your wanton promises?" he snarled.

"What?" she demanded. "I don't know what you're talking about, Evan." Travis had been right, she realized. There was something profoundly wrong with Evan Peterson. "You invited yourself to my home and you are not welcome here. I insist that you leave *right now.*" She struggled to keep her voice strong and steady. Showing any weakness now would be her downfall.

Evan rose from the swing and Chloe felt a twinge of alarm at the malignity she saw in his face. She wanted to back away, but knew she couldn't. Her only defense lay in remaining resolute. She met his look with one that she hoped was fiercer than his.

For a timeless moment she waited for him to either hit her or turn away. It seemed she had won, that her rage far exceeded his selfishness, because he broke their gaze and thundered down the steps. He went back down the road, dust rising from each step he took.

She watched him go and didn't take her eyes off his back until he was only a dot at the far end of the road. Then she sat hard on the swing, perspiration soaking her, and her hands began to tremble slightly. She scrubbed her lips with the hem of her skirt, feeling dirty. She looked at her wrist and saw that her cuff button had been torn off during her struggle to escape Evan's grasp.

Until this moment, like a faded flower pressed between the pages of a book, she'd harbored the idea that Evan must have cared for her, just a little, in spite of what Travis had said. Now she knew how wrong she'd been. Travis was gone and if she was to have no one in this world, then so be it. She'd learn to make her own way. It would be far better to be alone than have to endure a man like Evan.

The sun was a brilliant red-orange ball settling on the horizon, ending this day and this chapter of her life.

She stood up, sealing away in her heart the part of her that had once yearned for love.

Chapter 12

The sun was low in the sky when Chloe reached down and plucked three carrots from her kitchen garden growing next to the back porch. On the opposite horizon, a huge harvest moon rose behind the hills. Those last days of September were shorter as summer drew its last breath. In just the past week, the nights had turned crisp and in the mornings the wind had a sharp edge. A scent was in the air, the spicy aroma that signaled the change of seasons.

She crouched and shook the soil off two nice potatoes to put in her basket. Looking at them, remorse struck her without warning, as it often did these days. She thought of Travis living on these potatoes because she'd banished him from the house, and wished she had it all to do over again. He'd been everything she thought she wouldn't want: independent, rebellious, iron-willed, full-blooded, with his emotions alive beneath a carefully blank surface. Now she realized that those very qualities had drawn her to him.

Though she'd resolved to survive by herself, her memories of Travis gave her no peace. At least their bittersweetness was preferable to her last nightmare meeting with Evan. He, thank God, had not bothered her again since that dreadful evening he came to "apologize."

In the shadow of the porch, a chilly breeze eddied around her. It was time to bring out her down comforter and woolen rag rugs. It would be a long winter in this house. All her days seemed long now.

From the road, the sound of approaching hoofbeats slowed and stopped outside the fence, just in front of the shop. Rising from her chore, she tried to see around the back steps. She hoped it wasn't somebody wanting a blacksmith. Since Travis had gone, time and again she'd had to explain that he no longer worked there, that Misfortune was without a blacksmith once more. She heard someone open the gate, its hinges screeching. Spurs rang with each step the someone took across the yard, hurtling her memory back to a hot noon when a drifter with spurs had walked through her gate. Wild hope flared in her.

Travis . . . ?

She stepped out from beside the stairs and was confronted by a man she'd never seen before. He was not very tall, no taller than herself. He had long dark hair and the bristle of a one-day or two-day-old beard. He wore a duster that nearly reached his ankles and a wide-brimmed hat, and he carried a well-tended Henry rifle in his right hand. Strapped around his slender waist was a gun belt that seemed too big for a man his size. His face was young; she would have guessed him to be in his early twenties.

But that was the only indication of his youth. There was something ominous about him, something forbidding in his ice-blue eyes that gave her a sense of critical danger. She knew this man, somehow, but she was positive she'd never seen him before. His voice was low and husky when he spoke.

"Beg pardon, ma'am," he said. "I need to see the blacksmith. My horse is losing a shoe."

"My father was the only blacksmith in town," she replied cautiously, clutching her basket, "and he passed away last spring."

"My condolences, ma'am. I'm really sorry to hear that." The man looked around the yard and then back to Chloe. "What's the name of this town?"

"Misfortune," she answered, wishing he would leave.

He smiled a slow, private smile. "Sounds like a good hiding place for a man who doesn't want to be found. It would be a dandy place for a blacksmith who doesn't want to be found."

Chloe's heart stopped for a horrible, gasping second, then with a tremendous lurch, began beating like a bird's. She looked at the ground quickly, hoping her fear didn't show in her eyes, that he couldn't hear her breathlessness.

She tried to arrange her face in an expression of ignorant curiosity.

"I'm sorry—?"

He shifted the rifle to the crook of his left arm. Reaching into his pocket, he brought out a silver dollar, rolling it across the back of his knuckles as he talked. "You might be able to help me. I'm looking for a man I've been tracking for five months. He's always a jump ahead of me."

"A criminal, you mean?"

"We've got some business to discuss, him and me."

"Are you a marshal?" she asked with a calmness she didn't feel.

"Not exactly, ma'am. I get paid to find people who are wanted for one reason or another, people in some kind of trouble. My name's Jace Rankin."

Yes, of course. She'd known it without being told. Oh, God, oh, God. Chloe's memory dropped back to her conversation with Travis that awful morning he left. She'd been full of audacity and advice then, telling him he ought to face Rankin to find out what he wanted. At the time she couldn't imagine what he feared or why he was afraid. Yet now that *she* faced him, she was absolutely terrified for Travis. All she could think of was to protect him and keep his whereabouts a secret from the bounty hunter with a boy's face and an old man's eyes.

"You mean you are a bounty hunter, Mister Rankin," she specified coolly, trying to cover her panic.

"You might say that, Mrs.—" He waited for her to fill in the blank.

"Miss Maitland," she supplied.

"Well, Miss Maitland, have you seen any strangers around town in the last month or so? The man I'm tracking is a blacksmith by trade. Just spent a few years in prison. He's tall and thin, dark hair, light eyes. His name is Travis McGuire."

It felt like a knife twisted in Chloe's heart to hear Travis described by this mercenary who made his living from the capture of human prey.

She feverishly devised a desperate plan.

"Oh, Mister McGuire, is it? Yes, he was here. I took him in while he was ill with sunstroke, but he left town about a month ago. Good riddance, I say," she snapped, wagging her finger to emphasize her grievance. "He was rude and uncooperative, and gave me nothing but trouble. I have no idea where he went and I couldn't care less."

Rankin studied her a moment with those dead blue eyes, as if weighing the truthfulness of her story. She suspected he was as accurate in his character judgments as was Travis.

He didn't speak for several long seconds and she was just about to start nervously babbling when he said, "I thank you for your time, Miss Maitland." He put the dollar back in his pocket, then turned and walked toward the road, his spurs ringing again. The sound ridiculed her memory of the slender, dark-haired man she held in her heart.

When he reached the fence he paused, his hand on the gate, then faced her once more. "I don't suppose McGuire is still around these parts after a month. But just in case you should see him, or remember something else about him, I'll be around town for the next day or so."

"He'd better not come back here, if he knows what's good for him." Chloe matched him look for look. "Misfortune is not a town that welcomes strangers, Mister Rankin."

* * *

An hour later the sun was down and Chloe went out to the shop to saddle Lester. She knew it was a daring thing she planned, to try to find her way in the dark to a place she hadn't seen for ten years. To go to a man she wasn't sure would even be civil to her after the horrible thing she'd said to him.

She'd braided her hair and put on her oldest skirt. To stay warm she jammed Frank's old hat on her head and put on one of his plaid wool shirts as a jacket. In the kitchen she wrapped a loaf of bread and some leftover fried chicken in a dish towel to take with her.

Chloe hoisted the saddle to Lester's back. Jace Rankin must have possessed the instincts of a bloodhound to have followed Travis to this remote corner. She imagined being on the wrong end of that Henry rifle with those eyes above the sight, and she shivered. Rankin would shoot a man without a second thought. She tightened the cinch strap and quietly led the horse out to the dooryard. Lester did not want to leave her stall at this hour and kept trying to turn back.

"Lester, be a good girl," Chloe hissed as she held the reins tightly and looked up and down the road. At the other end of town, past Doc's, Chloe could make out the light in the saloon windows. Faint piano notes floated up the street, but otherwise the town was quiet.

She swung onto Lester's back and pointed her toward the hills on the south rim. "Come on, girl, let's go," she said and nudged the horse forward.

* * *

Far down the street in front of the dark silhouette of the old hotel, a match flared briefly before a pair of ice-blue eyes as Jace Rankin lit a cheroot. Leaning against the hitching rail, he watched the black-smith's daughter set a southerly course to meet the man he was searching for. That namby-pamby schoolteacher had been right. McGuire was still around and Chloe Maitland was going to lead Jace right to his hiding place. He smiled to himself with the knowledge that after five months, his search was finally over.

The moon was as bright as a lamp hanging in the starred sky. Chloe was grateful for the light but it offered no warmth against the chill breeze and she tightened the wool shirt with one hand. All around her the night was alive with sounds of nocturnal animals scuttling through the low brush and announcing her passage. Lester, realizing she had no choice in the matter, settled into a steady, dependable gait as they crossed the flat terrain to the hills.

Chloe tried to maintain an easy grip on the reins but nervous as she was, it proved a chore. She kept one thought uppermost in her mind—that she was only going to Travis to tell him about Jace Rankin, then she'd turn right around and go home. She would not try to read in his eyes whether he hated her or missed her. And this time he wouldn't be able to make her reveal her thoughts, as he had so often when they were together.

She reached the foot of the low rocky hills and

urged Lester on. They carefully picked their way up the old path, worn smooth by years of wagons and horses making the same trip. She searched for the scant landmarks her memory allowed her to recall but had trouble locating them. Once, she found she'd gone in a complete circle and came out at the same spot where she'd begun.

Finally getting her bearings she reached a pile of rocks marking the grave of prospector, Jim Clancy, who'd died twenty years earlier when a boulder broke loose from the cliff above and crushed him. After his burial, the boulder had been rolled to his grave where it sat as a headstone. Over the years superstitious miners would pass and throw another rock on Clancy's grave for luck, until a sizable mound was erected. Frank's claim was just beyond Clancy's.

It was getting too dark to let Lester find the path. She climbed down from the horse and carefully led her toward the parcel Travis was working on. She couldn't see much but in the distance she heard the faint rushing of water in El Diablo, the 140-mile trough excavated to bring in the water necessary for placer mining.

Gravel crunched beneath her shoes and Lester was getting skittish. She strained to see ahead, looking for a campfire or a lantern, anything. She was positive she was close to the claim. But the path was deserted and silent except for the bubble of El Diablo and the call of a lone night bird. Lester pulled back on the reins, her frightened whinny making Chloe flinch.

She was beginning to regret her impulsive decision to come up here at night. It had seemed like a good idea to use the darkness as a shield but it was working against her. She took one more step when suddenly, from behind, a crushing arm closed around her neck and she heard the click of a gun hammer right next to her ear. Lester shied but Chloe maintained a death grip on the reins. The cold point of a gun shoved against her temple. She froze, pulled up on tiptoe, every muscle stiff with a terror so great her heart felt like it would explode. Adrenaline flooded her and sent a prickling sensation to her armpits.

"You move one eyelash and I'll splatter your brains all over your horse," a low, furious voice warned. A voice she knew.

"Travis," she cried in a hoarse gasp, "please don't hurt me."

His arm fell away instantly and he holstered the Colt. Turning her roughly toward the moonlight, he knocked off her big-brimmed hat. He studied her, then swiftly touched her face and hair with both hands as if to confirm what his eyes told him.

"Chloe," he said finally, his voice husky with fear at what had nearly happened. He pulled her into his embrace for a brief moment, pressing her head to his shoulder. Then he held her back at arm's length, his tone and expression hard. "For a minute I thought you were Jace Rankin. I almost shot you. What the hell are you doing up here in the dark, dressed like that?"

Her legs, locked at the knees a moment before,

were now as rubbery as a newborn's. She wanted to keep leaning against his tall form, inhaling the familiar scent of him through his shirt, but he pushed her away.

"What do you want?" he repeated.

She took a deep breath and pressed a hand to her chest, trying to slow her heart, then rubbed her windpipe where his arm had bruised it. She'd felt encouraged in that instant when he recognized her and hugged her, hopeful that he still had some kind feeling for her, even if it was only gratitude. But now his anger had taken over. Just as she suspected, he despised her. Her back and shoulders tensed as she struggled beneath the weight of his punishing coldness. She would deliver her message and go.

"Rankin's here."

"What do you mean 'here'?" he demanded, looking over her shoulder into the darkness. His stomach clenched at the thought that she might be so vengeful about his leaving that she'd lead Jace Rankin to this hiding place. "Did you tell him where I am?"

"Do you really think I'd do that? Don't you trust me at all?" Chloe asked, her arms held wide to emphasize the question. She could see his frown in the moonlight that made him look as gray as a corpse.

Travis had forgotten himself in the moment of recognition, when he'd realized who she was. It had felt so good to hold her for that instant. But he remembered the expression on her face the morning he'd left her, the name she'd called him, the pain that had followed. "You know how it is. Jailbirds can't afford to trust anyone."

She winced as he added his razor-sharp sarcasm to her burden of guilt, but her back remained straight and tight. "Travis, I'm sorry for that—more than you know. I didn't mean it."

He ignored her penitence and returned to the subject. "What about Rankin?"

Wouldn't he even acknowledge her apology? This was how it was to be between them? Pride pulled her chin up and put an edge on her words. "He's in Misfortune, hunting for you, asking questions. I talked to him not more than two hours ago. I thought you'd want to know." She turned to leave, not wanting to spend another moment in his presence, loving him, hating him.

"Chloe, wait a minute," he said, gripping her elbow. She wasn't going to drop this stingy crumb of information on him and then go, leaving him to wonder about the rest.

"Let go of my arm," she snapped. "I'm going home."

"Back to your whiny mama's boy? How does it feel to be kissed by someone with no lips, Chloe?" His tone was scornful, but tense inquiry lay under the words.

She pointedly looked down at her arm where he held it, then up at this face. "What difference does it make to you? It's none of your business."

Travis softened a little then and released her. "No, it isn't. Come on, come and sit down."

She did not soften at all. "Why? So you can insult me again?"

He sighed. "No. At least come to the fire and give

me the details about Rankin." He looked into her set face. "Please."

At length she nodded. "All right."

He retrieved her hat, then led the way to his campsite several yards ahead through the brush. It was settled against the slope of another hill. There a small fire burned and he'd pitched his tent.

He tied Lester to a fence post he'd driven deep into the rocky soil for his own gelding. Then he sat Chloe on a weather-bleached stump near the fire and dropped to one knee in front of her.

The flames illuminated his upturned face. He was still shaving every day, she noticed, even though there was no one to see him up here. But he looked exhausted, like he worked hard and never slept. She felt such a rush of affection and tenderness her throat ached. She closed her eyes against the hurt for just a moment, resisting the urge to pull his head to her lap and stroke the heavy hair that brushed his shoulders.

"Tell me what happened," he said.

She explained Rankin's visit to her backyard, careful to keep her voice steady. "I'm not sure he believed me when I told him I don't know where you are."

He gazed at the ground and shrugged. "He probably didn't. I've never been able to avoid him for long. He's very good at what he does."

"Yes, making money on other people's troubles. I never once thought he'd find you in Misfortune, miles from nowhere," she said.

He glanced into her face. "I know you didn't but

I'm not surprised he's here." Then almost to himself, "Jace knows how I think."

Chloe caught this suddenly familiar reference, but he continued before she could remark upon it.

"Anyway, thanks for coming up here to warn me. Sorry if I scared you back there." He reached out and almost touched her hand but then pulled back, trying to squelch his feelings for her. He liked the long braid hanging down her back. Looking at her now, he wondered how he could have mistaken her for Rankin. Even in the dark, the plaid shirt and big hat she wore could do nothing to disguise her soft curves and feminine face. His nerves were beginning to fray, he supposed. "You look good, Chloe."

The compliment surprised her and she ducked her head, shy for a moment. She was glad to feel the tension between them ease, even if it was only temporary.

"You made the payment on the house?" he asked.

She nodded. "Yes, I'm safe for another year. How have things been going for you? Are you well?" He looked so tired and worn she was almost sorry for having suggested this lonely exile to him.

"I've scraped a few dollars out of the ground. No mother lodes. But you were right, it's hard work." He opened his hands to her like a supplicant to show her the half-healed blisters and calluses there.

She bent forward and held his wounded hands in hers to examine them. Their heads bumped. "I have an ointment for this."

He chuckled. "Yes, I know you do. I remember my experience with your ointment on my face."

She laughed, too, her face mere inches from his. "Oh, so do I! You swore at me with amazing energy for a man near death."

Then, it was as if they both remembered him putting the ointment on her hands.

His gaze dropped from her eyes to her lips and stayed there for several seconds. All he had to do was lean forward a little to cover those lips with his own. He knew they would be soft and lush, just like the rest of her. He'd find solace in her arms and he'd sleep the healing, dreamless sleep he had the first time they made love.

No. He wasn't about to ask her for anything. Being tired and lonely and missing her were not good enough reasons to ask her to spend the night. Deliberately breaking the spell, he pulled his hands away and rolled back off his knee and stood with his arms crossed.

Chloe felt the abrupt shift of his attitude and recognized his withdrawal into himself merely by his stance. When she lifted her eyes to look at his closed face, the memory of their last parting hovered like a specter between them. She would go home but not before she explained the wound she'd inflicted. She rose from the stump and took two steps closer to him.

"Travis, I have to talk to you about that day you left."

He nodded but didn't speak. His face was blank.

This was so difficult. It wasn't hard for her to apologize. She'd already done that. It was hard to risk telling him the secrets in her heart, both that day and now. What if he didn't feel the same? What if he didn't even understand? Well, nothing could be as bad as what she'd lived through since he left.

She took a deep breath and held it for a moment. "That day . . . oh, God, that day was so wonderful and so awful." The memory burned like a hot iron and made the words tumble out in a cascade of pain. "I woke up next to you, feeling really safe for the first time since I was a girl."

She thought she saw an instant of commiseration in his face, but the poor light made it hard to tell, and then it was gone. She lifted her eyes to look at the moon, now high and white and cold, and laced her fingers together. "Then you told me you were leaving, that you were running from Rankin. I couldn't understand it. Now that I've met him, I know why." She turned back to him, catching and holding his eyes with hers. "But I think you were running from me, too. And that hurt so much, I wanted to die. So even though I love you, I tried to hurt you back. I've missed you every moment you've been gone, but it took all the courage I have to come up here and see you again."

"I thought you were getting married. What about Peterson, your fiancé?" No one but Travis could make Evan sound like a disgusting affliction.

She stared into the yellow flames of the fire, trying to decide what to say. How could she tell him that when she'd given herself to Travis on that night, he'd forever consigned her to a life with two options, to be with him or no one?

"I couldn't marry him or even bear the thought of

him touching me after that night we ... after you ..."

Travis could not respond. The bleak honesty of her words and her small, quavering voice slashed through him. He wanted to take her in his arms again, to smother her in hungry kisses. But he didn't move. This matter of the heart was a frightening thing. Intense emotions that had been cold ashes for years now reignited in his soul: joy, passion, empathy, remorse for hurting her, and, most unbelievably, hope. And all these emotions added up to produce one inescapable truth.

He was in love with Chloe Maitland.

There could be no more denying this, no more hiding from it. He realized he'd fought it from the beginning. Even when she was the biggest pain in the neck he'd ever known, she had captivated him. Now it was more painful to imagine spending the rest of his years without her.

What could he offer her? he wondered bitterly. A life on the run with no security? He did not have the right to ask her to give up everything she'd struggled so hard to save to go with him. He jammed his hands into his back pockets and tipped his face toward the sky, as if the answer might be found there.

Misreading his silence, she despaired. He didn't care. She gave up her seat on the stump. "It isn't important now, I guess," she said. She walked over to Lester and untied her.

Her actions jolted him from his thoughts. "Wait a minute, where do you think you're going?" He couldn't let her leave. Not yet.

She faced him. He looked annoyed again and the firelight accentuated his frown. "I came up here to tell you about Rankin, and I did. Now I'm going home."

"You can't go back down there alone, in the dark." Surely she didn't think he would let her do that.

"I certainly can and I will," she retorted, Lester's reins in her hand. Then she waved her arm at the campsite. "There's no reason for me to stay here, is there, Travis." It was a flat statement, not a question, and she mourned inside at the thought. "Besides, I'm not afraid of anything, remember?"

Her haughty bravery was too thin to disguise the weary hopelessness he heard in her voice. The sound of it alarmed him; he'd known that kind of desolation and what it could do to a person. He half turned from her, pacing back and forth over a short track. Damn it, he hadn't meant to let her get so close to him. But she had.

Still, he wasn't sure he could lay his soul bare before her and knock down the last wall standing between them. Could he take that chance again? He turned back to her and looked again at the one person who'd given him trust and comfort when everything else in life had failed him. The hell with it, he thought, his mind made up. If he didn't tell her how he felt, she would be gone. And this time he knew he'd never see her again.

"I can think of only one reason for you to stay." Slowly he held his hand out to her and took a deep breath. "I love you and I need you."

She stared at him, awestruck. Blindly she put her

hand in his. Travis McGuire had not only said he loved her, but that he needed her as well. "That's two reasons," she pointed out.

"Not to me," he replied. "I need you because I love you." He examined her fingers as they lay across his calloused palm. They were still work-roughened, and he knew that he had contributed to at least a part of that. "You're the best thing that ever happened to me, Chloe."

His words, words she'd never expected to hear from him, filled her with such piercing joy, she nearly feared it. But as she studied his face she realized that at last, the mask was gone. The feelings he'd so carefully hidden he now allowed her to see. Warmth and compassion and vulnerability, enduring love and loyalty—she felt them flowing from him. They rested like a benediction on her heart. He took Lester's reins and retied them.

Chloe shivered in the autumn wind. He closed his arms around her and she raised her face to his. Her lips were close and they looked soft. That faint fragrance he remembered so well clung to her.

She heard an anguished sound in his throat, then he took her face in his hands and lowered his mouth to hers in a desperate kiss. His tongue slid around hers and she yielded to the aching sweetness of the touch she thought she'd never feel again. In between the kiss that became many kisses were their whispered words of love.

"I missed you so much, Chloe."

"Oh, me too, Travis, me too. I felt so bad for what I said. I didn't mean it. I never meant it."

"Shh," he soothed. "I know. I think I knew it then but I let it eat away inside so I could keep you out of my head. It didn't work, though."

"I don't want to be separated from you again."

"I wish I could give you everything you deserve." He shifted her to one arm, and walked her back to the fire. With his free hand he gestured broadly across the arc of the night sky, as though the world was theirs for the taking. "I'd catch the brightest stars in a net to make a necklace for you. I'd buy you a mountain of French milled soap to make you forget you ever stood over that washtub."

She basked in the light of his ardent illusions. For so long, she'd felt as though her only worth to others was in the service she could provide them, while they gave little in return. In his withdrawn silence, Frank Maitland had taken for granted that she cooked and washed and kept house for him. Evan, she knew, had expected her to do all that and provide the home as well. Travis asked for nothing. She nestled deeper into the curve of his arm.

The animation left his voice. "But I don't have anything to offer you if you come with me, except a life running from Jace."

Again she noticed the first-name familiarity. "It doesn't matter now, Travis. None of it matters if I'm with you."

"Yes it does!" he said emphatically, startling her. He held her away from him by her shoulders to look her in the face. His expression was stern. "That part of this hasn't changed and it won't. He'll probably never be far behind me. I want you to know that before we make any choices or decisions. To face him would mean I'd have to kill him or let him kill me. I can't do that."

"Why must it come to that? Will you let this man steal the rest of your life away from you? If you do, you're still a prisoner." There was a blank, a piece missing from his explanation. Suddenly, she remembered something he'd muttered earlier. "There's something you're not telling me. You said he knows how you think. Why?"

Travis sank to the stump Chloe had occupied earlier and pulled her down to sit on his knee. He knew she had the right to demand the rest of the story from him. It was painful to talk about, though . . .

"Jace Rankin was my best friend. And Celia's brother."

Chapter 13

The floorboards creaked under the weight of a figure that moved in stealth around Chloe Maitland's porch. Its wide overhang cast concealing shadows in the moonlight and the man took advantage of these as he crept from window to window. He looked in each one, trying to see beyond the lace curtains hanging over the glass. But the house was dark and he could detect no activity inside.

He moved to the front door and opened the screen. Its hinges screeched in the late night and he froze, listening. No neighboring dogs barked, no lamp was lighted. The only response was the wind sighing over the prairie. He breathed again, certain the noise had gone unnoticed. His hand closed around the doorknob and slowly turned it. It was locked.

He uttered a low, malignant curse.

Carefully he made his way down the front steps and went around to the back porch. With cautious movements he climbed the stairs and tried this door. When it opened, he felt the exhilaration of success and crept into the kitchen.

It would be impossible for her to escape. He had the advantage of surprise in his favor. He quietly closed the door behind him.

Travis smiled into the face of the woman sitting on his knee, enjoying the effect of his words. He'd never thought Chloe would be left with nothing to say, but now she stared at him, her jaw dropped slightly.

"Jace Rankin is your brother-in-law? That snake?" she demanded, finding her voice and shivering again.

He nodded, patting her backside to make her stand. He rose and went to his tent. "When I got to Salem after my family died, Jace was the first person I met." He disappeared inside the tent for a second and emerged with a blanket and his nail keg. "He was twenty-two or twenty-three, but he'd always looked younger than he was."

He still did, Chloe thought, except for those eyes—

"He was working for the sheriff. In fact, he'd just been made a deputy. He was a scrapper, mostly because bullies wanted to pick on 'the runt'. He's not very tall and it made him tough. In some ways, we were a lot like each other." He wrapped the blanket around her shoulders.

"I'd better move your horse, just in case Jace trailed you here," he said, and she followed him to hear the rest of his story. He paused a moment, his ear turned to the night, while he listened for the crunch of gravel, for rustling brush, a horse's nicker.

"Do you think he's here?" Chloe whispered guardedly. She stared into the darkness but couldn't really see much beyond the circle of firelight.

Travis shook his head, satisfied that they were alone. "He would have shown himself by now." Lester pushed her nose against his chest in recognition and Travis chuckled.

"Jace was the one who sent me to his stepfather, Lyle Upton, for a job. Jace was the closest friend I ever had." He pulled Lester around to a secluded place behind a rock outcropping, unsaddled her, and retied her.

"And he believes you killed his sister?" Chloe asked. "This best friend?"

Travis led Chloe back to the fire and sat her on the stump, then took a seat on the overturned keg next to her. He threw a few more chunks of wood on the fire, creating a shower of sparks and making it burn high. "Their mother died when Celia was born. He always protected her, watched out for her. Sometimes it seemed like *he* was her father instead of Lyle, and he was even more forgiving of her than I was. Of course, she was an expert at pulling all our strings."

Another stiff night breeze blew through the camp and Chloe pulled the edges of the blanket closer. Travis appeared unaffected by the chill while he stared at the flames. "When she was killed, Lyle convinced Jace that I must have done it. That was really hard for me to take." He glanced up at Chloe and gave her a crooked little smile. "I like to think Lyle had some trouble doing it."

Chloe returned the smile, wondering why life had double-crossed Travis so many times.

"Later, after I'd been in jail for a couple of years, I heard Jace had become a bounty hunter and was making quite a name for himself." He took her hand and smoothed his palm over her fingers. "He started chasing me about a month after I was released. I spend a lot of time wondering if he's going to sneak up and blow my head off while I'm asleep."

He said this so casually, it almost sounded like a joke.

She'd met Jace Rankin and he'd frightened her. If she had the threat of him hounding her, she'd be petrified with fear. Travis had never been more than cautious and watchful.

"You don't act scared," she said.

He gave her an even look. "I am, though. All the time."

Chloe gripped his hand and looked into his eyes. "Life leaves scars sometimes, and God knows we haven't been spared." Her voice grew earnest. "But if we're together, I know the old hurts will heal. I don't care about Jace Rankin. I don't care about anything but you. I belong with you. I never could have loved Evan. I'd always told myself he meant well, but now he's below contempt. You were right and I should have listened to you. He's weak and he's mean."

"What made you see that?"

She told him about both times Evan came to her house after Travis had gone. His eyes narrowed as he listened and she saw his temper begin to flare.

"Don't bother with getting angry," she went on impatiently. "See, that doesn't matter. We're everything we've got, but Travis, it's so much."

She was right, they had a treasure. He took her face between his hands. The fire reflected itself in her hair and he exulted in the fierce loyalty and love in her eyes, so different from what he'd come to expect from people. He pulled her into his arms and embraced her desperately.

"I came up here because I couldn't stay with you, but I couldn't leave you, either. Woman," he growled, "you kept me awake every night, thinking about you, missing you so bad." He put one hand at her waist and one on her back. "Tonight, I'm going to keep *you* awake."

"How?" she asked, entranced by the sudden change in his voice, throaty and dark with increasing passion.

"I could make love to you," he suggested and she shivered, this time in anticipation.

He nuzzled her ear while his hand moved up her ribs, his palm sliding to a stop at the side of her breast. "If I were going to make love to you," he continued, kissing her jaw and temple, "I'd start by giving you lots of soft kisses."

She sat like a mannequin, letting him do things to her that made her insides jumpy. She needed deeper breaths to get enough air.

"Then I'd unbraid your hair, so I could feel it falling around me while I held you." He pulled the ribbon off the end of her braid and worked his fingers through the plait to comb it out.

He took her earlobe gently between his teeth and

sucked on it, covering her body and scalp with goose bumps. His breath was warm on her neck and she realized she was leaning toward him, sideways. When he put his tongue in her ear, she uttered a low cry and sought his lips with her own. His mouth moved over hers, greedy and feverish, his tongue slick and probing.

He pushed aside the blanket and her old flannel shirt and unfastened the buttons on her blouse, and grazed her camisole with his fingertips. When he reached inside to fill his hand with her breast, his touch was flame-hot as though there was no fabric between and her nipple hardened under his palm.

He slid from the nail keg to his knees in front of her and pushed her legs apart. Gripping her backside, he pressed his hips to her and even with skirt and petticoat and jeans between them, she recognized as never before the evidence of his arousal. The passion she had once believed she lacked ignited with a sizzling energy. She closed her legs around him, bringing him up as close and tight as she could.

All the while he devoured her with frantic liquid kisses. His face was taut in the firelight, his eyes pale and intense. "Chloe," he groaned against her mouth. "Oh, Chloe, honey."

That sweet, magic endearment. She'd never thought to hear it from him again. It was as common as any word in the language but when Travis said it, she felt as though he'd created it just for her.

"What would you do then?" she questioned breathlessly.

He stood, pulled her to her feet, and put a guiding arm over her shoulders. "Next I'd take you to the tent where it's warmer and undress you so I could taste you all over."

Chloe was sure she would have fallen right then if he hadn't been there to lean against. "And who will undress you?" she murmured before he kissed her again.

"You're going to do that."

He held the tent flap for her and followed after her. It was a good-sized shelter, tall enough to stand in. The bright firelight cast their silhouettes. The floor was layered with two thick sheepskin robes and blankets.

Travis sat her down on the robes and felt for her boots, pulling them off and throwing them in the corner. She began to unfasten her camisole buttons but he stopped her. "I'll do that." He redirected her hands to his shirt, but as soon as she'd unfastened it she was distracted by the feel of his warm fingers on her bare flesh. He pushed her back and stretched out next to her, one leg thrown over hers. Then he opened her clothes to expose her full breasts.

"As smooth as rose petals," he intoned, gently squeezing the soft, fragrant flesh. She always smelled of fresh air and sun. If he were blindfolded in a roomful of people, he could find her by that sweet scent.

His jeans became unbearably tight when he dropped his lips to her stiff nipple. Chloe sucked in a short breath with the first touch and as he suckled she buried her hands in his long, thick hair. He could feel her chest rise and fall rapidly with her breathing and the moan that escaped her only served to fuel the heavy ache building in him. The days and weeks up there, lonely and thinking of her, had been torture. Nothing could satisfy the plaguing emptiness but her.

Travis lifted his head and kissed her soft mouth again, reaching beneath her skirt. He ran his hand over the inside of her leg up to the place he longed for and remembered so well.

As soon as she felt his touch brush her drawers, Chloe's hips began to move restlessly and Travis was enticed by her squirming. He wanted to take things slowly, to make this reunion last, but he feared it wasn't to be. This time his need was even more powerful than the first time they made love. Now he knew for certain the delicious pleasure waiting for him. When he pressed his palm to the juncture of her legs, high and sweet, Chloe pressed back hard and he could feel the dampness gathering under the fabric there. His heart beat like a drum as raging hunger licked through him.

She parted his shirt and pulled him down to her by its edges, anxious to press his bare skin to hers and feel the silky hair on his chest.

As soon as their flesh made contact, dire urgency ignited in them and their hands were busy at the rest of the fastenings on each other's clothes. Chloe felt his fingers at her waist, quickly opening her skirt and tugging it down. She pulled the ties on her petticoat and kicked it off.

Travis sat back on his knees and impatiently

yanked off his shirt, then paused to gaze at her pale form, naked and ethereal against the robes.

"I love you, Chloe," he said, and it sounded like a prayer.

Broad shouldered and beautiful, he knelt next to her. "I love you, too, Travis," she responded and held her arms open to him. He leaned over her and laid a line of fiery kisses from her throat to her navel, while her desire burst into flames.

She wasn't afraid like before. Now she wanted to give him as much pleasure as he gave her and she boldly reached for the buttons on his jeans. Through the denim she felt a furnace-heat, hard and full, and her fingers brushed tentatively over that hardness.

Travis uttered some wordless sound and sat up to pull off his boots. She heard his belt buckle open and knew he was pulling off his pants.

"Oh," she said in disappointment, but he took her hand and pressed it to himself to prove his point.

"Sorry, honey," he said. "I can't wait to feel you around me."

Thick and hot, he pulsed against her fingers. She closed her hand around him and heard his groan in her ear. He lay down with her and thrust a slow push-pull in her grasp while he put soft, damp kisses over her breasts and stomach. Finally he took her hand away.

"It'll be over before we can start," he whispered raggedly. "But you, I want to touch you . . ."

He let his hand drift to her hip where it smoothed and massaged her in an arc over her abdomen and down her other thigh. Then he opened her legs to gain access to the heated, sensitive flesh between them.

She was engulfed in the exquisite sensation of the hot, slick strokes as his fingers moved over her and within her, bringing her to the very edge of fulfillment. Then he withdrew his hand and Chloe moaned in equally exquisite frustration. "Travis . . . don't stop. Please don't," she begged.

But he needed her now, this instant, to feel her close around him. He was full and aching and at his flash point. "I'm right here, honey. It's all right." He hovered over her for an instant, preparing to join her body with his.

She looked up at him and knew such joy her throat closed with emotion. "Tell me again, Travis."

"I love you, Chloe. I love you so much." He slid one arm under her shoulders and the other under her waist and held her to him as he entered her with a smooth powerful thrust.

Chloe drew a sharp breath as he filled her, again overwhelmed with a sense of wholeness and communion that nothing else in life had ever given her.

Travis sank into the tight, warm glove of her. His strokes were hard and urgent, swelling the yearning that made her heart thunder in her chest and her breath come in short gasps. The fire, oh, the fire he kindled. God, this couldn't go on. There would be nothing left of her but cinder and ash. She sobbed his name once, twice, in her frenzy.

But he already knew what she needed. He had always known. His thrusts became almost savage in intensity, compelling her body to surrender to him in a series of contractions that began low in her abdomen and reached to grip him within her. Her high, thin cry floated away on the night.

The wild fever of her response burned in his blood and a deep, low-throated moan rose in him as he strained forward in one last powerful thrust. His release exploded in him, so strong he gripped the robe in both fists. His body was rigid over hers, his breath stopped in his throat. Finally he relaxed against her, resting his head on his forearm next to her, his breathing labored.

They lay limp and sated in their warm bed, their heavy limbs entwined. Travis rolled them over so they lay on their sides, facing each other. He felt baptized in her love, as all his pent-up rage and disgrace and hurt were washed away with the union of their bodies and souls. He kissed the point of her jaw and ran a fingertip around her nipple, watching it harden in response.

"I sure am glad you're too old for passion," he teased lazily. "If you were any wilder, you'd probably kill me."

She nipped his nose, self-conscious about her abandon. "Are you complaining?"

"Mmm, not me," he replied, his lips behind her ear. "I wouldn't have it any other way."

She went on thoughtfully. "I guess it was a pretty silly idea. That I'm old, I mean. I had no idea it would be like this. I just didn't know. I'm glad I was wrong about it." She nuzzled her face against his neck again and put her hand to his face. "But it could be like this only with you, Travis. Just you."

The last word was muffled by his mouth coming down on hers. He was part of her and she, part of him. Bound by more than any earthly consideration of mutual convenience or tolerability, they were bound by the heart.

Their coming together was lingering and tender the second time, while they smoothed wondering hands over each other's body to explore and relish and worship.

Chloe felt his sharp hipbones and the long bone and muscle in his legs. Travis dropped kisses into the curve of her waist and on the swell of her hip.

Soft, rounded flesh, smooth and firm. She was so beautiful.

Sinew and cord and strength. He was beautifully handsome.

Travis joined his body to hers with long, slow strokes and when they reached their climax, it was as soft and passionate as their lovers' whispers in the darkness.

Travis wrapped them more securely in the warm blankets, then reached for her hand, sandwiching it between his chest and fingers. She felt the slow, steady rhythm of his heart under her palm. There was nowhere else on earth she belonged but with this man.

He pulled her closer to him, savoring the joy of her body against his, her hair falling over him in a silky drape, her breath fanning his collarbone. He fought the perfect sleep he knew to be waiting for him, worried that this might be the night Jace chose to ambush him. And now Travis had Chloe to protect as well, but he was glad she was with him, soft and warm.

He murmured, drowsy-voiced, "If the world ended tonight and I died here in your arms, it would be okay. I have everything now."

"Oh, Travis," Chloe choked, but already his breathing was deep and smooth, and she knew he slept. She nestled more tightly to him, protectively, hoping he wouldn't feel her tears as they dropped on his shoulder.

"Chloe—honey, wake up."

Stop it, she told herself. There were lots of nights when she thought she heard Travis calling her. Or dreamed that he lay next to her, his long legs entwined with hers, his hand on her breast. To wake and find it was only her imagination was bitter disappointment.

"Come on, honey. It's getting late."

She rolled over, trying to shut out the sound. But when she felt his warm lips at her temple, his hand stroking her hip through the blanket, they were too real to ignore. Lifting heavy lids, she saw Travis next to her on one knee, already dressed. This was a more elemental Travis than the one who'd made horseshoes in the shop and danced with her on the porch. The edge of danger she'd always felt in him was far more apparent now. His gun belt was strapped to his waist with its holster tied to his thigh. His long dark hair accentuated the silver tint of his eyes. Though she was comforted by this strength, she realized that an enemy would have much to fear from him.

The gray-blue daybreak lay just beyond the open tent flap. She smelled fresh coffee steaming in the tin cup he held.

"It wasn't a dream. You're really here," she said, looking up at him in the low light. Relief coursed through her, pulling her from sleep. She put her hand on his booted foot. "Oh, Travis, I'm so glad."

For a suspended second, he looked at her with such wistful, unguarded devotion, the emotional intensity nearly took her breath. He reached out and smoothed her hair back from her forehead before leaning over to put a soft kiss on it.

"No more dreams, Chloe. From now on, it's all real. But if we're going to leave, you have to get up. Jace will be up here this morning." He said this as certainly as if they had an appointment to meet.

She sat up stiffly, not used to sleeping on the ground. She tucked the blanket under her arms but she shuddered when the cold morning air touched her naked shoulders and back. "Brrr, I'm freezing."

It took all his willpower to resist sliding his hands under the blanket to touch the ripe curves hidden there. She looked small and delicate in the tangle of covers, her features still sleep-soft. Her tousled hair fell around her in long burnished waves and as she looked up at him, she made him feel like he owned the world.

Travis draped her wool shirt around her, then with one finger traced a path across her bare skin at the point where the blanket covered her breasts.

"God, but you're beautiful," he intoned.

"I am?" She'd heard him say so before but it was while they were making love. She'd assumed it was something he was *supposed* to tell her. It surprised her to hear it now, especially when she was rumpled and uncombed.

"Don't you know that?" He shook his head then. "No, I guess you don't. There was no one to tell you and you never would have thought so yourself."

She offered him a shy smile. "No, but it's very nice to hear you say it."

Brushing her cheek with the back of his fingers, he handed her the cup. "Here, drink some of this." He cocked an eyebrow at her, his tender expression dissolving into a wicked smile. "I don't have time to warm you up, so you'd better get dressed.

He went outside where he was loading the pack-horse. She sipped at the coffee. It was too hot to really drink it. She scurried into her clothes, then groped through the bedding on all fours, searching for her boots. Last night their need to touch each other, to express their love had been so urgent, they'd flung garments everywhere.

She paused a moment and sat back on her knees, looking forward to a thousand nights and more like that to come, a lifetime's worth of fire and passion, tenderness and contentment. When she thought of how close they'd come to losing it all, her heart clenched in her chest. She shook herself out of the reverie and put on her shoes, then quickly rebraided her hair. This was no time to daydream. They weren't out of the woods yet.

She emerged from the tent, bringing the blankets and sheepskins with her, and Travis immediately began dismantling the shelter. He'd already saddled Lester for her and the horse stood waiting patiently, nibbling at the dry brush.

She looked around the stark, barren camp. Funny, but daylight made it even more isolated and lonely than darkness. A big water ditch that Travis had dug lay to the immediate west of the campsite. Beyond that and the sluice boxes he'd built, there was nothing—no trees, no birds, no greenery. There was nothing but dirt, rocks, and the faint rushing of water in the El Diablo behind them. To be up here for months or years on end with no one to talk to, why, a person would lose his mind. No wonder Tarpaper Bolen was a bit odd.

"Don't stop to fold that stuff," Travis said, indicating the blankets she carried. He pulled out the tent stakes. "Go back to town. Only pack what you think you need now. We can buy you other things later."

He dropped the canvas and walked toward her. The early sun glinted on his hair and lashes, bronzing their dark brown edges. Hard work had ripped the knees out of his jeans and his boots were scarred and dusty. His chambray shirt was missing a button. But she was positive there was no man more handsome than Travis McGuire. Again she marveled at his lean, natural grace—loose hipped and limber when he moved. In the better light, she could see how much more rested he looked.

Travis took her hands and raised them to his mouth, pressing a kiss on each while he watched those big green eyes. He tried to tell himself one last time that maybe he was a fool to risk everything—his heart, his future and freedom—on a woman. But he knew it was a lie. She was not simply "a woman." She was Chloe Maitland, his life-partner. She'd pulled him back from the edge of despair and she was worth more than he could risk.

"I wish you'd let me take you back to town," he said, feeling like the lowest chicken-hearted skunk he'd ever known. "But I really wish you weren't going at all. Isn't there anything I can do to talk you out of this?"

They'd been over this a half-dozen times late last night. They'd awakened and begun planning their future, making a picnic of the fried chicken and bread she'd brought along. He didn't want her going down there, alone, especially with Jace so close. But Chloe was adamant and she refused to let him risk himself to go with her. Despite his calm-voiced reasoning, he'd been unable to dissuade her. At one point he'd lost his patience and called her the most pigheaded, thick-skulled female he'd ever known. Then he'd felt bad for his hard words and made slow, sweet love to her, whispering over her body how sorry he was.

Chloe knew it was impossible for him to go with her. Jace Rankin would spot him for sure. But as certain as she was that going away with Travis was the only thing to do, she couldn't leave her home without seeing it once more. Chloe shook her head.

"No, Travis. I need warmer clothes." She looked down at the tops of her shoes, then back up into his eyes. "And—and I want to see the house once more. I—*we* worked hard to save it. I can leave it without looking back, but I'd like to see it one more time. You know . . ."

Travis nodded, trying to understand, but he really had no experience to draw on. None of his ties went so deep or so far back. The longest he ever lived in one place was in prison. Her life had been so different from his. Did she really know what she was doing by going with him? He pulled her into a fierce hug.

"All right. But go fast. Don't dawdle and try not to let anyone see you." He looked out at the brightening horizon. "It's already later than I'd like." He shifted her to one arm and turned her toward the plains below. They stretched out beyond the reach of their vision. He pointed to a ragged collection of tiny buildings on the flat prairie. "There's Misfortune. See that roof on the west end?"

She peered in the direction he indicated, trying to separate one building from another. They were all so far away and weathered, they blended into their surroundings. Finally, she was able to distinguish the roof she was supposed to see. She nodded.

"That's your house. I used to sit here and watch it sometimes while you were doing the wash."

She stared with more interest. "My house? You can't tell me you were able to see me," she asserted. There were so many amazing things about him, she half expected him to say he could.

"No, but I'd imagine what you were doing as you went through your day." He shook his head, looking at the packed earth at their feet. "I couldn't stop thinking about you, no matter how I tried. I made myself crazy from thinking, and I was burning mad with both of us for it."

She nodded. "It was so—so *silent* after you were gone." She glanced up at his handsome face and put her hand to his cheek. "I thought I'd never see you again. I felt like I was dead inside."

He walked her over to her horse. Chloe put her foot in the stirrup and swung herself into the saddle while Travis held the reins.

"I truly don't believe Jace will bother you. But it'll be better if he doesn't see you, so be careful." The breeze stirred his hair. He put his hand on her knee.

"I'll hurry," she replied, leaning down to give him a quick kiss. But as soon as their lips met, he let his hand slide along her leg to her ankle and took her foot out of the stirrup. Then he stepped into it to pull himself up to her. Lester stood rock-steady while they closed desperate arms around each other. All the torment and worry and peril they'd both known went into the kiss they shared.

Then he put his hands on either side of her face to tip her forehead to his mouth to put a kiss there, and pressed another to her chin and each cheek. "So the angels will watch out for you," he said, invoking Fiona McGuire's blessing. He jumped down, feeling helpless to do anything more.

"I'll be back in two hours. I promise," she said, urging Lester forward. She forced herself to smile brightly as she waved goodbye, and made a vow that this was the last time they'd have to separate.

* * *

After Lester picked her way down to the prairie floor, Chloe pressed the horse into a trot to hurry her along. Now and then she'd glance back over her shoulder at the yellow hills she was leaving. She actually felt less danger from Jace Rankin than pain of separation from Travis. It had been only a half hour since they parted and already she missed him. How had she lived through the last few weeks? The truth was, she hadn't.

She'd struggled to regain the familiar pattern of her life, and had convinced herself that she'd succeeded by gritty determination. But it was a lie. She'd only gone through the motions, dull-eyed and brokenhearted.

Chloe rocked along with Lester's steady gait, her thoughts drifting. Travis had said life wouldn't be easy for a while. No, it probably wouldn't be. It would be wonderful if they could carry on with the life they'd started over roast beef sandwiches on hot, hushed noons. With love and commitment woven through their days to strengthen them. With no threatening shadows lurking on the horizon. But she'd rather live in his tent for the next ten years than go back to the lonely emptiness she knew before he came to Misfortune. And to live without him was unthinkable now.

Up ahead she saw the rundown buildings and overgrown graveyard that marked Misfortune. "Come on, girl," Chloe said, urging Lester into a trot. "Travis is waiting for us."

* * *

After Travis packed the rest of his gear he sat down, cross-legged, to wait for Chloe at the point on the hillside that overlooked Misfortune. His muscles were tight with the watchfulness that never left him. Now and then he'd glance up to check the sun's relentless progress as it climbed the sky, then back to the flat plain between Misfortune and himself.

Watching for Chloe.

Watching out for Jace.

Almost three hours had passed since Chloe left. She should have been back by now. Behind him, the loaded horses pawed the ground restively. He turned to look at them, running his hand through his long hair.

Travis got to his feet and began pacing near the edge of the hill, his arms alternately crossed over his chest and clasped behind his back.

He'd seen a kind of yearning in Chloe's eyes when she left, as though she wanted to take a long look in case she never saw him again.

Doubts crept in to plague him. What if she'd changed her mind? The prospect made his stomach feel like it had dropped to his feet. Her life hadn't been easy, but it had been more secure than what he was offering her. Maybe she decided she'd be losing too much by going away with him.

Women, damn them, were always changing their minds, he seethed. How many times did he need to have *that* demonstrated to him? He picked up a handful of stones and began pitching them straight out over the hillside with brutal force, his arm stiff and locked. Maybe that story about loving him was just that, a story.

No! His imagination was running like a wild horse. No, she couldn't have deceived him so easily. Not Chloe, she wasn't a schemer. He glanced at the rocks clenched in his fist and slowly dropped them, dusting his hands on the seat of his jeans. The woman who lay beneath him deep into the night had surrendered herself completely, unselfishly. He knew there was no mistaking it. Miserable guilt at his suspicions welled up in him.

Then where was she? Why was she taking so long? She knew Jace was coming—

He looked up sharply. Jace! Sweat popped out on his forehead and scalp. He hadn't expected it, but yes, it was possible. Jace might have her, using her to force him out into the open. All because he believed Travis had killed his sister. Even his years in prison wouldn't satisfy Jace.

Through his mind flashed a familiar memory so bitter it had once threatened to poison his soul. Of years spent in a small dark cell, of endless rainy nights punctuated with dark dreams, of a raw wound on his ankle that never got the chance to heal.

But this time the images faded before those of a tall, slender woman with red-gold hair and green eyes, who smelled like sunshine and in every possible way made him feel like a man.

Travis took another look at the open vastness before him and at his horse behind him. All right, by God! He strode to the animal and untied his reins.

If Jace wanted him, he'd get him. But he couldn't have Chloe . . .

Travis rode up to Chloe's back fence, avoiding the main road into town. He dismounted and smoothed his hand over the horse's nose to calm him. Then drawing his big Colt revolver, he moved quietly and swiftly down the line of pickets, watching the house and the shop. In the corner of the yard where the maple tree stood, he hopped the fence and circled the edge of the property. Chloe's horse waited in the dooryard, her reins casually thrown over a bush. He crept to the kitchen garden next to the back porch where he crouched beside the steps, his shoulder pressed to the wall, his head down, listening, listening. For voices, for the squeak of a floorboard, for the sound of a gun hammer being cocked. There was nothing but the wind blowing over the grass and his own breathing.

Looking up the stairs he saw the door was open, the screen unhooked as it swung lazily on a vagrant northerly draft. Fear for Chloe pumped through him. He hadn't seen Jace for five years and didn't know what kind of man he was now. The man who'd been his friend wouldn't have stooped to use a woman to bait a trap. But time and circumstances could change a person. God knew, he'd felt the change in himself.

Damn it, why hadn't he come here with her? Better yet, he should have refused to let her return at all. He could have bought other clothes for her.

Automatically Travis checked the rounds in the

Colt, then made his way up the stairs, careful to stay on the far edges to keep their creaking to a minimum. He slipped into the kitchen when the screen door swung wide again, holding the revolver at chest level in front of him. From the kitchen he went through the dining room, finding no trace of Chloe and nothing unusual. He halted in the parlor, his throat suddenly dry.

A table had been overturned and the lamp it had held lay shattered on the floor. The smell of kerosene filled the room as it soaked into the braided rug.

He stepped around it, keeping his gaze steady on the incline of the stairs as he edged his way to the second floor. He saw a fallen satchel on its side at the top of the staircase, beribboned white underthings spilling from it. An old rag doll, the one he'd seen in Chloe's hands when he first woke up here, lay facedown below the bag, its arm torn off. At the sight of it, Travis stopped a moment and took a deep silent breath to steady his hands.

He continued on light footsteps through the rooms upstairs. With each empty room he struggled harder to suppress the rage threatening to erupt from his fear. She wasn't in the house . . . no one was in this house.

He bounded down the steps, two at a time, and strode to the back door. "Jace," he growled aloud, "we're about to have that talk Chloe suggested."

"Rankin!" Travis shouted. His own voice echoed back to him, bouncing off the silent, deserted buildings as he rode slowly through the center of Misfortune. Rankin may not be holding Chloe here, but for his plan to work, he'd have to be someplace where Travis could find him.

Now and then a face would appear at a window, then vanish again, as though the few residents knew a terrible conflict was about to take place.

"Here I am, Rankin," he called to the empty windows and shadowed doorways. "Come and get me but let Chloe go." The stillness was unnerving, broken by the squeak of an old shop sign swinging on rusted hinges in the wind, and the sound of his horse's hooves on the dusty, sunbaked street.

Up ahead, a man emerged from the Twilight Star and sauntered into the street, in no particular hurry. His stature was compact and threatening. He held a Henry rifle diagonally across his body. The weapon almost looked too big for him but he handled it with familiar closeness, as though it were a well-loved woman. As the man stepped into his horse's path, Travis heard the ring of spurs and he reined the animal to a halt.

A lengthy silence followed while the two men assessed each other.

Travis found no emotion in Jace's eyes as they glinted up at him. He didn't see hate or anger there, only an aloof detachment.

There really wasn't much about him Travis recognized. The easygoing openness he'd had as a younger man was gone. It wasn't just that he looked older. He looked *old*, in a way that only experience, not years, could bring about. He saw nothing in the bounty hunter to remind him he had been his closest friend. Now he was Travis's worst enemy. He climbed down from his horse, the saddle creaking in the quiet morning.

Finally, Jace spoke. "I was just about to ride out and see you, McGuire. Thanks for saving me the trouble."

Travis's hands hung at his sides, the revolver just inches from his grip. "You've fallen a long way Rankin—using a woman to get what you want. This is between you and me. It doesn't concern Chloe Maitland."

Jace watched him unblinkingly, like a blue-eyed cat outstaring its prey. "Hmm, yeah, the new lady-love. At first she told me she'd never heard of you. Of course I knew she was just protecting your hide. She's feisty but she's not a good liar. She finally broke down and admitted you'd stayed with her for a while." His ice-blue eyes narrowed slightly. "She must be pretty important for you to risk your chickenshit neck to tell me to stay away from her. Does she know you murdered your wife?" His voice was deliberate and smooth, as though he merely sought information.

Travis felt his fingers close into a fist. He wanted to knock that flat expression off his face. No, that wouldn't help, not yet. He opened his hand. "Why should I lie to her?"

The action was not lost on Jace. "Looks like prison was good for that famous temper of yours. It ties my gut in knots that my old man had you turned loose. I still don't know why he did it."

"What the hell do you want, Rankin?" Travis demanded, staring back. "I've had a bellyful of you following me over the last few months. Why did you do it?" Anger itched in his skin like a woolen union suit. Over Jace's shoulder he saw the DeGroots crowded against their shop window, watching them.

"You did a pretty good job of staying out of reach," Jace acknowledged with mild amusement as he stroked the blue barrel of the Henry. "But it was never quite good enough, was it? When an old mule skinner I met on the road told me this town would be a hard place for a man who didn't like being an outsider, I knew I'd find you here. You're used to being an outsider."

Travis frowned at him. In spite of his efforts to harness his anger, Jace's tactic was wearing on him. "You think you know me so well, but you never could get it through your head that I didn't kill Celia." His words grew louder. "I swear to God, sometimes she pushed me so hard, I was tempted. She slept with any man in town who asked. She even brought them home to our bed. I sure as hell would've had the motive if I'd known. You knew what she was doing. Everyone knew it but me." He wrapped his horse's reins around his gloved fist. "But I didn't kill her. One of her lovers did." He laced the word "lovers" with a bitter sarcasm.

A spark of rage lit Rankin's features then, animating his cool appearance. His hands tightened on the rifle. His voice rose on a wave of controlled fury, *"Don't"*— then dropped —"tell me that again. I heard that lie often enough five years ago. My old man helped you cheat justice and I'm here to see that you don't get away with it. One way or another, you're going to answer for what you did. No matter what, she was my sister!"

"She was *my wife!*"

They glared at each other, their faces tight with anger, breath coming fast.

"Goddamn you, Jace," Travis finally snarled, sick of this game. "Where is Chloe?"

Jace's brows rose in mystification, shifting his hat slightly, his cool exterior recovered. "How the hell should I know? I haven't seen her since last night when I watched her ride out to find you. Maybe she went back to the schoolteacher." A slow smile widened his mouth. "Although a fine-looking woman like her seems wasted on that crazy sissy. He told me you stole her from him and ruined her reputation. Doesn't surprise me."

Crazy sissy. Travis wondered if his heart had stopped. He got a funny empty feeling in his chest. He grew light-headed and his vision blurred for an instant while the sky seemed to change places with the ground.

He knew instinctively that Jace was telling him the truth. He might be relentlessly single-minded in his purpose but he still had a fragment of honor and Travis could feel it.

Jace hadn't taken Chloe. Evan had.

Evan Peterson. The man who hid behind Chloe's skirts and lost his future security when Travis won her heart. The man with the mean streak Travis had detected.

He grasped Jace's arm. "Help me find Chloe. I don't know where she is, but I know Peterson's got her."

Jace pulled back impatiently, clearly offended. "Why should I? Get the sheriff to look for her."

"He couldn't find salt in the ocean. I've got a bad feeling about this. Peterson could really hurt her." Travis hated the position he was in, but he had no choice. He didn't know anyone with Jace's tracking skills. "I need your help."

Jace's eyes gleamed with his advantage. "What's in it for me?" he inquired softly.

Travis clenched his jaw, then pulled his gun from the holster and held it out butt-first. "I'll go with you. Whatever you want."

He studied Travis speculatively. Finally, he nodded but didn't take the weapon. "That's an interesting offer. She must be worth a lot to you."

Travis looked up at Albert DeGroot, giving the nosy shopkeeper a menacing stare until he and Mildred backed away from the window. Then he returned his gaze to Rankin. "I owe her my life."

The bounty hunter was silent a moment. "You've got yourself a deal, McGuire. I'll decide how I want to settle this after we find the woman." He pushed Travis's gun back toward him. "Keep the Colt, you'll need it. But stay ahead of me. I can't have you shooting me in the back."

Chapter 14

Chloe twisted her hands in front of her. The rope chafed her wrists and two bright-red rings were appearing on them. She tried shifting her feet but they were tied even tighter. At least her stockings kept the coarse hemp off her ankles. She sat crosswise on a dusty iron bed, her back propped against the rough plank wall.

In this small room over the Rose and Garter Saloon, Evan paced feverishly before her, barely recognizable in his insanity. He'd ordered her not to speak and she willingly obliged—he was so agitated, she was afraid he might shoot them both.

She watched him warily as he strode back and forth, muttering to himself, answering questions she couldn't hear, seemingly deep in thought. Horrified by his bizarre behavior, she laced her fingers together to hide their shaking. He wore a wrinkled, dirty suit that looked as if he'd slept in it for several nights. His white shirt was graying and damp with sweat. His cravat hung untied around his neck.

She'd packed her satchel and was going down to the parlor when Evan had appeared at the foot of the stairs, waving a gun she didn't even know he owned. He grabbed her by the front of her shirt, hurling the accusations of a jilted lover. With surprising strength, he forced her to this place, taking the back path that ran behind the buildings.

Now he came to a sudden stop and whirled to face her, resting his chin on his fist. He studied her from several angles, as though she were a museum exhibit. His red-rimmed eyes were maniacal and accusing.

"You belong to me, Chloe," he said finally, "and I won't abide a whore. I know you went to that blacksmith last night. And I know what you did with him. I sat in your kitchen and waited for you all night. But you didn't come home. I cannot let this defiance pass unpunished. You were disobedient and you must be corrected."

You must be corrected. Through her fear her memory seized upon what Travis had told her about Cory Hicks and the bruises on his left arm. Cory had told Travis that Evan was "correcting" him.

She'd though she'd felt terror last night when Travis grabbed her in a stranglehold and pressed the barrel of his gun to her temple. That was laughable compared to the danger she faced now, but she had to venture a response, to try to remind him that she was an adult, not one of his pupils. "Evan," she began in a surprisingly calm voice, "it isn't your place to object. Won't you please untie me?"

"Silence!" he thundered. "How dare you address me by my first name? No student is allowed to do that!" He gestured recklessly with the gun. The weapon was clumsy in his hand and showed him to be a man who knew nothing about firearms. "Apologize at once!"

Chloe froze, paralyzed with fear. She lost any hope of reasoning with him. He was completely out of his mind. "I apologize, Mister Peterson."

He went on in a sly, confidential tone. "I know why you broke our engagement. You were pining for McGuire. When he left town, I thought you'd see how foolish and pointless your little infatuation was."

He stopped and grasped his head with his hands. His face contorted with great pain, as if his skull were too tight. When he spoke again, his voice was filled with raging sobs. "Instead you turned me away. Twice! You wouldn't let me touch you, but he got it all! I had a right, damn you! I had a right to marry you and live in that house. I courted you for six months. Did you suppose I wanted to live in the Tollivers' attic forever? You made me believe it would be mine."

In the next instant his voice was calm again and he smiled patiently at her. "But now that I've told Rankin where to find your blacksmith, he'll kill him for me." He squeezed her chin in a hard pinch, then let his hand drop to fondle her breast. Lust crossed his twisted features and she squirmed away from his touch. "McGuire won't bother us anymore and we'll never be apart again."

Chloe stared at Evan, overwhelmed, as boundless, gnawing fear licked through her. It would be foolhardy to remind him they'd never been engaged.

Travis had sensed Evan's instability from the first moment he'd met him. Why had she failed to recognize all the signs that now seemed so obvious? She'd only admitted that Evan was weak and mean. The idea of his insanity had been one that she'd skittered away from as though it were a grotesque insect. Now she was forced to face it.

She looked around wildly at her prison. Feeble sunlight penetrated the dingy lace curtains. The late morning breeze that blew through an open window couldn't dispel the years of mustiness closed in here. A hideous possibility formed in her mind: she might die in this room.

Fortune had made her the captive of a man consumed by madness, *a man she nearly married,* and no one—not even Travis—knew where she was.

"That's where he's got her, right up there," Jace murmured. They were on the east edge of town, standing in the doorway of a vacant apothecary shop. All the buildings on this side of Misfortune were abandoned.

He pointed to a second-floor window over an empty saloon on the other side of the street. A faded sign hung askew above the broken doors, telling any who cared that this had once been the Rose and Garter.

"How do you know?" Travis whispered.

"Wait a minute . . . there, see?" A lace curtain, pulled by the breeze, fluttered from an open window. "If the window was broken or had been open a long time, the weather would have shredded that curtain by now. But it's whole and still sort of white. They're up there, all right."

Travis pushed away the images crowding into his head of Chloe held prisoner by that lunatic. If he stopped to think about what could be happening, he'd be worthless to her.

He took a deep breath and let it out. "Thanks. I'll be back in a few minutes." He drew the Colt and stepped out of the doorway.

Jace pulled him back and leveled his dead stare at him for a moment. "Or maybe you won't. If you manage to save the woman, you'll be out the back door and I'll have to track you down again. Or that jittery teacher might kill you and I'll miss seeing it." He pulled off the duster and threw it over the hitching rail, then checked the rounds in the Henry. "No, I'm coming along."

"Thanks for the bighearted offer," Travis snapped back, wondering if there was any limit to Jace's cold hate. But he grudgingly accepted that the bounty hunter had more experience in this than he did.

"Then let's go. But use your head." Jace kept his eye on the window a moment longer. "If we spook Peterson and he's got a gun, someone is going to get shot. I don't plan for it to be me. Don't let your temper get in my way."

Travis glared back, fed up with Jace's icy arrogance.

"Get this straight, Rankin," he ground out, low-voiced. "If you want to help, fine. Otherwise, stay out here and wait. This isn't business—there's no reward. This is personal."

Jace finally nodded. "Okay, for the next ten minutes, we're on the same side."

They left the doorway and moved quickly to the Rose and Garter. Travis fought the urge to barrel through those doors and blow off Peterson's goddamned head.

Inside the dim saloon, the once elegant back bar and nearly every other structure were festooned with cobwebs. Weeds grew through breaks in the rotting floor, leaning toward columns of sunlight that shone through bullet holes in the walls and dirty windows. Overturned tables and broken glasses lay scattered around the room. In the dark corners, unseen creatures made scurrying sounds as the intruders crossed to the staircase.

Travis led the way up the rickety steps, staying close to the wall, his revolver extended the full length of his arm. He relaxed his fingers around the grip, forcing himself to maintain an easy, flexible hold.

On the second floor Jace looked up and down the dark hall. There were three rooms on each side of the stairway, all with the doors closed. He swore silently, then put a finger to his lips. They stood motionless, listening for the sound of voices. Finally, a low droning reached them. Travis headed toward the sound with Jace behind him.

In front of a door, Travis dropped to one knee and looked through the keyhole. He saw Peterson nervously pacing back and forth, like a wild dog in a pen. The room was small and each circuit brought him within inches of the door. Of Chloe, all Travis could see were her feet hanging over the edge of the bed, her ankles bound. If he'd hurt her, Travis vowed to himself, he'd riddle Peterson with the Colt and drag his miserable carcass to the prairie for the coyotes. Without looking away, he motioned to Jace to be ready, and felt him move into place behind him. They needed the advantage of surprise. As soon as that son of a bitch turned his back—

"Mister Peterson, couldn't you put the gun down and loosen the rope on my wrists? I can't feel my fingers."

Travis tightened his jaw and reached for the doorknob.

Peterson whirled to look at her. "Be quiet, slut! I ordered you not to speak. You still haven't learned obedience. You just added another hour to your punishment." His voice took on a whining tone. "I can't be lenient with you. If the other students hear of it, they'll suspect me of favoritism."

Now Travis understood why Evan had always made him feel as though he were looking into the bottom of his own grave. The man had hovered on the twilight edge of sanity all along.

Turn around, damn you—

Peterson paused to rub his eyes. "Just a little while longer," he said to Chloe, a satisfied smile on his pale, sweating face. "Then you can be my whore, Chloe, and give me everything you gave him—the smooth skin, those long legs, your soft breasts. . . ."

Every muscle Travis owned clenched in fury, and he felt Jace's warning hand on his shoulder.

"Just till I know for certain that the bounty hunter

has taken care of McGuire," Peterson continued. He pivoted toward the window—

Suddenly the door crashed open and Chloe saw Travis and Jace Rankin storm the room, guns drawn on Evan. Both men wore cold, deliberate expressions even more deadly than Evan's frenzied raving.

Travis spared her a glance as he ordered, "Don't move, Peterson." Then he rushed to Chloe and pulled her to the floor. There wasn't time to be gentle and she landed hard on her hip. He shoved her behind him and toward Jace.

The bounty hunter looped a strong arm around her waist and dragged her roughly along the floor to the hall like a sack of potatoes. From a sheath at his waist he produced a huge hunting knife and with two strokes sliced the ropes tying her.

Chloe gaped at him while she rubbed her wrists, trying to comprehend his presence. Each event, every passing minute, was more unreal than the last. She struggled to get to her feet, but they were numb.

"Stay down and stay out here," he instructed tersely. He turned his frightening blue gaze on her for an instant, then went back to Travis.

Chloe sat on the floor in the hall, her pulse thundering in her head while she strained to hear what was happening.

Evan stood staring at the two of them, nearly hysterical with fury and disappointment. "You," he said to Jace, waving his gun again. "I thought you'd kill him for me! Why did you let him come back?"

"Give it up, Peterson. It's over," Jace said.

"No, it isn't!" Evan howled and pointed at the doorway. "She's mine and her house is mine. I deserve them."

"Put the gun down," Travis commanded, sharpening his aim.

"No!" he yelled. The roar of the shot Evan fired was deafening.

Oh, God—Travis! Chloe scrambled on hands and knees to the doorway. She felt a scream rip through her throat as Jace sank to the floor next to her, blood gushing from his shoulder.

"Peterson, you bastard!" Travis snarled.

Chloe jumped as Travis fired twice and she looked up to see Evan fall backward over a chair in the corner. Travis's face was pale and set, his eyes narrowed to silver slits, as a twist of smoke drifted from the barrel of his gun. The smell of sulphur and a bluish haze hung on the abrupt silence. Travis bent over Evan and pulled the pistol from his lifeless hand. A bright red stain grew rapidly in the center of Evan's chest, marking the site where two .45 bullets entered his heart.

"Travis," Chloe called with a voice that trembled. She was too stunned to cry.

He went to her where she knelt, love and relief bringing life back to his face. They embraced briefly, fiercely, huddled in the doorway. A heartbeat pounded between them, whose she wasn't sure.

"Did he hurt you, honey?" he questioned anxiously. He scanned her face, then let his light touch follow the path of his searching gaze over her hair and cheeks. She felt the tremor in his hands. "Did he," he faltered, "do anything to you?"

"No," she gulped. "Is he dead?" She ventured a quick look at Evan's still form.

Travis nodded. "I didn't have a choice."

Lying on the floor, barely conscious, Jace mumbled incoherently. Travis turned his attention to him. "Is it bad?"

Chloe tore open Jace's blood-soaked shirt, trying to see how much damage Evan's bullet had done. The wound, high on his shoulder, was messy and he was losing a lot of blood.

Travis winced at the ragged bullet hole.

"I don't know—it *looks* bad. We need to get Doc Sherwood right away. What is he doing here, anyway?" she asked, gesturing at Jace.

"He said he didn't want to risk having someone else kill me."

White-faced with pain, Jace lost consciousness. Chloe glanced at the wound again and then back up at Travis. Their eyes locked as the same possibility occurred to them. "Do you think he—what if he dies?" she posed in a shaky whisper.

If Jace Rankin died, all the problems he'd created would die with him, Travis thought. He and Chloe would have a new start without Jace behind them. But not really. Travis knew if he let Jace die, the man would have more power over him than he did while alive. His conscience would torture him for the rest of his days and not even Chloe's love would save him from the ghost that would plague his sleep.

Travis stood and reached down to pick him up. "Come on, we've got to take him to Doc."

"No, Travis, wait," Chloe hissed. She gripped his arm urgently and pulled him back to the floor. "You have to get away and this is your chance. I'll get Doc and then meet you outside of town. We'll leave, just like we planned."

He shook his head and gave her a sweet, gentle smile that pierced her heart. "I can't do that. I made a promise."

"What kind of promise?" she demanded with sudden apprehension.

He stood again and lifted Jace to his shoulder.

"Travis, what kind of promise?" she repeated, her voice rising.

"I'll explain it all after we take him to Doc."

She followed him helplessly down the stairs. A sick foreboding rose in her to take the place of the fear she'd just left behind her.

The sound of voices and running feet reached them through the open doors. As they stepped outside, they saw a small group racing toward the Rose and Garter.

Albert DeGroot was the first to reach them. "Thunderation, McGuire! Did you shoot this man?"

Travis kept walking, with Chloe at his side. "No, I shot Evan Peterson. He kidnapped Chloe and you'll find him in a room upstairs. He's the one who shot Jace."

Everyone spoke at once, their voices a confused, questioning babble.

"Is Evan dead?" Albert called after them.

Travis stopped then and turned to face the shop-keeper. The question he posed carried easily on the still afternoon. "Could I let a mad dog live?"

"Chloe, you should go home." Travis sat hunched on the edge of Doc's old horsehair settee, his elbows on his knees, staring at the floor between his feet. His hair fell forward, concealing his face. Jace's blood soaked the back of his shirt.

They had just finished answering Fred Winslow's questions regarding Chloe's kidnapping and rescue. The sheriff had left, satisfied with their explanation that omitted the details about where Chloe had spent last night.

"No, I'm not going home! Why are you sitting in this parlor instead of riding away? You have to leave, now, while Doc is operating." She struggled to stay calm. It seemed that hours, not just forty minutes, had passed since Doc had taken Jace into his surgery room. But the grandfather clock in the parlor ticked on in tranquil accuracy. "Why won't you tell me what this is about?"

He lifted is head and held her with his gray eyes, then gave her that same poignant smile he'd shown her earlier. "Come and sit over here, honey. I'll tell you," he said, and held his arm out to pull her to him.

She sat in the cove of his embrace, her hands clenched in her lap. His touch was warm and vital, but inside a frigid shakiness gripped her. Something was desperately wrong.

"When you didn't come back, I went to your

house. I saw the broken lamp and your rag doll—"
He swallowed. "I thought Jace had stolen you, so I
went looking for him. But then I figured out it was
Peterson who had you. Without help, I knew I might
not get to you before it was too late." He touched
her long braid where it fell over her arm, letting it
slide through his fingers. "I needed Jace, so I asked
him to help me find you. Like I said before, he's
got—something—a sixth sense, I guess."

"But, Travis, you put yourself in terrible danger,"
she moaned.

"You were already in terrible danger. Peterson was
crazy. He could rape you or even kill you."

Chloe couldn't deny she'd had the same valid
fears. But Jace Rankin didn't strike her as the kind
of man who gave something for nothing. "What did
you promise? Did you have to pay him?"

"Not exactly." He looked away from her pale anxiety and drew a long breath. "I surrendered to him."

"What do you mean?" Chloe stared at Travis, ag-
hast.

He opened her cold hand and laced his fingers
with hers. His words were heavy with resignation. "I
promised I'd do whatever he wanted if he'd help."

Swamped with horror, Chloe didn't realize she
was crying until she felt tears splash on her wrist.
"You can't be serious! I won't let you keep a promise
like that. He'll kill you!"

He'd never really seen her cry until now and the
pain of it cut deep. "I would have done anything to
save you. Don't you know that?"

"But to hand your future—*our future*—to Rankin!"

"That's what I'm trying to save, Chloe." His expression was nakedly earnest, then settled into tired lines. "I'm fed up with running. There's a chance I can reason with him. You were right that morning, it's time to face him."

"But 'a chance' isn't enough," she argued brokenly. "And I was wrong to tell you so."

He shrugged. "I have to try. We were good friends once."

"Obviously friendship means nothing to a man like that!"

He pressed both her hands to his lips for a moment, his eyes closed. "Living on the run is just existing. You deserve better than that. We both do."

"I wouldn't care if we had to live in a tent for the rest of our lives," she appealed. "We still have time to go. You did the right think by bringing Rankin here and now your responsibility is finished."

"Chloe, please. I want you to go home and wait for me. I'll be there. I will."

"Come with me, Travis," she implored.

"No more running. Damn it, Chloe, I'm innocent!" He pounded his fist on his knee.

"I'm not the one who thinks you're guilty. You don't have to convince me. But you won't be able to convince Rankin."

He didn't reply. His set face told her his mind was made up. She suddenly realized that it had become very important to Travis to make Jace Rankin believe him, to redeem himself in the bounty hunter's eyes. The future was a secondary issue. There was nothing she could do to turn him from his decision. She looked around the room, remembering the last time she'd seen it. It was the afternoon she'd sprinted down here like her feet were on fire to bring Doc home to help a tall, slender drifter who'd passed out in her yard.

He'd given her a scant glimpse of life at its sweetest and its most unbearable, a life filled with passion and sorrow and joy. A life she hadn't dreamed of for herself. Now that she'd tasted it, she couldn't tell which was worse: having never known it, or losing it forever. But the result was the same.

"So Jace Rankin wins again," she mourned. "That man keeps tangling up my life and I don't even know him. I'm grateful for his help, but I'm not willing to offer you up as payment." She rose from the settee and swiped impatiently at her tears, then stared down at his handsome, weary face. "Travis, I love you so much—more than I know how to tell you. You want me to go? All right, I'll go. But if I walk out that door"—her voice broke—"I know I'll never see you again."

"You *will* see me again," he said, pushing his hair off his forehead. He stood and reached for her hand, then pulled her into his arms. "And when I come back, it'll be for good."

She clung desperately to Travis. She knew that he was only trying to soothe her fears and keep her calm. His promise to Jace Rankin made it impossible for Travis to keep his pledge to her. Her arms encircled his waist so well, her head fit against his shoulder so perfectly. How could she obey him and turn her back, leaving him to what could only be imprisonment or death? Surely as long as she stayed here she could protect him from the bounty hunter.

His arms slipped away from her and he reached around to loosen her grip, holding her fists against his chest.

She looked up into his eyes, trying desperately to find some weakening of his resolve, some hint that he might abandon this idea. How had circumstances swung so wildly from futile to exultant and back again? She'd found Travis again and discovered their love for each other, only to lose it all once more.

"Please don't send me away," she begged, barely over a whisper. She saw his throat work as he swallowed and offered her a crooked smile.

He pressed urgent kisses to her temple and cheek, then her lips. When he spoke, his voice was low and rough with emotion. "Go on now, honey. Everything will be all right." His hand on her shoulder nudged her toward the entryway.

She strode across the parlor to leave, hoping every inch of the way to hear his footsteps follow her, but she didn't. He wasn't coming with her. Her hand on the doorknob, she turned to face him.

For an instant while he stood watching her, raw, bare pain glittered in his eyes. Then the mask she knew so well dropped into place again.

"Goodbye, Travis," she choked. Not waiting for his response, she pulled the door open and ran down Doc's steps.

A huddle of people loitered outside the Rose and Garter, down the street, and Chloe hoped to slip to her house on the other end without being seen. She wasn't up to answering all the questions they would ask.

She headed home, her steps leaden. She glanced over her shoulder to see if she was spotted, but the group was too absorbed with discussing the afternoon's tragedy. It was certainly the most sensational incident Misfortune had seen in the last ten years.

A darkness lay on her spirit as she trudged along, stumbling over the ripped hem of her skirt. Her clothes were a mess, torn and bloodstained, but she didn't care. A sob flooded her throat and she struggled to keep it there. She wasn't about to let herself start weeping in the street, but dear God, it was hard not to. Guilt was a cruel burden and there was no question that she was guilty.

Every event that had happened today was her fault.

If she hadn't been so stubbornly blind about Evan's insanity . . .

If Travis hadn't felt compelled to stay in the hills to be near her . . .

If she'd swept into the house last night without talking to Rankin . . .

And the worst fault of all—if only she'd left with Travis this morning when he'd wanted her to.

No matter how she justified or cursed fate, she knew that Evan's capture of her and his resulting death, Travis meeting Jace again—none of these things would have happened if she hadn't been so bullheaded about returning to Misfortune today. Travis had tried to talk her out of it. He'd practically begged her not to go. But, no, she'd wanted to see the house one last time, to have her own way. Well, now she could sit in that house, without Travis, and review her regrets for years to come.

To have gained his love but lost him in the blink of an eye, added to everything else that had happened, was more than her mind could accept. And Travis's love for her ran so strong and deep, it had made him sacrifice his freedom or his life just to save her from a madman that he'd warned her away from months ago. Why hadn't she listened to him then?

There was a chance, she reminded herself, a chance he would survive this and come back to her. He'd said so, and she clutched at the fragile possibility. Still, she'd looked into Jace Rankin's eyes, and she'd seen no pity, no remorse. Remembering that, her skimpy faith died. What did Travis find there to give him hope?

Behind her, she heard the rattle of harness and iron wheel rims. When a wagon came abreast of her, she saw young Andy Duykstrom on the seat. On the flat wagon bed under an old blanket, lay Evan's body. A spontaneous shudder rolled through her at the sight of it.

"How do, Miss Chloe," the slow-witted youth called to her. He gestured with his thumb over his shoulder. "I'm just taking Mister Peterson to the undertaker." He grinned happily then, as a thought occurred to him. "Guess now that he's gone, I won't have to go to school no more."

The wagon rattled on with its grisly cargo, raising

a cloud of dust, and Chloe felt her burden of guilt weigh still heavier.

When she got to her gate, she stood looking at the house for a moment, her hands gripping two of the pickets. The wind tugged at her hair and torn skirt as she stared in silence, eyes dry.

There was certainly nothing lavish or majestic about this old place. The county was dotted with large, plain farmhouses designed very much like it. Yet it had touched several people and such battles had been waged over it. She'd struggled to save it from repossession. Evan had courted her in order to live in it. Travis had walked away from it, and so had she, briefly. But the path of her life brought her back to it again.

She slowly pushed on the gate and walked to the porch. Grief and the strain of the day's events settled over her and an icy tremor began in the pit of her stomach that spread to the ends of her limbs. Shivering, she tucked herself into a corner of the porch swing, wrapping her arms around her waist. The afternoon sun fell on her as she huddled on the swing, staring dully at the dry, treeless miles beyond the yard.

Chloe wondered if she'd ever be warm again.

Travis watched Chloe from the window until she was lost from his view and tried to block the despondency weighing him down. He'd seen the utter hopelessness in her face, and it shook him to his soul. If she didn't believe in him, how could he believe in himself? Couldn't she see how important it was that he make peace with Jace? He leaned against the window frame, feeling as tired as he could remember.

The clock was just striking four when Travis heard the door to the surgery open. He turned as Doc came into the parlor, drying his hands.

"That boy is tough," he remarked. "The wound was a nasty-looking thing. At first I was worried that he'd shattered his collarbone."

"He'll live?" Travis asked.

"Oh, sure. It cleaned up fine. He lost some blood, but he's awake and asking to see you." Doc fixed a serious eye on him. "Don't linger with him. He's weaker than he admits. If you've got differences to settle, they'll keep. He's not going anywhere today."

Travis nodded and walked down the dark hall to face his bygone friend, the man who would just as soon kill him. Doubt and determination were at odds within him. He pushed open the door and saw Jace lying on the table, still in his jeans and boots, his arm wrapped across his ribs with white linen bandages. The odor of carbolic acid was heavy in the little room. As Travis approached, Jace rolled his head toward him, his eyes drowsy with chloroform. His waxy pallor was unsettling.

"How are you feeling?" Travis asked quietly.

"I've been better." Jace's words were groggy and halting. "Did you kill him?" There was no question who he meant.

"Yeah. I didn't mean for you to get shot, you know."

"I didn't either." He paused, as though gathering

strength to continue. "I wanted to shoot *you* lots of times, but I never got close enough till now." Jace drew a breath, his voice barely more than a whisper. "Then you walked right into my hands. Why?"

Travis looked away. He hated having to explain himself to Jace. It required him to reveal his heart and that wasn't an easy thing for him to do. But if they were going to understand each other, he knew he had to be honest. "I told you why. I was willing to trade my freedom or my life to save Chloe. I'd have done anything to save her."

"Too bad you didn't feel that way about my sister," Jace said, weary bitterness in every word. "I've hated you since Celia died and I swore I'd get even when I found you."

Travis stared hard into Jace's hazy blue eyes to make sure he heard him. "You can take me back to jail or put a bullet in my head, but it won't change the fact that I didn't kill Celia and it won't bring her back."

Jace breathed a sigh and closed his eyes for a moment, then with obvious difficulty focused them on Travis. "You could have left me to bleed to death. But you didn't."

Travis glanced at the floor, then replied, "We go back too far for me to let that happen. It's one of the reasons I've never faced you till now. I knew I couldn't kill you.

"Celia—she was always so restless and unhappy— she said it was because of you."

His wife's flaxen-haired memory rose in his mind again, a female demon of temptation, faithlessness, and pretended innocence. "You know I was crazy about her, Jace. I gave her everything I had. Everything. But it was never enough."

Jace shifted uncomfortably on the table. "I think I always knew that. She was . . . spoiled and selfish." After a long pause, he added, "Maybe no one could have made her happy."

This was a stunning admission from a man who'd thought of Celia more as his child than his sister. Travis detected a glimmer of reason and gripped Jace's wrist. His voice dropped to a tense whisper. "You know I wasn't responsible for her death."

At length, Jace nodded slightly, his face suffused with resignation and fatigue. "I guess I needed someone to blame . . ."

Travis pressed his advantage. "I loved her but I had to try and let go of the memories. So do you. Pick up your life, Jace. If you don't, it'll eat you alive."

"Maybe. I don't know." A slight smile crossed Jace's face. "But one thing is certain. That Maitland woman has enough grit to ride a mountain lion bareback."

Travis chuckled and nodded.

"And she'd do it to save you," Jace added, serious again.

Travis felt his grin fade as he thought about the truth of his words. "I think you're right."

A frown creased Jace's forehead. "Oh, shit, this hurts," he groaned. His eyes closed then and his features smoothed out as pain and exhaustion conquered him.

Travis heard Doc's voice from the doorway behind him. "Come on, son. Let him get his rest."

Travis nodded and walked to the door. Even lying there swatched in bandages, Jace still made a formidable enemy, and Travis was thankful he was no longer one of his targets. There would be no more running or hiding, no more looking over his shoulder. He remembered nights sleeping in the open, holding his breath at the snap of every twig, his hand aching from gripping the Colt. Now Chloe would never have to live through that. Finally, it was over and he had his life back. He was free.

Knowing him as he did, he wondered if Jace would be able to put Celia's death behind him. He was wasting his life, trying to avenge his sister's murder. But Travis couldn't be responsible for the road he chose.

"Will you keep him here till he's able to get around?" Travis asked.

Doc rolled down his sleeves. "He's welcome to stay, but I suspect when he wants to leave, he will, whether or not I think he's ready. He seems every bit as independent and ornery as you can be," he observed.

Travis massaged the back of his neck, glancing back at Jace. "Yeah, people used to say we were a lot alike. Like brothers, they said. But that was years ago. Times change, men change."

"Not as much as you might think. Basic decency usually survives." Doc watched him and then said, "You've had a hell of a day, haven't you. Come out to the kitchen and I'll buy you a drink."

"Thanks, Doc," he smiled, "but there's a lady I need to see and I've kept her waiting long enough."

"Give her my regards," Doc called as Travis went down the front steps.

The shadows grew long and cool. Chloe considered going into the house but couldn't think of a reason. A rude magpie squawked at her from the porch railing but she stared it down until it darted away into the sky.

The smell of wood smoke floated to her on the late breeze, as kitchen stoves were lit for the evening meal. This morning she'd expected to be cooking tonight's dinner over a campfire, beginning a new life.

Earlier she'd cleaned up the broken lamp and put away in the chest of drawers the things she'd packed. After washing off the dirt and blood, she put on clean clothes and her shawl, and came out here again to sew the arm back on her doll.

Something about the poor thing, with its solemn button eyes and enduring smile, and the sawdust leaking out of its faded body, punctured the last of Chloe's defenses. It seemed to represent everything she'd lost—her parents, Travis, even Evan's life— and she'd succumbed to wrenching, gasping sobs that tore at her heart.

Now she sat here, drained and dull-eyed, with a handkerchief wadded in her fist and the doll on her lap, its arm mended. She tightened her shawl, then rested her head against the back of the porch swing and closed her eyes while she struggled to absorb the unbelievable twists her life had taken. At the same time, she did her best to shut out the prospect of the empty years ahead of her.

Once before she'd made up her mind to carry on the existence she'd known before Travis came along. She was strong and sensible, she could do it again. Time would take care of it, she told herself.

She felt the doll again in her hands and knew with profound despair that she was lying to herself.

This time it wouldn't work. Her tough shell was gone, stripped away by her love for Travis. In loving him, she was prey to every painful emotion she'd avoided all these years. She took a deep, shaky breath, trying to ease the bitter ache.

ching-ching-ching

Her eyes snapped open.

CHING-CHING-CHING

From down the street it came, with the sound of running boot heels. She rose from the swing, her hand pressed to the base of her throat. She could feel a pulse throbbing there, keeping time with her pounding heart.

Travis trotted to her gate, his dark hair flying behind him. He stood there, tall and wild, breathing hard, just watching her. The sunset washed him in rich mellow light. Astonishment rooted her feet to the porch flooring.

Travis looked at Chloe a moment, at the doll clutched in her chapped hands, at her wide-eyed expression, and felt as though he were seeing her again for the first time. Except now she'd been crying and he knew he was the reason.

"What are you doing here?" Her words were purposely harsh. Maybe their curt edge would prevent any hope within her from waking.

Travis vaulted the gate and walked up the short path to the bottom step. He started to reach for her, but the anguish in her face stopped him and his hand dropped back to his side.

"I have something for you," he said finally. "I left it in my saddlebag when I put the horses in the shop."

Ah, so he was only back to say goodbye. Since Rankin was in no condition to go anywhere today, Travis was here to collect his belongings and see her one last time. Why did he have to look so endearing, so painfully beautiful? Staring down at him, heartache kept her silent, but she sensed no torment roiling in him. Leaving never seemed difficult for Travis.

She nodded, her throat too tight to speak, and watched as he strode to the shop. Her legs felt like they would no longer support her and she carefully sat on the swing again.

A moment later he returned with the saddlebag and dropped to one knee in front of her. He opened one of the flaps and pulled out a heavy pouch.

"I know you think your father just left you bad memories and a mortgage," he said. He loosened the strings on the porch and opened it, holding it out for her inspection. "But there was something more."

She peered into the bag and saw gold dust winking up at her. She felt her eyes widen. There was a fortune here, more money than she'd ever dreamed of having.

"You got all this from that worthless plot?" she asked, her voice restored. She thought he was only making peanuts, like the other old prospectors.

He nodded. "Not so worthless. I panned twice this much, thanks to Tarpaper Bolen, and I want you to have it. But there's a catch." He pulled the strings tight, closing the pouch again. Then he lifted his head to look into her eyes. When he spoke, his voice was gentle yet seductive. "You have to marry me to get it." He leaned closer. "Will you, Chloe? Will you be my wife?"

She could hardly believe what he was saying. "But what about Rankin?"

"He's tired and bitter. But saving his life convinced him that I didn't kill Celia. I thought I could finally make him see reason." He put his hand on her knee. "I know you didn't understand. But before I met you, I had no future, nothing to fight for. I hated having him behind me, but it didn't matter enough to make me stop and face him. I only wanted to stay ahead of him. Nothing mattered very much except my freedom. Then you gave me back my life and I had to try to make Jace see the truth."

"You're sure he won't change his mind?" she persisted suspiciously. Twice before Jace Rankin had come between them. She would leave no possibility unchallenged. "Will he show up here again, looking for you, threatening you?

"I know he won't."

"So you really aren't leaving?" Her sleeping hope stirred.

"No, honey. Not unless you chase me off. Even

then, I'd sleep right here on the porch and sit in that chair outside the shop until you agreed to marry me." He glanced down at the floor. "Falling in love with you saved my life, but it wouldn't be much of a life without you. I'm through with drifting."

A lot had changed since that hot noon last summer. And now here was Travis, kneeling at her feet—the angry man who had claimed to need no one, who'd taught them both what love and forgiveness could do, the man who'd given her passion and fire—and he wanted to join her life to his. He was more important than mortgages or houses or any of the things she had once thought so vital.

Naked emotion and the fear that she would reject him were etched in his face, and he couldn't hide them from her.

"I would marry you if you didn't have a dime," she answered quietly. "There's nothing I want more on this earth than to be your wife."

She reached out to touch his cheek and he suddenly pulled her from the swing into his embrace. She fell on him squealing and giggling, in a flurry of skirts and petticoats, and he rolled her under him. With the desperate troubles they'd had, to laugh again was a wonderful release. But it faded away when his lips covered hers in soft urgent kisses that deepened as his hand slid from her waist to her breast. She smelled his familiar scent, felt the rasp of his beard against her face, the warmth of his skin under his shirt. When his fingers pushed her skirt up her leg to her thigh, she stopped him.

"We can't make love here on the porch," she

chided, pushing at his chest. Her voice lacked conviction.

After one more slow, moist kiss, he sat up. Leaning back on one of the porch uprights, he settled her against his long torso. "We could, if we wanted to give the crowd down at DeGroot's something to mull over." He opened her palm and pressed a kiss into it, then turned it over, running his fingers over the work-roughness he found there.

"I guess these people will have to learn how to do their own wash because you just went out of business." He reached for the gold pouch and put it in her hand. "Take a little of this and pay off that damned mortgage. Or we can go somewhere else, if you want. It doesn't matter to me."

She straightened away from him and raised a brow. "But you just said you were through with drifting."

In the blue twilight, his mind traveled down the years and roads that had brought him to Misfortune. After a moment of introspection, he replied, "Maybe I wasn't really drifting all my life." He pulled her back into is arms and rested his chin against her temple.

"Maybe I was always on my way home to you."

ANNOUNCING THE
TOPAZ FREQUENT READERS CLUB
COMMEMORATING TOPAZ'S
1 YEAR ANNIVERSARY!

THE MORE YOU BUY, THE MORE YOU GET

Redeem coupons found here and in the back of all new Topaz titles for FREE Topaz gifts:

Send in:

 2 coupons for a free TOPAZ novel (choose from the list below);

☐ **THE KISSING BANDIT**, Margaret Brownley
☐ **BY LOVE UNVEILED**, Deborah Martin
☐ **TOUCH THE DAWN**, Chelley Kitzmiller
☐ **WILD EMBRACE**, Cassie Edwards

 4 coupons for an "I Love the Topaz Man" on-board sign

 6 coupons for a TOPAZ compact mirror

 8 coupons for a Topaz Man T-shirt

Just fill out this certificate and send with original sales receipts to:

TOPAZ FREQUENT READERS CLUB-1ST ANNIVERSARY
Penguin USA • Mass Market Promotion; Dept. H.U.G.
375 Hudson St., NY, NY 10014

Name_____

Address_____

City_____ State_____ Zip_____

Offer expires 1/31 1995

This certificate must accompany your request. No duplicates accepted. Void where prohibited, taxed or restricted. Allow 4-6 weeks for receipt of merchandise. Offer good only in U.S., its territories, and Canada.